SCARLET

a novel by

Andrew Stopyra

THE HASLEWOOD MYSTERIES
Book One

This is a work of fiction. Though inspired by certain historical persons and events, it is ultimately the product of the author's imagination, and any resemblance to persons living or dead is wholly coincidental.

The Hello Girls of World War I were very real and their contribution to the war effort was extremely important. Nevertheless, any references to them, their training, or work in the field, have been handled with a certain degree of artistic liberty, though with the utmost respect for their service. Camp Franklin has since been absorbed by nearby Fort Meade.

The original Simplon Orient Express, an alternate branch of the Orient Express, operated from 1919 to 1962 (with a hiatus for WWII) and should not be confused with the modern Venice Simplon-Orient-Express, which attempts to recreate the experience.

ISBN: 978-1-7343805-0-7

Library of Congress Control Number: 2019919990

For Chrissy.

Soli Deo gloria

Five paintings are referenced in this book. You may find it helpful - and enjoyable - to have a look at them.

You can find all five at scarletcons.com under Paintings.

You'll also find a playlist under Music. There are a few songs there that I felt complemented various parts of the story - songs that were either going through my head as I wrote a given passage, or that I heard later and thought captured the feel of some moment or scene. I tend to be overly aware of the soundtracks to movies and television shows (I'm not sure why), so I guess I naturally imagined a 'soundtrack' running behind my book. It's nothing official, and it's definitely not essential to the experience by any means. You may even disagree with my choices! But I just thought I'd share them with you for the fun of it.

~Andrew

Scarlet

IN THE EARLY HOURS OF MONDAY, AUGUST 21, 1911, a former janitor at the Louvre Museum in Paris entered one of its galleries wearing a long white smock.

He removed one of the paintings from the wall, wrapped it up in the smock, and walked out with it in broad daylight a few minutes later.

Within days, it became the most famous painting in the world.

And what did he do with it?
He kept it hidden in a trunk in his apartment for two years.

Art theft is a billion-dollar industry.

If you can move it.

Chapter 1

Paris
April 1925

Outside *M. Fontaine* in the Rue de la Paix, a man leaned against the stone exterior, sipping a warm drink and smoking a cigarette. People passed by at regular intervals, not so many that it felt crowded but enough that it reminded you what a beautiful day it was, the first in well over a week. Women in particular were out to browse the many jewellery stores in the neighbourhood, few of which were considered as trendy or as chic as *M. Fontaine*. Inside, one was enquiring about a ring.

"And you say it's platinum, is that correct?"

"Oh yes, Madame," M. Fontaine himself replied. "In fact, it was Cartier that popularised the use of platinum in rings, and this is one of the finest examples I have on hand."

"And the sapphires," she mused, "their shape is rather unique." She slid the ring on and off of several of her fingers, admiring it in each position and happy to find that it fit more than one perfectly.

"You are quite right, Madame!" Fontaine said. "I assume you are also familiar with the latest tutti-frutti designs? Though this particular ring contains only sapphires framed with diamonds, the elaborate shapes are still very much in keeping with this new style. Can you tell what the sapphires are supposed to represent?"

The woman slipped the ring back on to the finger she most preferred it on, her left index, and turned her hand this way and that as she thought about his question. The light glinting off the ring and its overall appearance distracted her somewhat.

"I would have to say," she began, then paused for a moment. "I would have to say that they look most like leaves."

"Once again, Madame, you are quite right!" Fontaine replied, feeling that a sale was imminent.

Just then, another woman entered the shop. People had been coming and going all day - at least three had entered or exited in the last ten minutes alone. This woman, however, caught Fontaine's attention straightaway. She wasn't wearing the typical flapper dress that was so popular, like the one adorning the woman admiring the Cartier ring. The new customer wore a more ornate dress in a deep red colour, with embroidery and beading, cinched with a belt that sat higher than the current fashion and which helped to accentuate the flare of the bottom half of the dress. Her black hair wasn't bobbed and tucked away beneath a cloche either. Instead, it was loosely curled, pulled up at the back but still shoulder length, and topped with a beret that sloped gently to one side.

"My husband will be in tomorrow to pay for the ring, if that is acceptable?"

For a minute or two, Fontaine had forgotten entirely about closing the sale, distracted by the woman in red who began slowly making her way along the display cases.

"I said, my husband will come by tomorrow, say about noon, to purchase the ring," the first woman said in a more forceful tone. "That is, if you still feel like selling it."

The words caught up to him and Fontaine's mind snapped

4

back to the woman before him.

"Yes, yes, of course, Madame," he replied. "There is no rush. Monsieur Barre may come at his earliest convenience. I'll be looking forward to seeing him again."

"Thank you, Monsieur Fontaine. It has been a pleasure, as always." The woman collected her handbag from the counter, adjusted her hat, and left the shop.

As the jeweller began putting away the other rings that Madame Barre had been considering, the woman in red appeared before him.

"That is an outstanding example of Monsieur Cartier's latest designs, is it not?" she said. "It reminds me of one of his custom pieces I recently saw on the hand of an English duchess on holiday in Monte Carlo."

"Uh, yes, it, it certainly is, Madame," Fontaine answered. He was not accustomed to stumbling over his words.

"Might I have a closer look?" she asked.

Fontaine removed the ring from the display pad and handed it to her.

She slipped it onto her left ring finger and held out her hand at arm's length in his direction, turning it from side to side.

"It really is stunning," she remarked.

Fontaine was enjoying her enjoyment of the ring so much that it took him another minute before he remembered that he had actually just sold it.

"Sadly, Madame, I should inform you that the ring is now sold."

She sighed ever so gently, pulled her hand closer to her face for one last look, then smiled warmly and slipped it off her finger.

"Thank you anyway, Monsieur, for the pleasure of admiring it."

"Not at all," Fontaine replied. "Can I help you find something similar? Or is there something specific you came in for today?"

The woman thought about it for a moment, glancing back and forth across the display case that stood between them.

"Can I see something with rubies, perhaps?"

"Of course! I have several lovely pieces right here, as well as more scattered throughout the shop. Are you interested in rings primarily or would you like to see a range of options?"

"A range, most definitely," the woman replied.

"Excellent! Give me a few minutes and I will assemble some items for you to look at." With that, Fontaine flitted about the shop, pillaging his various display cases for the best and finest examples he had of anything containing rubies.

For the next hour, the woman in red carefully studied each piece the jeweller brought her, praising the designs, critiquing the cuts, and comparing the metals. And Fontaine did not tire of the process. On the contrary, amongst her other qualities, he admired the woman's knowledge of the finer points of his trade and would happily have continued the conversation for the rest of the day, with or without a sale. But eventually, amidst the sea of jewellery now lying between them on half a dozen black velvet pads, the woman in red made her decision.

She selected four of his six ruby rings, five of the seven necklaces he had shown her, three of the six pairs of earrings, two of the three bracelets, and the largest of the four brooches - fifteen items in all, their value adding up to more than Monsieur Fontaine had sold in the previous three months combined. He hardly knew where to begin.

"Madame, your taste is second to none! I would have chosen many of the same pieces myself."

"You are too kind, Monsieur Fontaine," she replied.

As he was sorting through her selections and laying them aside, he asked, "And when would Madame like to collect her items?"

"Well, I was wondering if you might do me a service?" she said, looking rather sheepish as she finished the question. "My husband is engaged in a great deal of work for the next few days and won't be able to leave his office, I'm afraid. However, if you would be willing to deliver the items yourself, he has said that he would be able to pay you on the spot - and even include a small gratuity for your troubles."

Fontaine had been in business for nearly three decades and was well acquainted with everyone in the community who would have been in a position to make such a large purchase. But oddly enough, he had never seen this woman before, and he certainly had no idea who her husband could be.

"I am very sorry, Madame, but I must ask to whom you are referring? I'm afraid that in the pleasure of serving you, I have forgotten to ask your name."

"I am Madame Dufour," she replied.

"Madame Dufour?" Fontaine repeated with a touch of confusion in his voice. "As in Monsieur Dufour, whose office is in Saint-Germain-des-Prés?"

"That is correct, Monsieur."

"But I did not know that the doctor had married! This is indeed a fantastic surprise! Though I do not know the man personally, he has been very highly spoken of by many of my customers - especially the young ladies! Thankfully, I have not as yet required the expertise of a psychiatrist, but I almost wish that I had, so I could finally have made his acquaintance."

"Yes, he is a most excellent man," said Madame Dufour. "The wedding was an intimate gathering only. The doctor was kind enough to keep it as such so as not to highlight my own lack of family and friends. I am quite new to Paris and have not formed many relationships yet."

"Well, my lady," Fontaine replied, "I cannot imagine that you will be long without many close friends - though I am sure you will find some jealous ones too! I can already tell from a mere hour discussing jewellery with you that you are a rare creature. The doctor is a very lucky man." He had finished setting aside her selections while they were talking, so that as he spoke these last words, he took her hand and kissed the back of it respectfully. "I wish you both all the best."

"Thank you, you are too kind indeed," she said.

"So then," he continued, "what day and time shall I call in to his office?"

"As it happens, Monsieur," she replied, "the doctor is currently working from home. There is some carpentry work being done in his office, so he is seeing patients in his study for the time being."

"That would be no trouble at all," Fontaine replied. "If you will leave the address for me, I would be happy to call on the doctor at his home."

Madame Dufour wrote down the address on a piece of paper and thanked the jeweller once again for his kindness, as well as for his help in selecting such beautiful pieces for her collection. He replied that he looked forward to seeing her wear them, and to meeting her husband the day after tomorrow.

Loud and frantic knocking disturbed the quietness of the morning at the Dufour residence. The maid hurried to answer the door.

"Can I help--" she began to say but was interrupted by the visitor.

"Oh please! Oh please!" she cried, "I must see the doctor this instant! It is most urgent! I beg you, please!"

The maid was a little flustered and wanted to ask more questions, as she usually did in screening unexpected visitors for Dr. Dufour, but she wasn't sure the woman was in a state to answer them. She tried a simple one.

"I am sure the doctor will want to help you, Madame. But first, may I please have your name?"

"He truly must help, or I don't know what will happen!" the woman replied. "It is my brother. He is in desperate trouble. My name is Madame Moreau. My brother is a Monsieur Fontaine, a well-known jeweller whose shop is not far from here."

"Please, come in and sit down," the maid said. "There are refreshments in the lounge. You may help yourself. I will speak with the doctor."

"Oh, thank you! Thank you!" the woman replied, still emotional but beginning to show signs of relief. She followed the maid to the lounge, just to the left of the front door. It was furnished with two matching light green velvet sofas, facing one another across a glass coffee table. There was a comfortable looking armchair at the end of the room beside a small drinks trolley. The woman seemed indecisive at first about where to set herself, ultimately choosing the armchair and then leaning over to pour herself a drink. Her hand shook as she handled the decanter but she managed to get a small amount of brandy safely into her glass.

After a few minutes, the maid returned.

"Madame, you are very fortunate indeed," she said. "The doctor has had a cancellation this morning and is free at the moment. He is willing to see you now, if you are ready."

"Yes, of course! Absolutely!" the woman said. "I cannot thank you enough! Thank you for not turning me away. Thank you!"

"It is no trouble," the maid replied. "Come this way."

The two walked back past the front door, across the beautiful marble entryway with a curved staircase that led to the upper floor, and arrived at the doctor's study. The maid tapped lightly on the door, then pushed it open.

"Monsieur... the woman I told you about."

The doctor looked up from his desk and then stood up quickly and walked over to meet them at the door. He was a handsome man of about forty years, dressed in a fashionable navy blue pinstripe suit, complete with vest and a red silk tie. His jacket lay over the back of one of the two armchairs that faced his desk.

"Yes, of course. Madame Moreau, is it?" he asked. He placed one hand on her shoulder and extended the other towards the armchairs. "Please, sit down."

The woman, who had composed herself while waiting in the lounge, began to get emotional once again in the presence of the doctor. She teared up and clutched her handkerchief tightly between her hands.

"Oh Monsieur! Oh, it is horrible, truly horrible," she said. "You see, I arrived in Paris last week to visit my brother, Monsieur Fontaine. We correspond often through letters and recently I started noticing..." The woman was overwhelmed for a moment and paused. "I'm so sorry, Monsieur! I'm so sorry!"

"It's ok," Dufour said, "take your time. The more accurately you relate the details, the better."

She wiped the fresh tears from her cheeks and continued.

"Recently his letters were... different. That is, when he still wrote them. I could usually depend on at least two every month. But since the start of the year, I have only received three letters in all. His tone, his style... they just seemed different. The way he spoke about his work, the way he enquired about me. Also, I think he started inventing things."

"Inventing things?" the doctor asked. "What do you mean by that?"

"I mean stories, memories," she said. "I think he was imagining things that were not real."

"I see," said the doctor. "Now, you said that you arrived in Paris last week, correct?"

"Yes, that's correct," she said.

"So what have you observed since your arrival?"

"That is why I have come to see you, Monsieur," she said, catching her breath abruptly to avoid crying. "I am now convinced that he is hallucinating."

"Hallucinating, really?" the doctor replied. "And what makes you certain of this?"

The woman related three examples for the doctor. The third of which applied to Fontaine's business and was clearly the most disturbing to her.

"He has arrived home twice in the past week with large quantities of jewellery from his shop," she said. "Oh Monsieur, I mean many thousands of francs worth of the finest pieces in his inventory. He wraps them carefully in parcels and tells me that they have been ordered by some of the most illustrious families in the city, and that he is going to hand-deliver them for their convenience."

The doctor squinted briefly.

"And is this not typical of his business?"

"Oh no, Monsieur! No, no! Not at all!" she said, clenching the handkerchief even more tightly. "My brother has never delivered an order before. He insists that customers collect their purchases themselves, or engage some courier service, in order to avoid responsibility should something unforeseen happen in their transportation."

"I see," the doctor replied. It made sense to him. "So what is happening to the items that he is supposedly 'delivering' to these customers?"

"That is the thing, Monsieur," she replied. "I believe this has only started since I arrived, and I have stopped the first two attempts. I returned the items to his shop and he promptly forgot the matter by the following morning. I am afraid, however, that because I cannot be with him constantly, my brother will eventually begin carrying out these imagined orders and see his business ruined. And if he could undermine his own work, what beyond that? What other things might he be capable of without even realising it?" Having articulated it as such, the woman finally allowed herself to cry without reservation.

The doctor, whose elbows had been resting on the arms of

his chair and whose hands had been folded in front of his mouth, dropped his hands to his desk, took a deep breath and said, "Then we shall have to help him, Madame."

The woman nodded, not yet able to form the words 'thank you' through her sobbing.

"I want you to ring my office or call in if you are in the neighbourhood, and make the first available appointment for your brother."

"Oh, Monsieur, how can I thank you!" she said. "I only hope it is not too late for him."

"Let's not think those thoughts yet," said the doctor. "I have seen many remarkable recoveries in my career. I have high hopes for helping your brother as well."

Madame Moreau thanked the doctor again and again as he led her to the door of his study. After another assurance of his confidence that he could help, and a reminder to make the appointment as soon as possible, the doctor said goodbye to the woman and shut the door behind her.

———————————

The next knock at the door of the Dufour residence was much more measured and deliberate.

"Monsieur Fontaine!"

"Madame Dufour! So lovely to see you again!" the jeweller replied.

"Please, do come in," said Madame Dufour. She led him around the corner and into the lounge. "Make yourself comfortable."

Fontaine sat on one of the velvet couches, placing a small parcel on the glass table in front of him. Madame Dufour sat opposite him.

"This is very exciting," she said. "The doctor and I have plans for a dinner party later tonight, and I am looking forward to wearing one of the necklaces and a pair of the earrings with my new dress. I think they will complement it perfectly."

"Madame," replied Fontaine, "I am sure you will look as beautiful as always, jewellery or not."

"You are too kind, Monsieur." Madame Dufour had inched forward and was now sitting on the edge of the couch. "I am so very sorry to have to do this, but I am running late for an engagement myself. If you would be kind enough to excuse me, I must finish getting ready and then be on my way as soon as possible."

"Of course, of course!" said Fontaine. "I would not detain you any longer! But is the doctor aware that I am waiting?"

"Yes, he is. He has been expecting you but is currently on a phone call. I will let the maid know that you are here. She is currently tidying up in the kitchen after an unfortunate accident, but she should just about be finished and will make sure you see my husband as soon as possible."

"Excellent!" replied the jeweller.

Madame Dufour picked up the parcel and thanked Fontaine yet again for his kindness, as well as for his assistance in helping her select her new pieces in the first place. Fontaine replied in his usual manner, praising the lady and assuring her that the pleasure was all his.

When the jeweller had been alone for about five or ten minutes, the maid entered the room.

"May I help you, Monsieur?" she asked.

"Yes indeed," he said. "I am here to see the doctor."

"And your name, Monsieur?"

"Why, Fontaine, of course. You are expecting me, I think?"

The maid's eyes widened.

"Monsieur Fontaine?" she repeated, "From the jewellery store?"

"That is correct," he replied.

"I see, I see," the maid said. "I think I know why you're here. Let me go see if the doctor is ready for you."

"Excellent! I am very much looking forward to meeting the man," he said.

Within another minute or two, the maid was leading Monsieur Fontaine across the marble entryway and into the doctor's study.

"Monsieur Fontaine!" the doctor said, his eyes also a little wider than usual. "Your timing is impeccable. Please, do sit down."

"I have always found that punctuality is appreciated by my customers," replied the jeweller, "especially when such valuable items are involved."

The doctor squinted slightly, then leaned back into his earlier position, elbows resting on the arms of the chair, hands folded in front of his mouth.

"You are referring of course to your deliveries, I presume?"

"Yes, of course," said Fontaine. "I like my customers - especially those with such taste and, well, means, if I may be so blunt - to know that I not only value their business but also their time."

"Certainly," said the doctor.

There was a pause and Fontaine looked around the room for a moment, feeling somewhat awkward. The doctor kept staring

15

at him and he was trying to figure out why. Then he thought of something else to say.

"Oh, I can hardly believe that I forgot to say it when I entered the room but I think congratulations are in order, Monsieur!"

The doctor turned his head a little to the side, his eyes still fixed on Fontaine.

"Are they?" he asked. "And what have I done recently that you would like to congratulate me for?"

"Oh Monsieur!" Fontaine replied, "you had best not let the lady hear you say such things!" He laughed after he said this. The doctor did not laugh along with him.

"Would she be upset by that, you think?" he asked the jeweller, curious to see where he was going with this.

"Would she be upset?" he repeated. "I think so, Monsieur... and not a little at that! But after her recent purchase, I know you are only having fun at my expense. A husband would not lavish such gifts on a bride to whom he is indifferent!" The jeweller laughed again. The doctor still did not join him.

Dufour decided it was time to be more direct.

"Of whom are you speaking, Monsieur?" he asked.

Fontaine's eyebrows lowered. He felt the slightest touch of anger as he began to wonder if the doctor was indeed this calloused toward his own wife - toward such a charming woman as Madame Dufour!

"I am speaking of your wife, Monsieur Dufour," Fontaine replied. "That most excellent and remarkable young lady! I spent only two or three minutes with her in the lounge just now and I was once again overwhelmed with the perfect pleasure of her company."

16

The doctor's hands fell to his lap, elbows still resting on the arms of the chair.

"Will you excuse me a moment, Monsieur?"

"Yes, of course," replied Fontaine.

The doctor got up from his chair and left the study, closing the door behind him. Fontaine looked around the room again and tried to remind himself that his visit was about business. He should not attempt to chastise the doctor, no matter how much he felt the urge to do so.

Dufour was gone for nearly twenty minutes, and the jeweller was getting restless. He had taken to browsing the doctor's bookshelves and flipping through random pages while he waited. But he was feeling as though he could wait no longer.

Just then, he heard the front door open and a few sets of footsteps enter the house. He returned to his chair just in time as the doctor finally returned. There were three men with him and they remained standing by the door to the study.

"Monsieur Dufour," Fontaine began, "I'm afraid I have taken up far too much of your time already. If you wouldn't mind paying me for the jewellery, I must be getting back to my store."

"I think it would be best if you accompanied my friends here," said the doctor, motioning to the three men by the door. "I would very much like to continue this conversation in a more suitable environment."

Fontaine was now not only confused but genuinely perturbed.

"Monsieur, I have no idea what this is about but I really must get back to my shop. May I please take payment for Madame Dufour's purchase?"

The doctor frowned, not out of anger or frustration but more out of pity.

"Monsieur Fontaine, you are ill," he said. "But do not worry, I have had a visit just this morning - in fact, not long before you arrived - from your sister. She has explained the matter to me and I am prepared to help."

"Ill?!" Fontaine exclaimed. "Ill?! I have scarcely been ill a day in my life, let alone with the kind of affliction that you are in the business of treating! And my sister, you say! My sister and I have not spoken in twelve years, which is also the last time she visited Paris."

"My dear Fontaine," the doctor said, "it's ok. She cares about you very much, I can tell. You will be treated with the utmost dignity and we will figure out how to get you back to normal as quickly as possible."

With that, he nodded to the three men by the door and they began to approach Monsieur Fontaine.

"Now, you listen to me doctor," he said, now thoroughly agitated and raising his voice. "I don't know who these men are or where you intend to continue our conversation, but I can tell you right now that I am not going anywhere, with anybody! May I suggest that you clear this up immediately with your wife. Madame Dufour can explain the whole matter. She was in my shop two days ago and arranged the entire purchase. If you were not agreeable to her decision, or she went behind your back, so be it. I will take back the jewellery and we will chalk the whole thing up to a rocky first year of marriage, eh? But as for this madness about my sister and some mysterious illness, I can assure you that you are gravely mistaken."

"No, Monsieur," the doctor replied, "unfortunately it is you who are mistaken. You see, I have no wife. I have never been

18

married and have no plans of becoming so in the foreseeable future."

Fontaine froze as he stared the doctor in the eye. His mouth moved slightly but he did not make a sound for half a minute at least. The doctor stared back with a look that communicated, 'See? You know what I'm saying is true, don't you?' Then the jeweller started speaking again.

"But that is nonsense, sheer nonsense! I saw Madame not five minutes before I entered your office!" he exclaimed. "I sat with her in the lounge, she said you were on a call and would be with me shortly, then she excused herself to get ready for an afternoon engagement. She even took the parcel with her!"

"What parcel?" the doctor asked. "Wait, a 'delivery' of merchandise from your shop, I suppose?"

"Of course! I always make it a point to hand-deliver such large orders for my customers."

"Always, you say?"

"Yes indeed, always!"

"I'm afraid you are once again mistaken, Monsieur," Dufour replied. "I am not sure who met you at the door but it has only been myself and my maid at home this morning. Your sister was here, of course, but we finished before you arrived. And as it happens, I had it from her that hand-delivery is not a service you approve of."

"Again with my sister!" shouted Fontaine. "I have told you already, I have not seen her in twelve years! She lives in Nice and hates Paris. And I can assure you as well that if she had decided to visit the city, she certainly would have nothing to do with me or my business!"

The doctor did not want Fontaine to get further out of hand, so he nodded again to the three men and two of them took him by his arms.

"Release me at once!" he cried.

"I'm sorry, Monsieur," the doctor replied, "but I cannot do that. You need help, Fontaine, and I will see to it that you get the very best."

The men escorted the jeweller out of the study and the echo of his protestations filled the entryway. The maid watched from the top of the stairs as the men led him outside, down the front steps, and restrained him in the back of their car.

Dufour stood in the doorway and remarked to the maid, "This is serious indeed, Daphne. For a man to be able to spin such elaborate tales and appear to believe them with complete confidence... and to compose himself with such a rational demeanour... I must confess, I have little hope of seeing him cured."

"It's terrifying, Monsieur" replied the maid.

The doctor shook his head and turned to walk back to his office.

"And what have you been up to all this time, Daphne?" he asked the maid. Dufour had always treated her more like a co-worker than hired help.

"Oh, nothing so exciting," she replied. "The man's sister, Madame Moreau, had asked to use our toilet on her way out. I showed her to the door and along the way, entirely by accident, she knocked over one of Monsieur's vases in the hallway. Poor thing, she was still so emotional that I think she was somewhat unaware of her surroundings. I spent a while tidying up after she left. In fact, I must have been so distracted by it that I did not even hear Monsieur Fontaine knock on the door. He appears to have shown himself in I suppose."

"Men in such a state," Dufour said, "they begin to lose their sense of propriety. Letting himself in and making himself at home in our lounge are the least of his problems!"

They both stifled a laugh, shook their heads, and returned to their work.

As the car carrying Monsieur Fontaine pulled away, across the street, on a bench beneath a beautiful chestnut tree that was now in bloom, sat a woman in a red beret, holding a small parcel wrapped in brown paper. When the car had vanished out of sight, she got up and strolled down the sidewalk in the opposite direction, whistling and running her fingers through a few low-hanging blossoms as she went.

Chapter 2

Venice
May 1925

"Signorina Haslewood! So lovely to see you again!" The waitress leaned down and exchanged a kiss on each cheek with a woman sitting at one of the café's outdoor tables.

"Maria, I have missed you!" replied the woman. "And I have not had a good cup of coffee or a quality pastry since I last saw you." The two women laughed and squeezed one another's hands briefly as they continued with a few more pleasantries.

"You have been travelling for work again, I presume?" asked Maria.

"I have," the woman replied.

"You must forgive me, Signorina Haslewood, but I have forgotten what exactly you do...?"

"I have told you before, Maria," the woman said, "you must call me Scarlet. I am not your employer."

"Oh yes, of course Sign--" Maria caught herself, smiled, and continued, "Scarlet!"

"And I am in the fashion business."

"That must be very exciting, I would think," the waitress replied. "Far more exciting than brewing coffee and baking bread!"

"Not necessarily," Scarlet replied. "Have you never considered how perfectly miraculous the powers of a finely brewed shot of espresso and a melt-in-your-mouth piece of brioche can be?"

Maria let out a surprised laugh. "I'm afraid I haven't," she said, "but I certainly like the idea."

"It's true," Scarlet continued. "The ideal coffee with the ideal pastry can wake you up and prepare you for the day ahead, or it can calm you down and settle you at the end of a particularly stressful one. The hope of its enjoyment can get you through a busy morning, or you can give in and steal away to the nearest café for a few minutes and reignite your soul with a spark of flour and butter. Yes, good coffee and good pastry transport us. They are gifts from above, Maria!" she said, glancing up briefly at the beautiful blue sky, then turning back to the waitress with a smile.

"You are a very charming woman, my dear," replied Maria. "You know how to speak to people, don't you?"

Scarlet shook her head. "If one is speaking a truth they know well, one doesn't need to think too deeply about how to say it," she replied.

"Well, you have inspired me my friend," said Maria, "so I shall return in a few moments with some heavenly gifts for you. Only, you must tell me where they have taken you once you are finished."

The two smiled at one another and laughed again, then the waitress went back inside the café. In reality, Maria was not only the waitress. She and her husband owned the small but exceptional Café Riparo that sat a stone's throw from the Piazza San Marco. Besides their coffee, they were known by the locals for their buttery brioche, perfect panettone, and sublime sfogliatelle, the latter of which were Scarlet's favourite.

23

A few minutes after she had left the table, Maria returned with an almond and chocolate-filled sfogliatella and a cappuccino with a thin layer of the most velvety foam on top. Scarlet savoured their appearance for a moment before biting into the pastry. It was still warm and the chocolate filling was perfectly gooey, being neither too runny nor too firm. The almond filled her senses and the chocolate made her whole body feel at ease. A sip of the cappuccino rounded off the experience of the first bite.

However, before she was able to take her second, Scarlet heard someone calling her name.

"Miss Haslewood! Miss Haslewood! You are back in town I see!"

Scarlet turned towards the voice and saw Signora Rinaldi making her way down the street. She was an older woman of about seventy-eight, who was still very active despite a limp which she offset with the use of a cane. Today she was carrying her grocery bag, which she had made herself and which was probably older than Scarlet. A loaf of bread and several stalks of celery peered over the top.

"Yes, I returned just a few days ago," Scarlet replied. "And how have you been, Signora Rinaldi?"

"I have been well! Very well!" the woman replied. "And you are looking as young and beautiful as ever, Miss Haslewood!"

"You are too kind, Signora."

"Have you met any young and handsome men in your travels my dear?" asked the woman, as if this were something the two had planned to discuss upon her return.

Scarlet gave her a crooked smile and tilted her head a little to the side, obviously having fielded questions of this sort from her before.

"Plenty!" she replied, "Shall I bring one back for you next time?"

Signora Rinaldi laughed. "He would be most disappointed, I am sure!"

"Nonsense, Signora," Scarlet replied. "You are as captivating now as ever. I have seen pictures, remember? Time has been kind to you! I only hope it will be as generous with me."

"Well, you have many years to wonder," said the woman, who had by now made herself comfortable at the table. Scarlet feared that neither her coffee nor the sfogliatella would be quite as warm the next time she was able to taste them.

Changing the subject, Signora Rinaldi continued, "I have a small matter I need to speak with you about my dear."

"Of course, please feel free."

"It is about your rooms," she said. "I need to know if you will be staying on after June. We had agreed upon twelve months and I can hardly believe that it is now already May! As you know, my building is a very desirable location and I often have potential tenants knocking on my door to see if anything is coming available."

Scarlet nodded knowingly and said, "Yes, I see. I certainly wouldn't want to inconvenience you. I am nearly certain that I will be staying on but can I just confirm this with you in a day or so?"

"Oh no, my dear," the woman replied, "you may take a few days to think about it. If you could just let me know sometime next week perhaps?"

"Absolutely, that will be no problem."

"Excellent, excellent!"

Despite the matter having been resolved rather quickly, Signora Rinaldi engaged Scarlet in another fifteen minutes of conversation that included everything from the weather she missed while she was out of town, to government corruption, to the shocking state of the celery at the local grocer. None of it required a response, so Scarlet was able to take a few polite sips of her coffee in the process. Eventually the woman seemed to run out of topics of interest and got up from the table.

"Well, it has been lovely to catch up with you, Miss Haslewood! A pleasure, as always!" she said.

"And you, Signora Rinaldi," replied Scarlet, "I have missed you these past weeks. I am glad to see that you are still as I remember you."

"Oh, don't worry my dear. There's no fear of that changing anytime soon!"

And with that, Scarlet rose up and gave the woman a hug before she was finally left alone with her now cold pastry.

Just then, Maria came out of the café with a plate in her hand.

"I could not help but notice that Signora Rinaldi was outside. I thought perhaps you might need this." She set the plate down on the table. On it was a fresh sfogliatella, still warm from the oven. "We wouldn't want your heavenly 'trip' to be cut short now, would we?"

Scarlet sighed with relief and thanked Maria more than once.

"And don't forget," Maria said as she left, not looking back as she said it but only raising her right hand and waving her index finger back and forth, "I want to know where you've been before you leave!"

Scarlet breathed in the wonderful smells and then had all the pleasure of another first bite.

Scaletta's was the finest hat shop in Italy north of Rome. And if you ever forgot this fact, all you had to do was visit the shop and Signor Scaletta would remind you. His family had been selling various kinds of cranial accoutrements for seven generations, from styles by famous designers to custom pieces made on site.

"Ah, Signorina, you are ready for a new hat already?" said the jovial milliner. He was a kind-hearted man of about sixty-five who enjoyed getting to know his customers as much as, if not more than, making a sale. In his mind, the latter would follow the former in due course if it were meant to be.

"I would be very suspicious of anyone that felt they had too many hats. Wouldn't you, Signor Scaletta?" Scarlet gave him a wink as she turned to look at the new designs hanging on the wall near the entrance.

"Oh, Signorina," said the man, "as I have told you from the first time we spoke, 'Signora Scarlet Scaletta' has a beautiful ring to it..." The man smiled and returned her wink. Normally, the almost forty years of difference between them would make such a comment feel rather creepy. But Scarlet had gotten to know Signor Scaletta over the last twelve months and had even been to his home on occasion for meals with his family. He was a very happily married man and this was only something of a game they played whenever she was shopping for a new hat. In actual fact, he had come to feel for her as though she were his daughter, because as it happened, Signor Scaletta had lost a daughter only two months before he first met Scarlet. Though they did not see each other more than once or twice a month, she had helped to fill the void just a little.

After some small talk, he enquired about how she had been.

"I have been well," Scarlet said. "I was out of the country for a few weeks but even though it was for work, it was still a very nice time. I met some interesting people and even had a few adventures along the way!"

"I am happy for you that you get to travel so much," the man said. "It is perhaps the best education a young person can receive, simply to see the world and learn about people."

"I could not agree more," Scarlet replied.

"And I trust your last hat served you well on the journey?"

"It certainly did! I have loved it since the day I picked it up from your shop. You tailored it perfectly. It fits like a dream!"

"Wonderful!" Scaletta said, genuinely pleased with a job well done and a satisfied customer, especially Scarlet. "I don't think I have ever made a hat of any kind in a richer, deeper red. And I am glad it fits so well. Berets can sometimes be tricky to keep on your head!"

"Oh no, not a problem at all," said Scarlet, "it never moved an inch. Not even when I was running from the gendarmes down the Champs-Élysée!"

The man laughed very heartily. "Oh, of course! Because they wanted to have a drink with you, I imagine!"

They exchanged a few more thoughts on hats in general, as well as more speculation about what Scarlet might be likely to do depending on the hat she was wearing. Finally she asked about one particular hat that was hanging behind the counter.

"Ah, this one," the man started, "this one is a design I am very proud of. It obviously follows the classic men's fedora but the brim has been widened and the crown lowered in order to give it a more feminine appearance. These changes are not exactly new, but I have been experimenting with dyes and various fabrics. I am extremely happy with the colouring I have achieved, as well as the very fine ribbon-work that forms the band."

The hat was not a single colour but had a marbled appearance. Scarlet had never seen anything like it. It was a deep, deep blue, with very tasteful streaks of white swirling along the sides of the crown and over the brim. The blue had bled slightly into the white so that the streaks really did appear like natural occurrences as opposed to discreet designs that had been painted onto a surface. The band was a very delicate ribbon in a muted gold colour, not too wide to overpower the hat. Sparsely scattered flecks of gold created the appearance of stars across a night sky, as when on a very clear night the Milky Way becomes barely visible.

"It's," Scarlet began, but could not finish her thought. After a minute or so, she concluded with, "magnificent."

"I am glad you approve!" said Signor Scaletta.

Scarlet tried it on more than once, alternating between looking at herself in the mirror and holding the hat in her hand, examining every intriguing detail.

"Well, I am quite upset with you, Scaletta."

"Have you found a defect?" the man asked, a little concerned.

"On the contrary," replied Scarlet, "I am upset because now I must have this hat. You know it's not my usual colours but this is too stunning to allow anyone else to have it. I must have it! I must wear it!"

The man laughed his hearty laugh once again and then began fishing out a hatbox from beneath his counter.

"No, no," Scarlet interrupted him, "you won't have to box it up. I will wear it out!"

"But you will still need a place to store it, my dear."

"Why? I can't imagine ever taking it off!"

Having paid Signor Scaletta for the hat, she returned to the mirror again to make sure she found the perfect angle at which to wear it. She played with it for a moment but then decided she would need far too long to get it just right, so she left it as it was.

"Thank you so much, my friend!" she said to the man.

"The pleasure is all mine, my love," replied Scaletta. "I only hope we have not found the last hat you shall ever buy!"

Scarlet smiled at him as she turned to leave the store, touching the brim of her new hat as she did and saying with another wink, "Signor, don't be silly."

———————————

A few days later, the sky was overcast and a light rain was falling. Despite the weather, Scarlet had gone for a walk in the early evening. The rain had never bothered her. In fact, she often preferred to walk in the rain rather than the sun. There was something about the atmosphere it created, between the rhythm of the droplets, the sheen on the paving stones, and the splish-splosh of the puddles beneath her feet.

Her walk led her past an old church, not that passing old churches was particularly unusual on an evening walk in Venice but this was one that she had been curious about. There was nothing overly ornate about it, nothing historically significant either, at least as far as she was aware. And perhaps that was why she was curious about it - because no one else was. It wasn't on any tours, no maps pointed it out, nobody stopped to admire it. So that evening she decided to go inside.

After she had yanked on the creaky wooden door, clopped along the stone threshold with her heels, then let the same door slam behind her, she suddenly realised that there was a service in progress. Despite the mini racket she had made, no one looked up and the priest was unfazed. He continued with his reading as she sat down in the back pew and took off her wet scarf.

"...all thy billows and thy waves passed over me. Then I said, 'I am cast out of thy sight, yet will I look again toward thy holy temple.' I went down to the bottoms of the mountains, the earth with her bars was about me forever, yet hast thou brought up my life from corruption, O Lord my God."

As he finished this line, he spoke a solemn "Amen" and the congregation, which, including Scarlet, numbered about seven or eight, responded in kind with another "Amen." Then the priest flipped over several pages in his book and said, "For our final reading, the opening verses of the forty-sixth Psalm. 'God is our refuge and strength, a very present help in trouble...'"

Scarlet was trying to show respect for the priest's reading but she was also trying to look around the room at the building and the people. The stone walls looked tired and worn, though she felt that it was a good tired, resulting from use and not neglect. The ceiling was a beautiful network of wooden supports and rafters, most of which looked similarly worn, as though they had spent their early days buffeted by the sea as the hull of some great ship before they found their true calling. Most churches she was familiar with had some piece of stained glass some-

31

where in the building but this one had none. The only decoration was an inscription on the wall to the left of where the priest was performing the service. It was in Latin: nunc dimittis servum tuum Domine secundum verbum tuum in pace. Scarlet wasn't sure what it meant but she felt that it added a certain gravitas (one Latin word she did know) to the room.

Just as she had started wondering about the people in the other pews, she heard the priest saying, "The Lord be with you," and the congregation responding, "And also with you." She caught on just in time to join them with the final "you." Then the service ended and the people were slowly shuffling out of their seats. Most of them were older, at least thirty years older than her, Scarlet guessed. She got to see all their faces as they passed by her seat in the last pew. Every one of them smiled at her, even if it was only a quick look. Then the priest disappeared through a side-door behind the inscription and Scarlet was alone. She tried to remember something of the reading, partially because she wanted to savour the experience and partially out of guilt for not only having barged in partway through the service but then having been distracted by the architecture and missing most of what she was present for. All she could remember was "God is our refuge... a very present help in trouble." She repeated it a couple of times in her head and then felt satisfied that somehow, somewhere, the priest was pleased.

Scarlet left the church and started walking back to her apartment. However, before she arrived there, she had one scheduled stop to make.

She walked along the waterfront on the Riva degli Schiavoni, an area that was busy during the day but virtually empty at night. A small café had left a few of its tables and chairs set up outside despite having long since closed for the day. A man sat at one of the tables, his right leg crossed over his left, arms folded, staring off over the water into the night.

Scarlet sat down at the table with him.

"The water washing against the brick and stone, that is the heartbeat of Venice. Don't you agree, Miss Haslewood?"

"You would know better than me."

"Huh, I suppose so," the man reflected, "I guess fifty-three years in a place and you should have some sense of how and why it ticks, eh?"

Scarlet lifted her satchel up to the table, set it down flat, and began to unbuckle it.

"So, what've you got for me tonight?" the man asked.

"Mostly sixes and sevens, maybe one or two eights."

"That'll do," he said. "The average stuff is easier to move anyway. When you start talking nines and tens, you need to be extra careful about putting them on display."

Scarlet pulled out a couple of boxes wrapped in brown paper. She gave them to the man and he placed them on his lap, resting his hand on top of them.

"Don't you want to look at them?" Scarlet asked.

"That's not necessary," he replied, "I know you have good taste, Signorina." He reached into the inside pocket of his coat and pulled out an envelope that he slid across the damp table to her. It got a little wet but she didn't bother to inspect it. She slipped it into her satchel and then stood up.

"Aren't you going to look at it?" the man asked.

"That's not necessary," Scarlet replied, "I know where you live, Signor."

The man let out a surprised laugh then nodded goodbye to her as she walked past him and headed back to her apartment.

The last ten minutes of her walk home was very cold. The rain, even though it had been fairly light, had caught up with her and she started to feel a chill. She drew her scarf tighter about her head and neck and picked up her pace.

Chapter 3

Venice
October 1925

Scarlet had gotten up early to make sure she had enough time for everything she needed to do that day. Tomorrow she was leaving for another trip. Although she had been coming and going often over the last year and a half, this time was different. She hoped that these next few months would be a landmark season in her life - and she wasn't sure if she would be returning to Venice when it was all over.

Her life in Venice typically involved late nights, even later mornings, and slow afternoons. After a year and a half, it had started to become something of a 'hometown' for her - that place where she could return during those days between the days, those downtimes that always outnumber the exciting ones. Scarlet had only planned to stay for a few weeks in the summer of 1924 but she had felt something here, something that stirred her. Romantic canals, beautiful architecture, rich culture... Maria, the Scaletta family, and even her sometimes wearisome landlady, Signora Rinaldi. All of it had sort of crept up on her without warning. And she wasn't sure she wanted it to end.

She was trying her best not to get bogged down in emotions as she prepared to head out for the day. Just before she left, she made a quick stop in front of the mirror that was hanging by her front door, to make sure her hat was sitting right. It was the blue and white one she had bought from Signor Scaletta and over the past summer it had quickly become her favourite.

Since she was up so early, she felt entitled to a trip to Café Riparo before running her errands. Despite the fact that Scarlet had spent nearly the entire summer in Venice, and had stopped by the café almost everyday, the familiarity had not diminished Maria's warmth and hospitality. She made Scarlet feel like she was a princess deigning to walk amongst the commoners, though never with vain flattery. Maria was one of those special people that makes you feel as though you have done them some great kindness simply by receiving the kindness they have shown you. She seemed to prove the maxim that it is more blessed to give than to receive.

"Ah, mia cara! How are you this morning?" she said as Scarlet arrived at the café.

"I'm well," she replied, "and how are you today Maria?" After a brief hug, Scarlet sat down at one of the tables in the front window.

"Better now that you are here," Maria said. "It's still very early but I'm already worn out for the day! We had a very late night last night. It was my cousin's daughter's thirteenth birthday. It was a lovely evening but a baker has no time to recover in the morning. The baking cannot wait. Sometimes I think it is worse than a newborn baby! But then comes Scarlet, mia stellina, and the day seems brighter already!"

Maria was about twenty years older than Scarlet and while they had become close friends, she also sometimes played the part of the doting big sister. Scarlet enjoyed it more than she would have admitted.

Without asking what she wanted, Maria went back behind

the counter and began making a cappuccino. She pulled a warm brioche from the wire racks where they were displayed and spooned some freshly made crème pâtissière on the side. When the coffee was ready, she brought everything out.

"The crème is for a batch of éclairs that are not quite done yet but you must try it. It's pistachio. I think it will go well with the chocolate in the brioche. But then, what doesn't go well with chocolate?"

"Glorious!" said Scarlet. Maria went back to work and Scarlet tore off the top of the brioche, spooned a big dollop of pistachio crème pâtissière on top, and was dead to the world for the next fifteen minutes at least.

When she had finished, Maria returned to the table.

"So, my dear," she said, "what are you up to today?"

"Nothing special," replied Scarlet, "just a bit of shopping perhaps." She had not confided in Maria about her upcoming trip, though she had usually kept her in the loop about her comings and goings, at least generally speaking. But this time she didn't want any goodbyes.

"Well, enjoy your day and if you run out of energy, those éclairs should be ready a little later this afternoon!"

"I should be ok," Scarlet said, giving her another hug and kissing her once on each cheek. "You always manage to fill me up just enough."

Maria laughed and then said, "See you tomorrow!" as she went back to work. Assuming, not asking.

Scarlet only smiled and waved as she started to walk away, glancing back once or twice before she turned down the next alley.

"Signorina, please forgive me for asking but why would anyone want to cover up such healthy, full hair like yours? That rich, deep black. It would fetch a high price if it were in my shop!"

"I appreciate your concern, Signor," Scarlet replied, "but have no fear, this is not a permanent change. I am attending something of a ball. Well, more of a private affair amongst a group of friends. Anyway, some of them had the rather silly idea that we should all come in costume! I must admit, I'm not fond of these sorts of things... but I do love my friends."

"Ah, I see, of course," said the owner of the wig shop. His usual clientele were a fair bit older than Scarlet, or those who were ill or had suffered some kind of accident. It was actually a relief to be selling a wig for a more joyful occasion.

"Well, what colour were you thinking of?"

"I would be willing to consider a few options," Scarlet replied. "The right one will jump out at me, I'm sure."

She tried on several wigs before eventually settling on an auburn one. It was long and pulled to one side, the gentle waves twisting around one another and then folding beneath themselves so that the ends were invisible.

"This is perfect!" she said.

"Now I do sell a piece that I think complements this style particularly well," the man said. He went over to a small display of costume jewellery he kept in the back corner of the store and returned with a very unique headband. "Please, allow me," he said, and he attached it to the wig while Scarlet was still wearing it.

"It's stunning!"

The headband was actually more like a very thin tiara with several layers of low-hanging swags that ran from the right side to just a little past the back of the head, each tastefully adorned with rosettes and faux sapphires.

"Truly, Signor," Scarlet said, "this is far more than I hoped for."

"I am happy to help," the man said. "You're going to be the centre of attention at your party!"

"What?" Scarlet replied, then caught herself and said, "Oh, yes, definitely! My friends will be very jealous, I'm sure!"

The cleaners, her favourite stationer, and a shoe store were all crammed into her day before Scarlet arrived home in the early evening to finish packing.

With the exception of a brief trip to Berlin, she hadn't left Venice at all since she had returned from the 'incident' with Monsieur Fontaine last April. Scarlet preferred not to think of such transactions as 'jobs', and especially not as 'cons'. To her they were works of art. Like a composer arranging pieces for an orchestra, she was sensitive to the qualities of each individual instrument. She wrote parts for them that suited their temperament and highlighted their strengths. She gave them each their moments to shine and then brought them together for a touching harmony or a resounding crescendo. And to ensure they followed their brief, she was ever the conductor, maintaining the tempo and signalling each new movement.

Her upcoming trip was to include what was by far her most ambitious design yet. The scene in Paris last April was fairly straightforward. It was something that had taken comparatively little planning, maybe two months, and was primarily aimed at netting her some easy money to provide for a mostly restful summer. The man from the table on the Riva degli Schiavoni was Signor Luzzatto, a local businessman with a string of jewellery stores, half of whose inventory was stolen property. Scarlet felt like the whole enterprise was rather crude, especially his numbering system, reducing such beautiful craftsmanship to "5's, 6's, etc," as a way to indicate what quality of items he was looking for. It all felt very wooden and mechanical, lacking a certain elegance, like a massive smash-and-grab instead of the way she liked to operate. Scarlet felt a bit foolish even being a small part of it and she avoided getting involved beyond selling a few pieces here and there just to supplement her income, though Luzzatto had made her plenty of offers. In contrast to the Fontaine affair, her next 'arrangement' had been a year and a half in the making, with this last summer in Venice giving her space to reflect on the details and make sure all the angles were covered. If all went as planned, the result would mean never having to deal with another Luzzatto ever again.

She would be travelling by train on the Simplon Orient Express, leaving tomorrow afternoon and arriving the following morning in Paris, which was only her first stop. She would be there for roughly four or five weeks before taking the same train to Calais and then the ferry to England. After another five or six weeks in London, she planned to return to Paris. There were several variables that were simply outside the realm of planning and might keep her a little longer in either place but that was to be expected. At the end of it all, she hoped that she would be able to return to Venice.

At the moment, her bed was covered in clothing with more still hanging in her closet. She also had to sort through her beloved hats and substantial collection of shoes (though Scarlet would have considered it barely sufficient). Her desk was strewn with photographs, notebooks, and three passports from different countries alongside small stacks of corresponding currency. There were also about ten letters she had written. They were essentially rough drafts that formed the basis of the five she would be sending soon after she arrived in Paris. Underneath the papers there was a stiletto, its handle made from a beautiful ivory inlaid with two rubies on each side. Scarlet always brought it with her on her trips. Though she had never used it for anything more than opening mail, it made her feel a little safer.

The hardest part was not being sure if she would be back for the rest of her things, so she needed to choose carefully but also practically, keeping in mind what would be required over the next few months. Whatever was left behind, Signora Rinaldi would probably sell or donate once she realised she was gone. Either way, Scarlet had prepaid her rent until the end of February, so her things were safe at least that long. As for what remained to be packed, her luggage consisted of one large case, one medium case, an average-sized steamer trunk, and a generously-sized hatbox, all of which combined might accommodate about half of her wardrobe, not including the shoes. It was going to be a long night.

Scarlet was finally able to lie down around six o'clock in the morning. Her mind and body were vibrating from the stress and activity of the last twenty-four hours as she tried to breathe deeply and relax herself. She hoped that the sun wouldn't rise high enough to peak in around the curtains until after she had fallen asleep.

Without even realising that she had drifted off, Scarlet awoke to the sound of her alarm at ten o'clock. She had about an hour until the two valets she had hired should arrive to attend to her luggage. The train didn't leave until three but she wanted to be early.

She was understandably groggy and made her way into the bathroom to start getting ready. She splashed cold water on her face a few times before rubbing her eyes and then looking in the mirror.

"Well, mia stellina, it's time," she said to herself. "Let's go sell the *Mona Lisa*."

Chapter 4

The Simplon Orient Express 1457 to 1920 hours

Scarlet had been so engrossed in her packing, and then fallen asleep for the entire morning, so that she hadn't even realised that an *acqua alta* had occurred. It was fortunate that she had allowed herself three and a half hours to get to the station because she ended up needing almost all of it. It wasn't an extreme *acqua alta*, so only a portion of the city was flooded, but she did have to pass over some of the gangways that had been set up in order to help facilitate the morning commute. Scarlet had been in Venice long enough to have seen these events before but it was always a little unsettling. It really did make you feel like the city was sinking, a sensation that one normally wouldn't associate with a traditional jungle of concrete, stone, brick, and mortar.

When she arrived at the station, she had another surprise.

"Signorina Haslewood, I presume?" asked the conductor. She had been easy to locate as there were only three passengers scheduled to board at Venice and the other two were men.

"That's correct," Scarlet replied.

"Signorina, I am very sorry but there has been a terrible mistake."

Scarlet squinted slightly. "Mistake?"

The conductor proceeded to explain to her that there had been a mix-up in Belgrade and that her compartment to Paris was no longer available.

"Unavailable? How can it be unavailable?" she asked. "But I booked my ticket well over a month ago. I don't understand."

"I cannot understand it myself, Signorina," the conductor replied. "I can only offer my sincerest apology and assure you that every enquiry will be made into the source of the confusion."

Scarlet's schedule for her upcoming trip left only a small cushion for unexpected circumstances. She had not imagined that her compartment being sold out from under her would be one of them.

"As much as I appreciate your sympathy" she said, "I must be in Paris tomorrow morning. Surely there is something that can be done?"

"Let me see if I can accommodate you," the man said. She could see him flicking through some papers in his hands as he walked away from her down the platform. He stopped to speak with another member of the crew but they were too far away for Scarlet to make out what they were saying. She could only see the conductor reach into his pocket, pull out his watch, and check the time. The train was due to depart at 1457 and it was now 1451. Scarlet shook her head in frustration and then paced back and forth a few times as she waited, trying to remain calm.

At 1455, the conductor returned to her with a smile on his face.

"Excellent news, Signorina! I have secured you a compart-ment in one of the cars bound for Calais. Only you must be sure to exit the train at the Gare de Lyon when you arrive in Paris or you shall miss your stop completely."

Scarlet was of course relieved and thanked the man for his help, though not profusely as she still felt that they had merely corrected their own error and not exactly done her some great favour. However, when she was finally shown to her compartment, she realised that they had at least corrected their mistake with interest. This particular car was far more luxurious than any she had been on previously. The compartment had gorgeous wood panelling, a beautiful banquette upholstered in a cream-coloured fabric dotted with emerald green fleurs-de-lis, and an elegant oval mirror mounted above a small wash basin.

"I hope this is acceptable, Signorina," said the conductor. "This is the newest sleeping-car design that is expected to enter regular service in a few years time. This is something of a trial run. You are very lucky to be travelling today, I think!"

Suddenly the annoyance she had felt only a minute ago out on the platform had melted away. She smiled warmly at the conductor.

"Thank you. I think I shall be quite comfortable, Signor."

While the rest of Scarlet's luggage had been loaded into one of the train's fourgons, she had brought the medium case with her into the compartment. She had planned to freshen up and then make her way to the dining-car for some coffee but instead she spent the first half-hour doing little more than staring out the window. Somehow at the same time she was both exhausted and excited, drained and yet full of anticipation. It is a strange mix of emotions and physical responses that comes over one when a journey, long in the making, finally begins.

At around quarter to four she eventually made it to the dining-car. Only one other seat was occupied, so Scarlet sat almost as far away as she could in an effort to enjoy the quiet and avoid conversation. As a general rule, she wasn't antisocial or opposed to friendly small-talk with a stranger. There were always interesting people to meet, and con, on the Simplon Orient. But this afternoon Scarlet wasn't interested in surveying the room for marks or letting the moment take her where it will. She was trying to keep her mind still and focused.

"Good afternoon, Mademoiselle," the restaurant attendant said. He was an older French man, perhaps in his mid-fifties. "Can I bring you some tea or coffee?"

"Coffee, please," Scarlet said.

"I can also offer a small selection of afternoon snacks," the attendant continued. "We have pain au chocolat or butterkuchen, as well as Turkish delight fresh from Istanbul less than three days ago."

"Nothing at the moment, thank you," she replied.

"Very well, ma chère. I will bring your coffee straightaway."

When the coffee had arrived, Scarlet sipped it slowly and returned to staring out the window as she had done from her compartment. The scenery passing by to the rhythm of the train on the tracks was rather mesmerising, so much so that Scarlet hadn't noticed someone sitting down at the table immediately behind her. She only became aware of them when they started speaking to her.

"Interested in a date?" the voice said, in a very clear American accent.

Scarlet was not unaccustomed to being approached by men

but this was certainly a new low as far as she was concerned. She looked to the side, unwilling to acknowledge such barbarism with the courtesy of eye-contact, and said in a very stern voice, "Excuse me?" She wasn't asking, she was telling.

The voice would not be dissuaded however.

"I said," it continued, "are you interested in a date?"

Scarlet realised she would have to be a bit more obvious, since Americans tended to struggle with the more arcane aspects of communication, such as tone of voice.

She set her coffee down with a hint of force and turned halfway round in her chair, prepared to meet the offending party with a withering look. Instead, she found a man staring back at her, his face filled with a humble cheerfulness that caught Scarlet off-guard.

He lifted his right hand to reveal a bag of dried fruit. "Would you like a date? I bought them just before I left Istanbul. They're really quite something." Then, as if to convince her, he popped one into his mouth and smiled as he proceeded to chew it awkwardly, eventually spitting out the pit while Scarlet watched him and remained silent.

'What exactly is going on here?' she thought to herself. Then she decided to respond, partially out of a mild sense of pity.

"No, thank you, I'm quite alright," she said, employing a more civil tone than she had originally intended.

"That's fine," the man said, "I didn't mean to pressure you or anything. I suppose I can't expect everyone to get as excited about things like dried fruit as I do. But if you change your mind, feel free to ask!" He turned back around and faced his own table just in time to receive his cup of coffee from the

French attendant.

"Thank you, my good man!" he said, a little more energetically than Scarlet thought necessary.

She had spent another forty-five minutes or so in the dining-car, finishing two cups of coffee and alternating between thinking about the first things she would need to do when she got to Paris, and how much she already missed the coffee at Café Riparo. Due to its volume, she also learned from the voice behind her just how much it loved pain au chocolat but didn't like the way "that Turkish delight stuff" stuck to its teeth. She consoled herself that at least it wasn't talking to her.

When she had returned to her compartment, she slipped off her shoes and used her luggage as an ottoman as she attempted to get comfortable on the straight-backed banquette. Despite feeling like it would never really happen, before she knew it she had fallen asleep. It was a broken sleep as she woke intermittently to adjust her position or due to some jarring from the tracks, but it was somewhat restful nonetheless.

Eventually the train came to a stop at Milan around seven o'clock. Scarlet and a few other passengers stepped outside onto the platform to stretch their legs and take in some fresh air - as fresh as the air around a train station platform could be. When they boarded the train again, it was time for dinner.

Scarlet went back to her compartment to check her hair and make-up, and also to change her scarf. She had on a black dress she had purchased only a week ago and which she had been looking forward to wearing on her trip. The front of it was embellished with a floral design in the centre, also in black but accented with fine metallic sequins that made it sparkle depending on the light. A fringe, roughly six inches long, picked up where the irregular hemline left off just above the knee. Scarlet loved the way it swayed gracefully as she walked. Her hair was pulled up in a loosely hanging chignon, above which she was wearing a beautiful white silk scarf tied on the left side of her head. As for jewellery, she wore only two pieces that evening: a string of pearls about her neck and a stunning ruby and diamond band on her left index finger - somehow it had failed to find its way from M. Fontaine to Signor Luzzatto.

Scarlet had lost track of the time when she had returned to her compartment to get ready for dinner and was now the last passenger to enter the dining-car.

"Ma chère, may I show you to your seat?" the attendant asked.

"Please," replied Scarlet.

It was a matter of course that one expected to share a table in the dining-car, especially if one was travelling alone. Normally, this didn't bother her. But this evening, Scarlet wasn't happy with the arrangement. It happened that the only seat left was opposite the American and his bag of dates.

"Mademoiselle," the attendant said, as he pulled back the chair and motioned for Scarlet to sit down.

"Merci," she replied, giving him a smile and trying her best to leave the acknowledgement of her table companion to the very last second.

"Ah, we meet again!" the man said.

"I'm not sure we ever met a first time," replied Scarlet, hoping to brush aside their earlier encounter and respond coldly enough to distance herself from any further conversation. But as the words left her mouth, she immediately regretted having provided him with an opening to introduce himself. And he did not fail to capitalise on it.

"Well, allow me to correct the situation," he began. "My name is Thomas White. And you?"

Scarlet answered him reluctantly.

"Dana Greenley."

Chapter 5

The Simplon Orient Express
1921 to 2237 hours

"Delighted to make your acquaintance, Miss Greenley," said Thomas.

Scarlet only nodded and gave him a polite smile, trying to focus on the menu, or her silverware, or her glass, or basically anything other than Thomas. This task became harder once they had ordered their food and the menus were removed.

After a minute or so of silence, Thomas said, "So, Miss Greenley, may I ask what brings you aboard the Simplon Orient this evening?"

"I have always found it to be faster than walking to Paris," replied Scarlet.

"So you have walked from Venice to Paris before then?" replied Thomas with a mischievous smile.

Scarlet raised her eyebrows briefly in acknowledgement of his attempt at breaking the ice. For the moment, she was quite fond of the ice. Her failure to reciprocate with questions as to the nature of his journey did not discourage him from volunteering the information.

"I've just come from Istanbul myself," he said. "Have you ever been there? Lovely city. The Hagia Sophia in particular is simply breathtaking."

Scarlet had been to Istanbul more than once and adored the Hagia Sophia, but she maintained her commitment to minimal conversation and said only, "Yes, it's a very nice place."

"I also enjoyed the archaeological museums," he said. "I suppose I'm a bit of an armchair historian. I haven't had any formal training but I take every chance I get to read about the current work going on in the East, and to visit sites whenever I'm in the region."

Frustratingly, Scarlet was actually finding his conversation rather interesting. She enjoyed history. And what did he mean by 'whenever I'm in the region'? Did he go there often? If so, why? She faltered for a brief moment, just long enough to hear herself ask, "How long were you there?"

"This trip was five weeks," he replied, "but part of it was spent in Aleppo as well."

'Damn him!' Scarlet thought, now terribly curious about what had taken him to Syria.

As if sensing her inner struggle, he shared a little more information.

"I actually work for the rail companies, both here and in America," he said, "so I'm often on the move. And Wagons-Lits is one I work with fairly regularly, so I'm no stranger to the Simplon Orient."

Scarlet was a little confused. Her impression of Thomas from their first encounter was of a fish out of water - the way he spoke to the restaurant attendant, his silly face as he ate that date in front of her. None of it spoke to his being a cultured, well-travelled individual. She had imagined this was his first time in Europe but apparently she was wrong. This unsettled her since she made her living reading people and situations. She was debating about asking another question when their food arrived.

"Monsieur, Mademoiselle," the attendant said as he set their plates in front of them. Dinner was a wonderfully fragrant coq au vin with boiled potatoes.

They had gotten through about half of their meal before Thomas continued the conversation with a question.

"So, Miss Greenley," he began, buttering a slice of the perfectly crusty baguette that had been placed between them, "you don't sound like you're originally from Venice. If you don't mind my asking, where is home for you?"

Scarlet was actually American as well, but she had been living in Europe for the past seven years and had developed one of those neutral, some might say 'mangled', accents that develops in such circumstances where interactions with people from your native land are limited. Though she had made it a point from her first months in Europe to become as Continental as possible, she had also become adept at playing various roles for her work. Dana Greenley was one of a handful of persistent identities she had developed for use in certain circumstances. It was her default role, so to speak, typically employed to protect herself from accidentally sharing something that might make her vulnerable.

"I was born in Chichester, in the south of England," she said.

"You'll forgive me for saying it but you don't have a very strong English accent."

"When I was six, my father passed away," she continued. "My mother couldn't raise all five of us, so when I was seven she sent me and one of my brothers to live with her sister in America."

"Ah. And where was that?"

"New Haven, Connecticut. I was there until a few years ago when I decided to move back to England to be close to my mother who had become ill. Unfortunately, she passed away last year."

"Oh dear," replied Thomas, setting down his knife and fork to focus more fully upon her. "I'm so sorry for your loss."

"Thank you," said Scarlet. His compassion was so genuine, his eyes so warm, that it made her feel for a moment as though she had actually experienced the things with which Thomas was empathising. In one brief moment, he had breathed more life into her Dana Greenley than Scarlet had in years of acting the part.

They finished their meals and the restaurant attendant returned to clear their plates.

"Would Monsieur or Mademoiselle like coffee or tea?" the man asked.

"Yes, please," said Scarlet rather eagerly, "I'd like some coffee, thank you."

"None for me, thank you," replied Thomas.

Scarlet let slip a surprised look but quickly returned to a more even expression.

"I have always enjoyed the Simplon Orient's coffee," she said. It was a lie but she was making the boldest move she was willing to make at this point to keep him at the table a little longer.

"It is fine stuff," he replied, "but I'm afraid I need to make an early night of it. I have a stack of papers to look over to prepare for business in England the day after tomorrow and I really should make a start before bed."

Scarlet only smiled and nodded in agreement.

"It was lovely to make your acquaintance," Thomas said, pausing before adding, "for the first time, of course," with that same mischievous smile.

Scarlet couldn't stop herself laughing just a little.

"Good evening, Mr White," she said as he left the table.

She spent the next hour or so alone, sipping her coffee, occasionally eavesdropping on her fellow passengers, and trying to sort out her feelings after her conversation with Mr. White.

Scarlet had long ago resigned herself to the fact that her 'activities', so to speak, had consequences for other people. She was not ignorant of the fact that Monsieur Fontaine would have a terrible time restoring his reputation and the reputation of his business. And he was certainly not the first. For Scarlet, however, who they were before or after was largely irrelevant. They were as blank canvasses onto which she would paint her scene and afterward discard. She formed no attachments beyond what was required to carry out her plans, but even then the attachment was more about the appearance of attachment and never anything truly meaningful.

Tonight, however, for the first time in a very long time, she had felt guilt as she lied to Mr. White. She had been moved by his interest in her - or rather, in Dana - and although she did nothing to hurt him, she felt as though she had trespassed upon something sacred. She was imagining the priest from the little chapel in Venice giving her a thoroughly disapproving look.

At this point the restaurant attendant appeared next to her and asked if she would like another cup of coffee.

"No, thank you, Monsieur," she replied.

She took the opportunity of the interruption to shake off her thoughts and clear her mind. She had too much to think about and too many details to stay on top of over the next few months to worry about the priest's opinion, or Mr. White and his love of dried fruit.

Scarlet got up from the table and returned to her compartment to review her notes and go over her plans for the next few days.

Around quarter past ten, Scarlet was ready to lie down and asked one of the attendants to prepare her bed. Her compartment was at the end of her car, so she strolled along the passageway to the opposite end while she waited. She was looking out the window trying to make out any stars in the sky when the attendant interrupted her.

"Mademoiselle, I, um..." The man was younger, maybe in his mid-twenties, and he had a very nervous expression. He continued, "I am so sorry, Mademoiselle, but I cannot get the bed in your compartment to fold out."

Scarlet raised an eyebrow. "Are you serious?"

"I am so sorry," he repeated.

"Well, is there someone else that can fix it?"

"My colleague is bringing the matter to the conductor as we speak, Mademoiselle."

Scarlet looked back out the window and sighed, then told the attendant that she would wait in the dining-car until the situation had been resolved.

About fifteen minutes later, three of the train's crewmen

found her and announced the bad news.

"Mademoiselle, it appears as though your banquette is faulty."

"Faulty? What do you mean faulty?"

"The hinges have not been assembled correctly, meaning that it is impossible to fold out your bed," said the one that was obviously the leader of the small team.

"Wait a minute," Scarlet said, shaking her head in confusion, "Fold out? I thought single compartments just needed the rear cushions removed? What are you folding?"

"It's a new design."

Scarlet rolled her eyes, then muttered quietly to herself as she looked down at the floor. "You've got to be joking."

"Again, I'm very --"

"I know, I know. Ok, so then where am I to sleep?"

The three men looked at one another and then told her that they would have to speak with the conductor.

After a couple of minutes, the conductor himself came to discuss the matter.

"Ma chère, I don't know where to begin. This is a most unfortunate circumstance."

"Yes yes, I know," said Scarlet, less concerned about everyone's apologetic sentiments and more concerned with getting some sleep. "So what can be done?"

"That is the thing, Miss Haslewood," the conductor replied, "there is nothing that can be done. I have no available compartments. The train is completely full until Paris."

Despite the fact that earlier she had dozed off for a while on the banquette, Scarlet knew she wouldn't be able to sleep on it for long. Certainly not an entire night. After her long day of errands yesterday, followed by very little sleep and a difficult journey to the station through the flooding that morning in Venice, she had been looking forward to a good night's rest on the train.

"Very well then," she said to the conductor, "can I at least request some coffee if I'm to spend the night awake?"

"Anything you want," said the conductor, "please, do not hesitate to ask! We will make every effort to make the night as comfortable as possible for you!"

"Thank you," she replied. Then Scarlet laughed and said, "I suppose at the very least I've helped Wagons-Lits with the testing phase of their new sleeping-car design, eh Monsieur?"

The conductor laughed and then looked serious again, not sure if he should laugh with her or continue apologising.

"The company certainly owes you a debt of gratitude, ma chère."

Chapter 6

Brooklyn, New York
August 24, 1911

"Gina, have you seen this story coming out of the Louvre?"

"I don't think so."

"Apparently," started the man, pausing as he flipped through the pages of the newspaper to find the right column. When he had found it, he continued, "Apparently one of their important paintings has gone missing."

"How did that happen?" asked a young girl who was sitting opposite him. They were both seated in matching mustard-coloured wingback chairs, reading quietly to themselves but enjoying each other's company. The girl looked up from her copy of Andrew Lang's *Red Fairy Book* and added, "Did they misplace it?"

"Seems as though someone has simply walked off with it," the man replied with a slight laugh.

"Really? But don't they have guards, and doors with locks for that sort of thing?"

"One would think so. I guess the staff just showed up on a Monday morning and the thing was gone. They've shut the museum down and the police are investigating it."

"What's the painting of?" the girl asked, now glancing back and forth between the man and her book.

"I don't suppose you've heard of it," he said, "but the

French call it *La Joconde*. It's a portrait of a Renaissance woman by Leonardo da Vinci. In English, we call it the *Mona Lisa*."

"Hmm. That doesn't sound familiar. Is it worth a lot of money, do you think?"

"Well now, there's the rub, eh," the man responded, setting down his paper on his lap.

"What do you mean?" she asked, mimicking him and placing her book on her leg.

"For this fellow - or fellows, perhaps - who took it, the value won't matter much now that the theft has made it into the papers halfway around the world!"

"Why's that?"

"Well," the man continued, "the real value in anything is only whatever someone is willing to give you for it, isn't it? I can tell you my jacket is worth three million dollars but if nobody out there is willing to buy it for that price, then what does that really matter?"

"But aren't paintings by da Vinci *actually* valuable?" the girl asked. "And your jacket has a hole in the sleeve."

"Oh, of course they are. But who's going to give this chap ten million dollars - or ten thousand! - for a painting that the whole world is looking for? It's not like he can just hang it on his wall over the fireplace and show it off to his friends. And you'd have to be a peculiar person indeed to spend millions of dollars on something you could never tell anyone you had."

"So why do you think he took it then?" the girl replied with a confused look.

"Well, Gina," the man said, raising his eyebrows, "maybe he just wanted to see if he could."

They both laughed and then the girl said, "Can you imagine

what the guards thought when they found out? And their bosses!"

"They probably all felt a little silly, I would say."

They both got comfortable again in their chairs and picked up their reading materials. But before they had gotten too far, the man added one last thought.

"Now, if someone could sell it without actually stealing it, that would be the real trick. Millions of dollars for nothing. Sounds pretty good to me."

"But who would be dumb enough to give someone money for something that the other person didn't even have?" the girl asked, shaking her head as she finished the thought.

"Ignorance and stupidity are not necessarily the same thing," the man replied, "though I suppose both can be put to the same use by the right kind of criminal - or politician!"

The girl wasn't sure that she had completely understood what the man meant but she felt as though she had gotten the gist enough to laugh along with him.

Just then a woman popped her head into the room and asked, "What are you two talking about in here?" with a big smile on her face.

"Oh, you know honey," the man replied, "Renaissance paintings, international crime, manipulating people for our own personal gain. Just the usual."

"Well how about you continue this sophisticated and fascinating conversation in the kitchen over some chocolate cake?" the woman said. "We have a birthday to celebrate!"

The man looked over at the young girl and their eyes widened. They set down their newspaper and book on the round table that sat between their chairs and headed for the dining room. A perfectly-frosted chocolate cake stood proudly atop a jade green cake stand, flanked by three plates and three glasses filled with a deep red raspberry cordial.

"You take dad's seat, Gina," said her mom as she pulled back the chair at the head of the table. The young girl sat down eagerly and pulled the chair as close to the table as she could.

Her dad sat down on her left and her mom started to cut the cake. When she had removed a big slice and plated it, she set it in front of the girl.

"Perfect!" said her dad, "I suppose we get the rest then, eh honey? Half for you, half for me?"

"No!" said Gina, "I don't think so mister. But if you behave yourself, I might let you have a piece." She finished her warning with a sideways glance and a cheeky grin.

"Oh, I see!" said the man, raising his hands as though he were under arrest. "We turn thirteen and we're the lady of the house, eh? Well, Madame, may I please have a slice of your lovely chocolate cake? Pretty please?"

"I suppose," replied the girl, "but I may require some favour in return."

"Oh, and what is that?"

"I shall inform you when the time comes," she said, giving him another look and throwing in a wink this time.

"Well, I shall do my best to be of service, Madame," her dad replied, bowing his head solemnly for a moment and then taking a big bite of his cake.

———————————

"So did you enjoy your new book?" Gina's dad asked as she settled into her bed and pulled the covers over herself.

"Yes! I only read three tales so far but it was very exciting. Thank you so much!"

"Of course, my dear," he replied, tucking the covers up under her chin and leaning down to kiss her forehead. Before he got there, she stopped him.

"Wait a minute. I think I may require that favour now," Gina said, pursing her lips and then smiling.

"Now?" her dad replied, "Would you like me to do your chores for you while you sleep or something?"

"Ha! I should have thought of that myself! No, I was actually wondering if you would read one of the stories in my new book to me as I fall asleep?"

Her dad looked surprised for a second but was more than happy to comply. He used to read to Gina often when she was little but as she had gotten a bit older, she had become a rather voracious reader all on her own. He was glad that the beauty of this moment resonated with him before it had passed so that he could savour every minute.

He picked up the *Red Fairy Book* from her nightstand and opened to the table of contents.

"Which one would you like me to read?"

"Hmm. I don't know. Surprise me," Gina said as she rolled over onto her side and burrowed down into her pillows and deeper under her blankets.

Her dad read over the list for a second and then said, "Oh yes, this one will do just fine."

"Which one is it?"

"You'll find out soon enough," he said as he flipped to the right page.

"You're so mean!" Gina laughed.

Her dad cleared his throat.

"And now, my little starling, your story."

He started reading:

"There was once upon a time a husbandman who had three sons. He had no property to bequeath to them, and no means of putting them in the way of getting a living, and did not know what to do, so he said that they had his leave to take to anything they most fancied, and go to any place they best liked. He would gladly accompany them for some part of their way, he said, and that he did. He went with them till they came to a place where three roads met, and there each of them took his own way, and the father bade them farewell and returned to his own home again. What became of the two elder I have never been able to discover, but the youngest went both far and wide..."

Chapter 7

The Simplon Orient Express
0056 to 0542 hours

The coffee was failing at its job of keeping Scarlet awake. As she sat alone in the dining-car, attempting to read in order to keep her mind engaged, her eyelids began to close. She shook her head and opened her eyes as wide as she could for a few seconds. Her body seemed to rebel against this move by prompting a massive yawn.

Of course, sleep was what she needed and wanted most of all. However, she felt that dozing off in short bouts throughout the night, her head in her hands or leaning against the vibrating wall of the train car, would only leave her in a stupor by the time morning came. Sometimes a little sleep is worse than no sleep at all.

Nevertheless, in her desperation, she was contemplating how she might arrange a few of the chairs, in the vain hope of getting comfortable enough to sleep for a couple of hours, when the train began slowing down. They were pulling into Lausanne for a scheduled stop.

Scarlet got up and stretched, then stepped out of her slippers and into her shoes. She pushed the slippers under her chair with her foot, wrapped a shawl around her shoulders, and made her way out to the platform.

The night air was cold and crisp. Scarlet felt a chill but welcomed it as a way to revive her tired body. With the exception of the train, everything around the station was still. It was very peaceful but Scarlet was trying to stay awake, so she walked to the opposite end of the platform to keep herself moving.

She was on her way back when another passenger stepped out of one of the sleeping-cars. It was Mr. White.

"Oh, Miss Greenley!" he said. "I hadn't expected to meet anyone out here this time of night."

"Neither had I," she replied. Exhaustion coupled with surprise made her feel nervous. "I would have thought you'd be sound asleep by now after reviewing your papers."

"They are certainly an excellent tool for helping one get to sleep," Thomas replied, "but unfortunately they haven't been able to keep me in that state. I felt the train stopping so I figured I might as well take the air for a few minutes."

They walked together along the platform as they continued talking.

"And what about you?" Thomas asked.

Scarlet wasn't sure she wanted to divulge the fiasco she had been through earlier that evening and the fact that she was essentially 'camping' in the dining-car.

"Oh, I sometimes find it hard to sleep on trains. When we pulled into the station, I thought I would see if a little walking about might help."

Thomas nodded in agreement but Scarlet could tell that he was suspicious of her clothing. He glanced over at her briefly, quickly looking her up and down.

'Surely he is going to ask why I'm still dressed as I was at dinner,' she thought. Much to her relief, he never did. Eventually the conductor signalled with his hand from down the platform and they boarded the train again.

Scarlet walked as though she were returning to her compartment, hoping that Mr. White would head in a different direction.

"Well, g'night, Mr. White," she said, "I hope you are able to sleep through the night now."

"I hope so too!" he replied, offering her his best wishes for her own rest.

Despite the fact that they had said their goodnights, Thomas was still awkwardly following Scarlet down the sleeping-car. As each compartment passed, she thought, 'The next must be his, surely!' Much to her chagrin, however, it appeared as though Mr. White had his lodgings directly next to hers.

"What are the chances?" Thomas said, lifting his eyebrows for a second and giving her a final smile as he disappeared into his compartment.

Scarlet had sat on her banquette and given Mr. White half an hour to fall back asleep before she ventured out to the dining-car, not wanting him to hear her and ask any questions.

The combination of the cold night air and the adrenaline from having felt both nervous and awkward around Thomas was more than enough to keep Scarlet awake - for a while at least. She picked up her book again and stretched her legs out across the chair next to her. She was several pages along and fairly engrossed when she suddenly noticed someone out of the corner of her eye.

"I'm just wondering," Thomas asked, "was the dining-car an

upgrade or a downgrade from your compartment?"

The embarrassment was palpable but Scarlet found herself ready to acquiesce to it. Instead of trying to salvage her dignity, she remained seated as she was, feet dangling over the edge of the chair, shawl bunched up behind her head as a pillow, empty coffee cup and pot beside her on the table.

"I'm surprised someone as well-travelled as yourself hasn't heard of Buffet Class," she replied. "It's all the rage."

"Oh, right, of course. Buffet Class. Everyone's been talking about it but I've never had the pleasure. May I join you for a little while?"

"I suppose," said Scarlet.

Thomas copied her position on the opposite side of the table, stretching out his legs across the chair next to him and resting his head against the wall.

"Ah, yes," he said, shuffling back and forth a bit in an attempt to get comfortable, "I can certainly see why this is so popular."

Scarlet returned to her book, pretending to be still engrossed in it despite the intrusion.

"She is a great reader and has pleasure in nothing else!"

Scarlet looked up slowly and gave him a half smile.

"I deserve neither such censure nor such praise," she quoted back to him.

"Then you are a great reader!" he laughed.

"One doesn't have to be too great a reader to have come across Jane Austen."

"I suppose not," he said. "So what has so gripped your imagination tonight that you would rather sit here and read than sleep comfortably in your compartment?"

"It's more that the latter isn't an option."

"What do you mean?"

"It appears as though my banquette is faulty," she said with a sigh. "The crew were unable to prepare my bed so I've been left to spend the night as a vagrant."

"Faulty banquette? You've got to be joking?"

"That's what I said to them. Something or other about the hinges, I don't really know."

"Would you mind if I had a look? As I said before, I do a lot of work with trains. Perhaps I might see something the crew has missed."

"By all means," Scarlet replied, waving her hand as if to grant him leave.

Thomas was gone for about fifteen minutes before he came back and resumed his position opposite her.

"Well," he began, trying to get back into a slightly less un-comfortable arrangement against the wall, "what do you know, they are faulty."

"At least now we know they haven't made up a story to amuse themselves at my expense."

"Speaking of stories, may I ask what you're reading?"

Scarlet turned the book towards him so that he could see the spine.

"*The Best Tales of Edgar Allen Poe*," he read out loud. "Very exciting!"

"Have you read much from him?" she asked.

"Just the odd poem, but I'm vaguely familiar with some of the tales."

Though Scarlet was enjoying the company, she couldn't help wondering why Mr. White was still here. 'Is he intending to spend the entire night at the table?' She glanced over at him. His eyes were closed as he leaned against the wall.

After about five minutes or so of silence, he said, "Do you feel like sharing one of those stories with me?"

Scarlet was a little surprised but was still trying not to seem fazed by the events of the evening.

"I suppose I could," she replied.

"No pressure at all, Miss Greenley. I'm already quite content. The jostling of the train and the gentle knocking of my head against the wall is quite soothing. I can't wait to popularise Buffet Class once I'm back in the States."

Scarlet decided she would give it a try. 'Why not?' she thought to herself, 'At least it will pass the time.'

She flipped through the book, thinking about which story to read. When she had settled on one, she cleared her throat, more out of nervousness than necessity, and started reading:

"At Paris, just after dark one gusty evening in the autumn of 18--, I was enjoying the twofold luxury of meditation and a meerschaum, in company with my friend C. Auguste Duphin, in his little back library, or book-closet, au troisième, No. 33, Rue Dunôt, Faubourg St. Germain. For one hour at least we had maintained a profound silence; while each, to any casual observer, might have seemed intently and exclusively occupied with the curling eddies of smoke that oppressed the atmosphere of the chamber. For myself, however, I was mentally discussing certain topics which had formed matter for conversation between us at an earlier period of the evening; I mean the affair of the Rue Morgue, and the mystery attending the murder of Marie Roget..."

Scarlet finished the story and, much to her surprise, Mr. White had actually fallen sound asleep. She didn't know whether to think it rather sweet or just infuriating, since she was unable to do the same.

After she had spent close to an hour alternating between sitting at the table and pacing up and down the car, Thomas woke up.

"I say," he began, rubbing his eyes and shaking his head, "how does one fall asleep to Poe?"

"Shall I take that as a complement or a critique?"

"At this hour, I wouldn't give it a second thought," he replied, yawning as he spoke.

"I'm just thinking," he continued, "it seems as though this arrangement suits me rather well. Perhaps you would like to make use of my compartment and get some sleep before we arrive in Paris."

"No, I couldn't," Scarlet replied quickly.

"No no, hear me out," he said. "I'll have a few hours between Paris and the ferry when I can get a bit more sleep, then a full night in London before I'm expected to be worth anything the following morning. You, on the other hand, are arriving in the early hours in Paris with the whole day ahead of you. You should really have the better chance of getting some quality rest now."

"You're very kind, Mr. White, but I simply couldn't."

"Well, that's a shame," he said, "that bed will be a great waste with the two of us sitting out here until Paris." Then he closed his eyes and tried to doze off again.

Scarlet did not want to be in his debt but at the same time she knew it made sense. His reasonableness and her tiredness overcame her reluctance more easily than she would have liked.

"Ok," she said, "I think I'll give it a try."

"Excellent, I'll find an attendant to change over the linens for you."

"That won't be necessary," replied Scarlet, a little too eagerly. She checked herself and then continued, "I'll change them myself. Mine are in my compartment anyway, left there after their failed attempt at making up my bed. I'll sort it out."

She knew this would be awkward, and Thomas certainly gave her a raised eyebrow, but she didn't want to risk the involvement of any crew-members that might know her as Miss Haslewood.

"But why? It is their job, you know."

"Don't trouble yourself about it," she replied. "What was it you just said? At this hour, I wouldn't give it a second thought."

He nodded in agreement, closed his eyes, and leaned his head back against the wall again, falling asleep before Scarlet had even finished changing the linens.

Once she had gotten comfortable in the bed, it was still a while before she was able to fall sleep, being not a little distracted by the presence of Mr. White's luggage and other odds and ends in the compartment. When she had finally cleared her mind, she was out cold until they arrived at the Gare de Lyon.

Chapter 8

Gare de Lyon
October 25, 1925

Scarlet had gotten up with only four minutes to spare before the train pulled into the station that morning. She had slipped out of Thomas' compartment and into her own, changing her clothes as quickly as she could. As she looked at herself in the mirror, she wished she had even just two extra minutes to do something, anything, with her hair. She grabbed a red scarf from her suitcase and donned it more out of a sense of utility than fashion, spreading as much of it as possible over the top of her head to hide the chaos. There was no time at all for jewellery or make-up.

'Well, if I should see Mr. White on my way out,' she thought, 'I shall be truly forgettable! Perhaps it's for the best.' As the thoughts crossed her mind, she frowned at herself in the mirror. "And what does it matter anyway?" she said to herself out loud, turning to her case and pressing it down hard in order to latch it closed. She cinched its two leather straps tight and buckled them in place.

An attendant came and collected the bag while Scarlet went to the dining-car to find Mr. White and thank him for his kindness. When she got there, however, he was nowhere to be found. Just then, the conductor entered the car from the other end and started walking towards her.

"Ah, bonjour Miss Haslewood! I am glad to see that you re-membered to get off. We will be removing the cars bound for Calais very soon. I hope that you were able to get some rest in Mr. White's compartment."

Scarlet's heart skipped a beat.

"I'm sorry?" she asked.

"I came into the dining-car earlier this morning, expecting to greet you at your table, when instead I found Mr. White fast asleep!"

Scarlet had been careful about the attendants the night be-fore, wanting to avoid them calling her by name in front of Thomas, but somehow she had completely forgotten about the conductor. She was used to improvising but suddenly she felt her palms beginning to sweat.

"Oh, that must have been a surprise!" she replied casually. "Whatever did you say to one another, I wonder?"

"It was nothing, really," the conductor said. "He awoke as I approached the table and made a joke about still waiting for his dinner from the previous night. I said that he was not who I had expected to find, at which point he said that he had allowed you to use his compartment."

"I see," said Scarlet, still unsure about what Thomas might have heard.

"I must say though, Miss Haslewood," the conductor contin-ued, "I was very disturbed by one thing in particular."

"And what was that?" she replied. Still aiming for a casual demeanour, Scarlet pulled her handbag up in front of her and pretended to be more concerned with finding some small item than with the conductor's disturbance.

"Well, ma chère," he said, hesitating a bit, "I wish that you had not made up the bed yourself. You really must allow my men to do their jobs."

Her heart slowed and her hands suddenly felt stronger and cooler. Her left one dropped to her side with her bag in it while she extended her right one to touch the conductor's shoulder as she replied.

"Oh Monsieur, it was no trouble at all, I assure you! I just felt too terrible about making your crew fuss with sheets and pillows at that hour of the night when I was perfectly capable of handling it myself."

The conductor smiled and said, "You are a perfect lady, Mademoiselle. I hope that we will have the pleasure of serving you again soon." He bowed slightly as he finished speaking and then excused himself to attend to his business.

Scarlet hadn't been able to locate Thomas before she stepped off the train. 'Where could he have gone?' she wondered, trying to remind herself that all she was interested in was thanking him for giving up his compartment.

The station was quite busy that morning with crowds pushing this way and that to get to their trains on time. Scarlet found the attendants gathering her luggage from one of the fourgons and began making arrangements to get her things loaded into a taxi as soon as possible.

While she was still waiting for her bags and staring off across the sea of faces passing by, someone tapped her on the shoulder.

"Madame Moreau?"

Scarlet's heart may have skipped more than one beat this

time as she slowly turned around. Before her was Dr. Dufour's maid.

"I'm sorry?" Scarlet replied, acting somewhat confused. Though it did not often occur, this was not the first time she had encountered someone involved in one of her cons after the fact.

"Madame Moreau," the maid repeated, "surely it is you. You probably don't remember me but I am the maid at Dr. Dufour's residence. We met last April."

"I am afraid you have mistaken me for someone else," Scarlet replied, smiling warmly and giving no signs of being uncomfortable.

"But it must be you," the maid insisted. "Even your red scarf, it instantly called to mind the red beret you wore that afternoon. I must confess, I think I remembered it because after I saw yours, I wanted one of my own!"

"It certainly sounds like the prefect beret, Madame, but I can assure you that I neither own any such hat nor am called by the name Moreau."

"Monsieur Fontaine was cleared of any diagnosis of insanity, I'll have you know," the maid continued, largely ignoring Scarlet's protest. "Both he and the doctor attempted to contact you but you failed to respond to any of their letters."

Scarlet could only assume they had contacted Fontaine's actual sister. Their estrangement had been something she had counted on should any such follow-up be attempted. After the ordeal on the train, she was glad of the reminder that not all her plans ended in such a muddle.

"I wonder if you would consider stopping by Dr. Dufour's office while you are in the city?"

"Madame, I mean no disrespect but I do not think you are

listening to me," Scarlet replied. "I am not, nor ever shall be, Madame Moreau."

"Then who are you?" the maid asked with a hint of frustration in her voice.

As Scarlet was opening her mouth to speak, a voice called out above the noise of the crowd passing by on her left.

"Miss Greenley! Miss Greenley!"

Both she and the maid looked over and saw a man shoving his way through the mass of would-be passengers. It was Thomas.

"Miss Greenley, I'm so glad I caught you!" he said. "I have barely a minute to spare before my car is removed for shunting onto the Calais line, but I did not want to let you get away before I had the chance to make sure you were ok after such a long, gruelling night."

Scarlet hesitated for a second, glancing back and forth between Thomas and Dufour's maid with her mouth still half open. More than anything, she wanted to freeze the moment and laugh for a while at its absolute perfection and absurdity.

"Mr. White!" she said as cheerfully as possible, "I thought you had vanished. I'm glad you found me."

"I suppose I did, only for twenty minutes or so. There is a fellow that sells the most delightful pain au chocolat just outside the station and whenever I pass through at this hour, I always make a run for it. I once missed my connection! Ah, the things we do for a good pastry, eh ladies?" He gave her a wink and opened the bag, inhaling the fragrance with a look on his face that Scarlet understood only too well.

"Mr. White," she said, "may I introduce you to... I'm sorry, I don't think I ever got your name?"

"Uh, yes," the maid stumbled, "it's, um, Daph-, I mean, Mademoiselle Faucheux."

"It's a pleasure to make your acquaintance, Mademoiselle," Thomas said with a nod. "And how do you two know each other?"

Scarlet looked at the maid, opening her eyes a bit wider and raising her eyebrows inquisitively.

"I'm afraid you caught us in a moment of confusion, Monsieur," the woman replied. "I mistook Madame for someone else. My sincerest apologies."

"There's no apology necessary," Scarlet replied, only because the maid's discomfort was satisfaction enough.

"Indeed!" added Thomas. "In fact, it was by something of a fluke that Miss Greenley and I crossed paths only yesterday. Misunderstanding and confusion sometimes have a happy ending!"

Dufour's maid was nevertheless embarrassed by the situation and Scarlet wasn't about to let her regain her confidence. She added nothing to what Thomas had said, only nodding and leaving a measure of awkward silence for the maid to excuse herself from the conversation. She did so and Scarlet and Thomas were left alone.

"I'm very sorry that I don't have more time but I do hope you get on well in Paris," he said.

"I'm sure I will," Scarlet replied, "especially after the great kindness you showed to me last night. I cannot thank you enough for the few hours of good sleep."

"Nothing at all," he said, glancing back over his shoulder toward the train. The conductor was checking his watch and Thomas clearly needed to hurry.

"You had better go, Mr. White. If you're much later, they may reassign you to my old compartment as punishment!"

"I think you're right!" he said with a laugh. "All the best Miss Greenley. I shall keep an eye out for you wherever there's a Buffet Class!"

With that, he took off at a slow jog back towards the conductor and his sleeping-car. Halfway there, however, he stopped and turned back towards Scarlet.

"Here, Miss Greenley," he said, handing her the bag with the pain au chocolat inside. "You spent most of the night in a dining-car, the least you deserve is a good breakfast!"

Then he turned back and disappeared onto the train for Calais.

Chapter 9

Paris
October 26, 1925

Scarlet dipped her toast into her boiled egg, which was perched atop a decorative egg server. The yolk was perfectly runny, the white just firm enough to keep it in place. As she took a bite, she lifted her head to admire her surroundings.

The garden at the Hôtel Ritz was quiet that morning. It was too cool for most guests to consider dining in the outdoors, and this was precisely why Scarlet had decided to take her breakfast there. She had wrapped herself in a woollen shawl but left her head uncovered so as to absorb as much of the sun's warmth as possible. The ivy cascading over the walls gave a sense of motion to the space, while the yellow flowers of the helenium continued to provide colour when most other flowering plants had retired for the season. The stalks of lady's mantle interspersed throughout lent a certain wildness to the large stone planter beside her table. She was really quite content.

After a leisurely morning that included an after-breakfast walk around the Colonne Vendôme and over to the Jardin des Tuileries for half an hour or so, Scarlet returned to her room. She went to her closet and pulled out a black and white dress and hung it on a hook in the bathroom. She stepped back from it for a moment and winced. It was a flapper dress, mostly in black but with a white V-stripe beginning at the shoulders and ending in front, just above the waist. Then there was a matching white stripe several inches further down that formed a low, artificial waistline, below which were wide pleats until the whole thing ended just below where the knee would be. In keeping with the style, the dress fit loosely and was largely linear in shape from top to bottom. Scarlet felt that she had rarely seen anything so hideous.

Next she pulled a black cloche from her hatbox. It was wool and shaped vaguely like a bowler, with a stubby brim curling out at the bottom beneath a black band. She planned to break up the monotony of colour with a silver, fern-shaped brooch set with diamonds and garnets. She loved that brooch. She hated the hat a little less than the dress. Lastly, she got out a pair of white leather heels with a t-strap, about which she had no feelings either way.

While the entire outfit was certainly not to her taste, she often found that dressing outside her normal preferences helped when it came to playing certain roles that were similarly outside her normal demeanour.

She slipped on the dress and started working on her makeup. She was aiming at something garish, and after thirty or forty minutes she felt she had achieved just that. Not that she would frighten away children or anything, but she applied it all far more generously than usual, from her rouge to her dark red lipstick, and even her deep blue, almost black eyeshadow. "I certainly wouldn't trust you!" she said to her reflection.

The last piece was her auburn wig that she had purchased in Venice a few days before. She adored the accompanying headband too much to sully it by including it in this ridiculous ensemble, so she left it with her other jewellery.

In reality, Scarlet's attire and overall appearance was rather trendy, which was the reason she had chosen it. But she felt herself somehow above 'trends', or perhaps just above the people who followed them. Perhaps it was pride or some other character defect. She liked to think of herself as classy, sophisticated. Secretly, she always kind of hoped people were quietly wondering if she were some long-lost countess, or the daughter of some foreign millionaire travelling about as inconspicuously as possible.

When she had finally gotten the wig set just right, topped off with the hat and brooch, she was ready to set out for the first step in her plan.

"Bonjour, Madame. What can I help you with today?"

"Bonjour! I am interested in a Maltese."

"Excellent choice, Madame," the woman replied. "I have several at the moment, all with full documentation. This way, please."

The woman led Scarlet back to a large room divided into quarters by the use of low-standing barriers, like fences, with a path running down the centre for them to walk along.

"Ah, yes, there they are," said the woman, pointing to the area on the far left. "Take your time and see if --"

"I'll take that one!" said Scarlet, hurrying a few steps up to the fence and pointing to a little white dog that was running circles, quite literally, around the other dogs. "He looks perfect!" she added, with a burst of energy almost equal to that of the dog.

"Oh, but are you sure?" the woman asked. "Would you like

some time to --"

"No no," Scarlet interrupted, "he'll do just fine. More than fine!"

"Well then, I suppose I should begin the paperwork."

"Yes, do!" said Scarlet, again with an eagerness that almost made herself feel a little nauseous. "I must take this little cutie home today!"

"Despite his energy, he certainly is adorable," the woman said, warming up to Scarlet a bit more as she put aside any expectations of grace or refinement.

"Indeed he is!" Scarlet replied. "Positively adorable!" As she picked the kicking, barking, tail-wagging little monster up into her arms and looked down at him, she wondered if she disliked him more or less than the dress.

After about twenty minutes, the shop owner had finished filling out the appropriate paperwork as well as selling her a collar, a leash, and a small baggy of dog treats, over all of which Scarlet continued to effuse with the same nauseating level of excitement.

When she was ready to leave, the shop owner wished her a happy new life with her new best friend.

"If there is anything else you need, or if you have any questions along the way, please do not hesitate to --"

"Oh, no no," Scarlet said, "we shall be just fine! More than fine!"

"Yes, I'm sure you will be," the woman said. "Best of luck, Miss Greenley! Oh, but before you go, I am very curious - what will you call him?"

"Just look at him!" Scarlet said, rubbing his head and getting her face as close to his as she was willing to get, even for the sake of a con. "I think he's a perfect little Vincenzo!"

The shop owner had never met a dog named Vincenzo, but then she had never sold a dog to a woman quite like this Miss Greenley.

"Of course he is," she replied. "Best of luck to the both of you!"

Scarlet had attached the leash to the dog and was walking him as fast as his little legs could carry him. Once or twice she picked him up only as long as she could stomach holding him, just so she could move a bit faster. As they passed through the Tuileries, he was walking on his own and attracting the attention of various passersby - mostly women dressed similarly to herself.

"Oh, he's delightful!" one of them said, pausing a moment to bend down and pet him. Scarlet kept walking.

Eventually she arrived at the Louvre.

She made her way to the receptionist's desk that guarded the offices of the various curators and the director himself. The woman at the desk was on a phone call when she walked up. Scarlet milled around in front of her as closely as she could while she waited. The receptionist was clearly uncomfortable but Scarlet didn't mind.

Behind the main desk were several other desks at which sat various museum employees whose jobs and titles were of no interest to Scarlet. She didn't need to know. She just kept pacing around, waiting for the woman on the phone and glancing over all the desks she could see.

Finally, the receptionist was ready for her.

"May I help you?" she asked, purposefully skipping over any

pleasantries.

"I certainly hope so," said Scarlet, acting more than a little perturbed. "I must speak with the director this instant!"

The woman frowned.

"I am afraid Monsieur is unavailable at the moment. May I know the nature of your business?"

"You may not!" Scarlet replied forcefully. The dog squirming in her arms and her constant need to keep him under control helped to communicate an overall sense of irritation, which wasn't far from the truth.

"Well, Mademoiselle," the receptionist continued, "I am afraid I cannot help you if you will not give me --"

"You're 'afraid' this, you're 'afraid' that!" replied Scarlet, now raising her voice. "It is your director that ought to be afraid, Madame... what is your name?"

"Martin."

"Yes indeed," continued Scarlet, taking her voice up another notch, "it is your director that ought to be very much afraid, Madame Martin!"

The receptionist was obviously unsure exactly how to handle this bizarre situation.

"I want to speak with him now!" Scarlet demanded.

"As I told you, Madame, he is not available at the moment. I cannot change that."

"Of course he isn't!" Scarlet laughed. "Well, he was only too available three weeks ago at Le Dôme!"

The woman raised her eyebrows. Any of the museum staff behind her who were not already watching them were now fully engaged. Apart from stimulating conversation and emerging trends in art and literature, Le Dôme was also well-known as the place for meeting or showing off one's latest liaison.

"Mademoiselle, I - I cannot --"

"No, you cannot, can you?" Scarlet was now only a tick away from yelling at the top of her voice. "No one can, can they? Ah, but isn't it always the way! These men! Animals, all of them!"

The woman made no attempt to speak but appeared to be sympathising with Scarlet as she nodded ever so slightly.

"And speaking of animals," Scarlet continued, "you may tell your director that his 'gift' has been rejected!" As she finished speaking, Scarlet lobbed the Maltese right into the receptionist's lap. The woman, who never expected such an escalation of the situation, lifted her arms and recoiled at the sight of the flying dog, which landed briefly on her knees and then slid down to the floor.

The receptionist and the rest of the employees stood up and watched as the little ball of white fur ran around and under their desks, barking loudly and jumping up on their shins as it passed them. Some of the staff just watched it while a few tried to catch its attention and pet it, though little Vincenzo wouldn't stand still long enough for anything like that. After a few laps around the room, one of the clerks caught the dog and handed it to the receptionist, who clearly did not want to be in charge at that moment. She did her best to restrain the fidgeting dog in her arms and return it to its owner.

But when she turned around, Scarlet was gone.

———————————

Scarlet found a bench on her way back through the Tuileries and sat down to enjoy the afternoon. She leaned back, looked up at the trees arching over her head, took a deep breath, and then let it out slowly. A starling flitted down from one of the branches and landed by her feet. She pulled the dog treats from her bag and broke off a few pieces, rubbing them together in her hands to make them finer, then spreading them out in front of the little bird. He hopped over and started eating them, not simply grabbing a few bites and fleeing but lingering, as if to share the afternoon with her. She would have tried to rub his head with her finger if she didn't think it would scare him off.

After half an hour or so, Scarlet reached into her bag to inspect her prize. She pulled out a small stack of mostly blank papers, about twelve or fifteen sheets. On the top they read: Musée du Louvre, Bureau du Directeur.

It was a simple but unique seal design. Most importantly, however, it was official.

Chapter 10

Paris
October 27, 1925

The previous evening, Scarlet had begun carefully copying over five of the letters she had prepared beforehand onto the Louvre stationery, using a typewriter the hotel manager supplied on request. She had gotten too tired to finish them that night and was now working on the last two in the morning after breakfast.

Each was essentially the same, just addressed to a different person. Their names were as follows: Lord Abernathy, Sir Peter Coleridge, Sir Henry H. Culpepper, Gerald Milliner, Esq., and Dame Angelica Fernsby. Each one of them had been selected over the last eighteen months based on Scarlet's careful research, including through discussions with art dealers and auction houses, as well as with less savoury players in the art world. She needed marks who were not only art lovers but who also had the resources to acquire whatever they wanted. A questionable moral compass was also a plus.

To each of these, she wrote the following letter:

Dear _____,

It has come to the attention of those charged with the oversight of such matters, that the Musée du Louvre is in need of assistance. If the Great War that ravaged our men, women, and children, as well as our homes and the very land upon which they are built, has taught us anything it is that civilisation is in need of preservation. As we continue to heal and restore what was lost, it behooves us to look with humility to the highest achievements of our ancestors. If we are to find renewal after great war, it will come through the inspiration of great design, great sculpture, great writing, and great painting.

Unfortunately, the Museum is keenly aware of its limited resources and inability to expand its collection in response to this need. With the exception of certain donations, particularly in the last decades of the previous century, major acquisitions have not taken place in over sixty years - not since Winged Victory herself came to rest in our halls as you see her today. Furthermore, the failings of 1911 still haunt our galleries, with the untimely death of Signor Peruggia not three weeks ago serving as a fresh reminder of darker days. The crime perpetrated by this man was not only a crime against the Louvre but against all humanity. And while every effort is being made to ensure that such an act is never again repeated, those in authority are concerned that it may only be a matter of time.

With these things in mind, the Director has proposed an ambitious plan to reinvigorate the collection and improve upon its dwelling place. This proposal having found support at the highest levels, we have now been charged with the task of setting it in motion.

The plan is this: to sell da Vinci's Mona Lisa.

The Museum is not ignorant of its value, which has only been enhanced by its recent fame. Nevertheless, the decision has been made to sacrifice a single masterpiece for the preservation, protection, and acquisition of many more.

A small group of potential buyers has been assembled from the Museum's private research over the past year. It is hoped that you will consider this correspondence an honour and a privilege, the latter being particularly important as the Director himself has requested that this proposal be handled with the utmost discretion. It is imperative that you not speak of this matter with anyone outside of those with whom consultation is required for the arrangement of funding.

We ask that you take some time to reflect on these things and consider participating in further discussions. As a representative of the Société, I will arrive in London on the 8th of December and will be staying at Brown's Hotel until just after the New Year. Please leave any correspondence with the manager and I shall respond as soon as I am settled.

Sincerely,

Comtesse Aurélie d'Auvergne
Société des amis du Louvre

That afternoon, Scarlet deposited the letters at the nearest post office and then stopped by Ladurée in the Rue Royale. The Hôtel Ritz had many charms, but for Scarlet the list began with its proximity to Ladurée. She might have told you she spent ten or fifteen minutes there that afternoon but in reality it was a little over an hour.

She sat by the window so she could watch the people and

cars passing by outside. The waiter brought her a cup of coffee and two small plates, one bearing three macarons, the other a beautifully-piped chocolate religieuse. He probably hadn't imagined that she wasn't planning on sharing them with anyone.

As she was enjoying her 'lunch', without any particular prompting, at least as far as she could tell, Scarlet's thoughts drifted to Thomas and their first meeting on the train. She smiled to herself as she recalled his awkward question and her initial indignation. Was it strange that she was sort of craving a date at the moment? Or any dried fruit really.

She sipped her coffee and watched a man outside the window stop and light a cigarette.

'He's not a very handsome fellow, is he?' she thought. She started to break one of the macarons in half but then decided just to pop the whole thing into her mouth while no one was looking.

Despite quoting *Pride & Prejudice*, Mr. White was no Mr. Darcy. He was only an inch or two taller than Scarlet, with brown hair and brown eyes, and features that meant he was more likely to blend in with a crowd than attract ladies at a ball. Not that he was particularly unattractive either. One might have said he was a perfectly average man in every respect.

The smoking man passed on as a taxi pulled up to the curb. A young man stepped out first, then reached back and took the hand of a young woman whom he helped out of the car. With his hand on her back, he shut the door behind them. The driver pulled away and the couple started down the street, the woman slipping her arm through the man's as they walked.

But would the perfectly average man give up his compartment to a complete stranger? Perhaps not. Though the average man may do any number of unpredictable or unexpected things when a woman is involved!

She pulled the top off of the religieuse and bit into it, trying to keep the filling from bursting out the sides. She was mildly successful.

A few small crowds brushed past and between one another outside her window and her view of the street was obscured for a minute or two.

Would he really have spent the entire night at the table with her if she hadn't taken him up on his offer? Surely most men who make such grand gestures for a woman do so where there is at least some hope of forming, or furthering, a relationship, no matter how vague or improbable that hope may be. He knew she was getting off at Paris, didn't he? Of course he did. Was he expecting her to change her ticket and continue on to Calais or London? How ridiculous!

In a lull between crowds, the smoking man passed by her window again headed in the opposite direction. This time he was carrying a newspaper and a brown bag that he was clutching like the top of a bottle of wine, which was probably what it contained.

What did she really know about Thomas anyway? A few words exchanged on a boring train ride...

Her mind was still for a while as she continued watching the world go by outside her window. For a few minutes, the clanking of motor cars was broken up by the clip-clop of a horse's hooves as a fiacre ambled down the street.

'He was right though,' she thought, taking another sip of her coffee. 'That really was the most delightful pain au chocolat.'

Chapter 11

Brooklyn, New York
August 25-30, 1911

Hank Parker had worked for Fenimore's Grocers for the last seventeen years. He was a living example of hard work and integrity paying off over time. From washing fruit and delivering crates of vegetables to neighbourhood restaurants, he had worked his way up to store manager in only eight years. With Hank at the helm, business was booming and the shop was the most popular grocer in Brooklyn. Mr. Fenimore was considering opening two more stores to branch out into the other boroughs, and there was a very real chance that he would bring Hank on as a partner to help oversee the entire business.

So when his employees showed up for work that morning, they certainly didn't expect to find Hank lying unconscious on the floor of his office.

"Mr. Parker? Mr. Parker! Someone get help!" cried Jenny, the store's bookkeeper and a dear friend of Mrs. Parker.

"What is it?" asked one of the boys that was starting out in the same job Hank had all those years before. The younger men in the store looked up to him - successful at work, a friendly guy, a lovely family - he was exactly where many of them hoped to be by the time they reached his age.

"He's not responding!" said Jenny. "I can't wake him!"

One of the two boys that were there that morning ran to get

help, stopping the first policeman he saw along the way. The other didn't really know what to do but knelt down by Hank's side and squeezed his shoulder.

"Mr. Parker? Mr. Parker, can you hear me?" he asked.

It was about fifteen or twenty minutes but eventually the policeman and the boy showed up with a local doctor who worked a few blocks away.

"Mr. Parker, if you can hear me, it's Dr. Greenley," he said, kneeling down and pressing his stethoscope against Hank's chest. He grabbed his wrist, feeling for a pulse. Then he pulled up Hank's eyelids and looked carefully for a few seconds.

"I think Mr. Parker is dead," he said, turning to Jenny, then the policeman, then the two boys.

"Dead? No, no that's not possible!" said Jenny. "Check him again. Do something!"

The doctor looked sincerely grieved by the situation but he knew there was nothing he could do.

"Someone should fetch his family right away."

"I'll go," said one of the boys, "they only live a few blocks from here. I'll run."

"And I'll get an ambulance down here as soon as I can," added the policeman as he followed the boy out of the shop.

Most of the employees were in shock, some of them pacing about the room and staring blankly at whatever their eyes fell upon, others sobbing and sitting on the floor several feet away from the body. Jenny continued to kneel beside him until the boy returned with Mrs. Parker and Hank's daughter.

"Oh, Evelyn!" she cried as his wife entered the shop.

Evelyn Parker had been running as quickly as she could but when she entered the store and caught sight of Hank's shoes in the doorway to his office, she slowed down. Her knees weakened and her hands began trembling. The boy that had fetched her had never experienced anything like this before and didn't know what he was supposed to do. All he knew was that Mrs. Parker looked like she might stumble, so he got beside her and held her arm just firmly enough to steady her. As she entered the office, he helped her fall softly to her knees.

"No," she whispered almost without a sound. Then the tears started to stream down her face. She took her husband's hand in hers and brought it up to her face. The doctor motioned for the employees in the room to step outside. Then he motioned for one person to step inside. Hank's daughter was standing at a distance, as far away as she could be without losing sight of her father. She wasn't crying yet but later the doctor told his wife that he had never seen such brokenness in someone's face before. He stopped waving her into the room and went to her himself.

Getting down on his knees in front of her, he took her hands and looked up at her eyes. They were fixed on her father and beginning to glisten with the first of many tears. Dr. Greenley had the sense not to speak, only to be there for the girl so that she wasn't standing alone. He stood up and moved beside her, putting his arm around her shoulders and holding her tightly. Then the tears began in earnest.

She turned her head and buried her face in his side as she cried. She stayed at Dr. Greenley's side as the ambulance arrived and they placed her father on the stretcher. She walked with him to the street as they slid her father into the back of the wagon and slammed the doors. Her mother hadn't let go of her husband's hand until that moment, then she turned and ran towards Gina, and the two hugged as tightly as they ever had before.

———————————————

Jim Greenley had been the Parkers' doctor since Gina was born. He had gotten to know them well over the years, though he had never introduced them to his family, as much as he had wanted to. Jim was an easy person to get along with but he took a very disciplined line with himself and his work. He always felt that it would be easier to maintain an objective opinion in difficult situations if he refrained from becoming too friendly with his patients outside of the office.

After that morning, however, he was beginning to rethink his position. Of course, Hank wasn't his first patient to pass away. But he had always felt a special connection with the Parkers since the day they told him that Evelyn was pregnant. Perhaps it was because his own wife had become pregnant with their daughter at just about the same time, and he had gone through all the new experiences of parenthood and family along with them over the last thirteen years. Despite his professional distance, he had felt a bond with them, an understanding of sorts.

He had asked his wife to prepare a meal that evening that they could take over and share with Evelyn and Gina. The Parkers had no family nearby and Jim figured that preparing food would be the last thing on Evelyn's mind. So at around six o'clock, the Greenley's knocked on their door.

Evelyn answered, her face worn and wearied.

"You don't have to say or do anything," Mrs. Greenley said quickly, "we've only come to make sure you keep up your strength." She held the casserole dish up in front of her and then nodded towards the loaf of bread in Jim's hands. Evelyn nodded gratefully but didn't speak. She opened the door wider and let them in, then closed it and went into the sitting room.

"Dear, why don't you find some plates and silverware. I'll keep an eye on the Parkers. And why don't you help your mom?" said Jim, turning to his daughter. The two Greenley women went into the kitchen while he hovered just outside the sitting room.

Evelyn was sitting on the sofa, her legs pulled up on an ottoman and covered with a blanket, her arms clutching a pillow. She was looking out the window at the end of the room, watching the people and cars passing by.

Gina sat in her wingback chair with the newspaper on her lap, her arms folded and her ankles crossed. She was looking intently at the front page but it was obvious that she wasn't reading. Jim wanted to sit with her but he felt like somehow it was a sacred space. So he remained outside the doorway like a faithful night watchman until Mrs. Greenley called them in for dinner.

Two days later, Evelyn went down to Fenimore's to pick up her husband's personal items. The boys at the shop had offered to bring them over to her but she said that she wanted to pack them up herself. This was partially true. She also just wanted to spend some time in a space that had been important to Hank.

When she arrived at the store, Jenny greeted her with a long hug.

"This is good timing," she said, "Hank's cousin is here as well. Maybe you two can --"

"Hank's cousin?" Evelyn asked, interrupting her.

"Yes, Margaret Parker," replied Jenny. "She just got here a few minutes ago."

Evelyn was trying to think clearly through the veil that deep sorrow often casts over the mind. She blinked a few times and frowned.

"Hank doesn't have a cousin named Margaret," she replied. "In fact, Hank doesn't have any cousins, as far as I'm aware. At least, not any first cousins."

"Well maybe you should just go talk to her," Jenny said. "She's in Hank's office."

Evelyn walked over to the doorway and looked inside, trying to focus her thoughts and figure out who it was that was sitting at her husband's desk.

The woman was holding a glass paperweight, turning it in her hands. Then she set it down and looked up at Evelyn. She didn't say anything for a few seconds.

"You must be Mrs. Parker?" she finally asked.

"Yes," replied Evelyn, her voice quiet but steady.

"I never expected this would happen," the woman said. "I mean, I suppose it was going to happen at some point but I never expected it would be like this."

Evelyn was trying to get her head around what the woman was saying.

"What do you mean, 'going to happen at some point'?" she asked.

"This," the woman said, looking at Evelyn. "Us, meeting."

"Jenny said you're Hank's cousin? Margaret Parker? Hank never mentioned you before."

"Oh, I told her that to make things a little..." she paused, looking for the right word. "Simpler."

Evelyn's heart was beating harder now and her hands were shaking slightly, but her voice grew a little louder and her tone more firm.

"Then who are you, please? And what business do you have here in my husband's office?"

"My name is Gloria Brown," she said, standing up and throwing her purse over her shoulder. "Hank and I have been seeing each other for a few years now."

Evelyn's body swayed as she reached up and grasped the door frame. She glanced around the room, not knowing where to focus her eyes. Her mind was racing, her thoughts converging and colliding, words forming then dissolving.

Gloria was speaking to her but she heard nothing. She turned and started making her way through the store to the exit. Jenny saw her using the shelves to keep herself walking straight and rushed over to her, as did one of the boys, the same who had helped her two nights ago.

"What is it dear?" Jenny asked, but Evelyn wasn't responding. They helped her to the front door and then Jenny looked back to see Gloria standing in the doorway of the office, watching them.

"What happened?" Jenny asked her, leaving the boy to help Evelyn walk home.

"She's grieving, can't you see?" Gloria replied.

"But something changed after she spoke to you. What did you say to her?"

"Something Hank should have told her a couple of years ago."

Jenny's eyes narrowed and somehow, like a revelation, she

ANDREW STOPYRA

felt that she knew exactly what was going on. And she was right.

Her initial thought was to tell the woman to leave and never come back. But she was able to retain the presence of mind, despite her rage, to ask a few questions before sending Miss Brown on her way. She would have preferred not even to look at the woman, but she also knew it was important to make sure she was telling the truth.

They didn't speak that long but Jenny learned enough, perhaps too much. Eventually she did what she had wanted to do and told her to leave and never come back, which is exactly what happened.

———————————

Later that evening, Jim Greenley paid another visit to check in on Evelyn and Gina. This time, he only brought his daughter along.

"Hi, honey," he said to Gina, who had answered the door. "Can we come in for a few minutes?"

"Sure," she said, moving out of the way and letting them through.

Evelyn was in the kitchen, sitting at the small table where she and Hank used to have coffee in the morning. She wasn't crying, she was just staring at the empty chair opposite her, hands folded on the table.

Jim didn't have the same feeling he had two nights ago about sacred space, so he pulled back the chair and sat across from Evelyn. Their daughters had gone to the sitting room together.

"I know it's a silly question," he started, "but how are you doing?"

She was quiet for half a minute and then looked up at him.

"I'm fine."

They sat together in silence for a while before Evelyn decided that she needed to talk to someone. And for the next three hours, that someone was Jim.

Out in the sitting room, Gina and Jim's daughter were sitting in the wingback chairs, talking about two of Gina's books that were on the little round table.

"I asked my dad for the *Red Fairy Book* but I haven't gotten it yet," said Jim's daughter. "Is it good?"

"You like fairy tales too?" asked Gina.

"Of course! Who doesn't?"

"Do you like *Grimm's Tales*?"

"Most of them. Sometimes they're a little creepy but then sometimes I like them because they're creepy. That probably sounds strange."

"No no," said Gina, "I feel the same way. 'Aschenputtel' is my favourite, even though I can never understand why her dad didn't stop her stepmom from tormenting her."

While their parents were talking in the kitchen, the girls continued discussing the finer points of various stories in the Brothers Grimm and Andrew Lang, and Gina forgot about her grief for a little while.

"Hey you two," said Jim from the door to the sitting room.

"Hey," they both said, almost in unison.

"Honey, I was wondering if I could speak with Gina for a little while alone?"

"Sure," his daughter said, getting up and walking towards the hall.

"Wait," said Gina, grabbing the *Red Fairy Book* and bringing it over to her. "You can read this while you wait if you want."

The girl took it with a big smile and went into the hallway, sitting on the last two steps of the staircase as she waited for her dad.

Jim sat down in the mustard chair opposite Gina. He thought her eyes looked softer and more peaceful than they had two nights ago. He always had a feeling she would get on well with his daughter.

"Gina, I need to talk with you about something difficult. It's about your dad."

"Ok," Gina said, her mind slowly coming back to where it had been prior to the diversion of the last few hours.

For better or worse, Evelyn had asked Jim to tell Gina about what she had learned that day. Perhaps it was out of anger but she didn't want any time to pass without Gina knowing the truth, no matter how painful it would be. She also hoped that if Jim spoke with her, there wouldn't be any chance of her daughter pushing her away. When it was over, she wanted them to grieve together, to be angry together.

It only took about ten minutes. Gina didn't cry. In fact, Gina barely gave any reaction at all. Jim noticed the peace slipping from her eyes, replaced by pain and desolation. He thought she looked... wounded.

They came out of the sitting room together and Gina stepped past the Greenley girl on the staircase to go up to her bedroom.

"Wait," the girl said, "your book!"

"Keep it," she replied, not looking back. Then she stopped herself. She was barely thirteen but in that moment she was able to see that Jim's daughter had nothing to do with this. She had been nice to her and Gina felt the urge to reciprocate.

"I'm sorry," she said calmly. "Thank you for the evening, I had a very nice time."

"Me too," said the girl.

"I want you to have the book," Gina said.

"Are you really sure?"

"Yes, definitely. But I completely forgot something," she continued. "I never even asked you your name?"

"Oh," said the girl, smiling, "it's Dana."

———————————————————

Three more days passed and then it was time for the funeral.

Hank was well-loved around the neighbourhood, not only because he managed Fenimore's but because he was always willing to be neighbourly. Some people showed up who knew him little more than from a single occasion in which he had helped them with some chore or given them a break on groceries when times were tough.

Evelyn decided to leave things as they were. Only the Greenleys and Jenny were privy to the real story. The priest shared things that were true regardless of Hank's character or behaviour, things of life and death, and how to reconcile the two. But neither Evelyn nor the Greenleys paid much attention, and Jenny had refused to attend the service altogether. Friends cycled through the pulpit, sharing stories and impressions, all of it washing over them like they were at a movie watching fictional characters in a far-off world.

But the service was having an impact on one person who knew the whole story. Gina sat at the back of the room beside Dana, listening intently to every single word that was spoken. Every tear, every sigh, every expression of sorrow and mourning in the room, she felt as though she were absorbing all of it. Whenever someone would share a funny anecdote about her father, she felt every vibration of everyone's laughter pulsating inside her head. It was like she was feeling too much, overwhelmed by feeling itself.

And then she stood up.

The service wasn't finished. In fact, there were still about four or five friends lined up beside the small stage, waiting for their turn to speak. Then there was music planned and an opportunity to pass by the casket and pay final respects.

But Gina was finished. She walked across the back of the church, her heels clip-clopping on the stone floor and echoing throughout the room. Then she pushed open the doors and let them slam shut behind her.

Chapter 12

Paris
October 29, 1925

Scarlet was up early and took her time getting ready that morning. She gave herself three hours to dress, do her make-up and hair, have breakfast, and make it to her meeting on time. She was due at the Louvre at ten o'clock.

She had spent the previous day shopping for today's outfit. Sometimes she knew in advance what she would wear for a particular job but other times she enjoyed finding something as she went. It helped her capture the moment. Besides, a new outfit always made her feel just a little more confident, and she needed all she could get for this particular con.

When she had robbed Fontaine last April, she had dressed to disarm him. She had aimed for a sophisticated attractiveness that she had hoped, and was right, would catch his attention without making a scene. She wanted him to notice her when she entered the shop but not dismiss her as some kind of floozy.

Today, however, she had a different agenda. She still aimed at dressing attractively but she wasn't after attention - she wanted respect. She would need the director to take her seriously and not dismiss her as simply a charming woman playing at a man's job. Of course, she would still be charming. It never hurt to grease the wheels a little.

She wore a long, white crepe silk frock, embroidered above

the hemline in black thread, giving it an elegant texture that contrasted with the plainness of the rest of the dress. She had decided on crepe because she felt that its weight communicated a certain gravitas that chiffon and taffeta simply couldn't achieve. It was sleeveless with a medium neckline, though she layered it with a black jacket that hung down below the hip. The jacket was pulled tight at the waist and secured with a single button so that the bottom half flared and opened up. The lapel was wide and plain like the dress, except for a stunning diamond and sapphire fleur-de-lis she had pinned on the right side. The jacket also had two large pockets, one on each side, and a vine-like embroidered design in white thread running along the bottom and then sweeping up around either side of each pocket.

She had curled her hair the day before yesterday and left it as it was that morning, the curls having opened up, creating a wavy appearance. She pulled it up in the back and fastened it in a bun, then wrapped her white silk scarf several times around the base of it, the same scarf she had worn for her dinner with Thomas on the Simplon Orient. She topped it all off with a headband, less flashy than a proper tiara but still adding a silver highlight to her dark black hair.

Her make-up was much more tastefully applied than the last time she prepared to visit the Louvre. Everything was done in touches, just enough to accentuate her face but not enough to look as though she were off to a club directly after the meeting. To this she added diamond stud earrings, a black pearl necklace, and a ring set with five small sapphires that matched her pin exceedingly well.

She stood in front of the mirror one last time, turning this

way and that a few times, making sure every detail was just
right. She pulled up a chair and sat down as if she were meeting with the director, crossing her legs and experimenting with
how she looked in different positions. When she was quite satisfied, she slipped on a pair of medium-heeled shoes in a deep
blue colour, completing her sapphire accents.

Allowing for twenty minutes' walk to the Louvre, she went
down to breakfast with half an hour to spare. It was a peaceful
morning despite sharing it with other guests in the dining room.
The wind was whipping up outside and had prevented her from
enjoying the gardens that morning. In fact, she would probably
end up engaging a fiacre for the short trip to the museum in order to preserve the last two hours of work she had spent on her
appearance.

At least that would give her another ten minutes or so to
squeeze in a second cup of coffee.

"Let me just check his schedule." The receptionist flipped
open a book and slid her finger about halfway down one of the
pages. "Ah yes, here it is. Miss Davenport, is it?"

"That's correct."

"He is expecting you. Please have a seat and he will be with
you momentarily."

"Merci."

No sooner had Scarlet sat down and folded her hands in her
lap than the director came through the door behind the receptionist's desk.

"Is she here?" he asked.

"Yes, Monsieur," replied the woman, pointing toward Scarlet.

"Ah, Miss Davenport! So lovely to finally meet you in person!" the director said, coming out from behind the desk and opening his arms to welcome her.

"The pleasure is mine," she said, standing up and shaking his hand.

"Please, follow me," he said, gesturing toward the door from which he had just emerged.

The office of the director of the Louvre was spacious and comfortable but not luxurious. At the far end of the room was a large wooden desk with a green leather chair behind it, but nearer the door was a small sitting area made up of two chairs, a loveseat, and a coffee table.

"Please, Miss Davenport, make yourself comfortable," the director said. He moved toward one of the chairs, offering the loveseat to Scarlet. She nodded, walked past him, and sat in the other chair. The director hesitated for a second, then shuffled his chair a little to the left so he could face her. Then they both sat down.

"I hope the trip from London wasn't too exhausting."

"Not at all," Scarlet replied.

"I have been looking forward to our meeting since I received your letter back in September. As I wrote in my reply, you are quite right that the Louvre has had many lean years since the war. Any assistance is most welcome."

"The society I represent was formed with revitalisation in mind," Scarlet said, "not only for Britain but for our allies on the Continent as well. It also doesn't hurt that several of our founders are quite the Francophiles."

"Well, you will find no complaints here!" the director said with a laugh. "We are happy to work with --"

"So, as for our proposal," Scarlet said, cutting him off without acknowledgement, "our financial supporters are willing to offer a large donation in exchange for a gesture of solidarity from your museum."

"Yes, I recall a similar statement from your letter," the director replied. "What sort of gesture are you thinking of?"

"The society is interested in a special exhibit. Something that would be a boon for the British Museum and draw in tourists from across Great Britain."

Scarlet paused for a moment, maintaining eye contact with him, then continued.

"We would like a loan of three of your Italian masterpieces from the Grand Gallery. A Raphael, a Correggio, and a da Vinci."

The director's eyes widened as he raised his brow and sat back in his chair. He crossed his left leg over his right and rubbed his chin thoughtfully.

"You understand, Miss Davenport, that the shadow, so to speak, of 1911 still haunts us. I'm not sure I would feel comfortable removing any works of such stature from the museum. There may also be some resistance from those above me."

"We certainly understand your concerns, Monsieur," Scarlet replied. "We anticipated that you might find the request difficult but our supporters are willing to compensate you generously for your troubles."

The director looked curious, as though he were not entirely sure how to take Scarlet's last statement. She didn't alleviate his curiosity immediately, allowing his thoughts to wander where they would. Eventually, she continued.

"We value discretion, Monsieur, and we trust that you will

feel the same way."

She pulled out a piece of paper from her bag, only half a sheet, and slid it across the coffee table. There was a number on it.

The director leaned forward and his eyes widened once again.

"We assume that the bulk of this donation will go towards the acquisition of new works and the improvement of facilities and security." Scarlet cleared her throat and then continued. "Of course, we don't expect an exact reporting of expenditures."

The director picked up the piece of paper and stared at it again.

"I am a little confused, Miss Davenport," the director said. "I feel as though the donation exceeds the request."

"That's because I haven't supplied you with the details yet. The society would like Correggio's *Marriage of St. Catherine*, as well as Raphael's *St. George Fighting the Dragon* --"

While Scarlet was still speaking, there was a knock at the door.

"Excuse me, please," the director said, folding the piece of paper in half and then calling out, "Yes, come in."

The door opened slowly and a man poked his head into the room. He was maybe in his early thirties, with glasses and brown hair that was unfortunately already beginning to thin.

He was about to start speaking as soon as he leaned through the doorway but when he saw Scarlet he paused for a moment. She was leaning over, shuffling through something in her bag.

"Oh, I'm so sorry," he sad, "I did not realise you had a guest, Monsieur. I can come back later."

"It's ok, Luc," the director assured him. "It's not the lunatic from a few days ago!" They both laughed. "You missed a show, Miss Davenport, I'll tell you that! So, what did you need?"

"I just wanted to speak with you about the Rubens."

"The Rub- oh, yes, I remember," the director replied. "The Berlin thing, eh?"

"That's correct Monsieur."

"Yes yes. Can you please give us another ten minutes or so?"

"Of course." The man nodded toward each of them as he left but Scarlet was still bent over, never having looked up at him.

"My apologies for the interruption. That was one of my curators. So, where were we?" the director continued as Scarlet sat up straight. "Oh right, the Raphael and the Correggio. I believe you mentioned a da Vinci as well?"

"Yes, that's right," Scarlet replied, "and da Vinci's *Mona Lisa.*"

The director breathed in sharply, as though he had just stubbed his toe on the doorjamb.

"And we would like them on a twelve-month loan."

The director rolled his eyes to the side this time and shook his head.

"Please, Madame," he said, "you ask too much of us. The theft aside, *La Joconde* has not left the Louvre since it arrived here over one hundred and twenty years ago. We do not simply share such paintings as though they were gloves or hats. I think my curators would resign if I were to agree to such an arrangement!"

Scarlet looked down and smoothed her dress over her

crossed leg. Then she shifted her position a little and looked up at the director. When he made eye contact again, she nodded towards the paper.

"As I said, exact accounting is not expected."

The director looked down again at the paper. It read only '200M'. This was francs of course, a little over two million pounds, or roughly ten million dollars at the time.

"I am still a little curious," he replied. "Are your backers really such pure art lovers that they would spend so much for a temporary exhibit? Do they expect nothing further in return?"

Scarlet smiled and adopted a tone that exposed the director's naiveté.

"Monsieur, the rich and powerful have very few things withheld from them. While philanthropy contributes to the good of humanity, it also allows them the thrill of overcoming new boundaries. The historic nature of this arrangement and the challenge of fulfilling it has not escaped their notice."

The director seemed satisfied with this response and nodded in agreement. His protest was short-lived. Scarlet knew that the promise of loose accounting practices would be extremely enticing, but she had counted on 'the historic nature of the arrangement' to appeal to his sense of pride. He took another breath, this time slow and deep.

"Well then, Madame," he said, rising from his chair and extending his hand, "let us make history!"

Scarlet smiled as she stood up and shook his hand.

"I believe we shall, Monsieur."

Chapter 13

London
December 9, 1925

There was a thin haze of smoke in the room that might not have been so obvious were it not for the light streaming in through the windows. It was an unseasonably clear and sunny December day in London, though there was still a chill in the air.

Scarlet sat alone at a corner table in the tea room at Brown's Hotel, sipping a cup of dark Assam. A Victorian three-tiered service stood before her, complete with cucumber sandwiches and a few small scones, as well as some currant jam and clotted cream. Also before her were four responses to the letters she had sent out from Paris back in October. Only Sir Peter Coleridge had failed to reply.

Whenever she was in London, Scarlet always stayed at Brown's in Mayfair. The suites were comfortable and the tea-room was second to none. But what she valued most was their discretion. High profile guests could rest assured that details of their stay and appointments would remain private. It was the kind of place where she could check in under one name but receive mail and visitors under another, and no one batted an eye.

The first letter Scarlet opened that afternoon was from Lord Abernathy, or rather, from his business manager. It read as follows:

Dear Comtesse d'Auvergne,

While we appreciate the significance of such an offer, we feel that it does not align with our present interests. We must respectfully decline.

You may be assured of our silence on the matter.

Sincerely,

H. M. MacIntyre

This was disappointing but Scarlet hadn't expected positive responses from all of her marks. Of course, to be down two already worried her a little.

The next letter she opened was from Dame Fernsby:

Dear Comtesse d'Auvergne,

I must confess, your letter took me by surprise. I would like to meet with you to discuss this matter further - though I make no promise as to the results of such a meeting.

Please call on the 12th of December at 2 o'clock in the afternoon. I will request lunch to be ready for us in the conservatory.

I look forward to making your acquaintance.

Sincerely,

A. Fernsby

Scarlet was encouraged by this response and immediately made a note of the date and time. She thought this called for a minor celebration, so she cut one of the scones in half and smothered it in jam, followed by a heaping dollop of clotted cream. She took a bite and then washed it down with another sip of Assam. 'Heavenly,' she thought to herself.

The next letter in the pile was from Gerald Milliner. It read as follows:

Dear Com.,

Jolly good. Will call on the 14th, say about noon-ish? We'll grab a spot of lunch - I know a good place near you.

Toodle pip,
Mill.

Scarlet read it twice, not because she didn't understand it but because, well, where to begin? At least he was willing to talk, that's all that mattered. And at the very least she was certain it would be an interesting lunch.

She had a cucumber sandwich next, then moved on to the final letter. It was from Sir Henry Culpepper:

Dear Comtesse,

I am intrigued. I never imagined she would be removed from her current dwelling except by force - or a short janitor with a long white smock. I would very much like to discuss this matter further with you and am happy to meet at your earliest convenience. Please ring my office anytime to arrange a meeting.

I look forward to hearing from you.

Sincerely,
H. H. C.

When she had finished her tea, Scarlet rang the office of Sir

Henry and arranged a meeting with him for December 17th at eleven o'clock in the morning.

She was delighted that her schedule was set. After a pre-dinner walk over to Berkeley Square and back, which may or may not have included a stop at Tiffany's, she dined at the hotel that evening and then retired to her room.

She read more of Poe as she lay in bed that night, recalling how Mr. White had fallen asleep to 'The Purloined Letter' on the train.

'What kind of work does he do?' she wondered. Would they really send an engineer back and forth between America and Europe? Surely there are competent men on both sides of the Atlantic?

She shook off her curiosity and returned to her reading.

"You perceive that aperture, Pompey. I wish to look through it. You will stand here just beneath the hole- so. Now, hold out one of your hands, Pompey, and let me step upon it- thus. Now, the other hand, Pompey, and with its aid I will get upon your shoulders..."

Chapter 14

Surrey Hills, Westhumble
December 12, 1925

Scarlet was two minutes early when she rang the bell at Dame Angelica's home in the Surrey Hills. She had traveled down by train that morning to the station at Box Hill & Westhumble, then gotten a taxi out to Haverford, the estate of the late Sir Allan Fernsby. Angelica was his sister and as Sir Allan had neither children nor wife, she was his only living relative and had inherited his estate after he died.

The house was a very large Tudor, with five gables on the front and a stately port-cochère marking the main entrance. The building had a rustic feel from the outside due to the red brick set between the usual half-timbering, as well as the puffs of smoke rising from more than one of its many chimneys.

Allan Fernsby had been heavily invested in manufacturing and shipping, having amassed a substantial fortune in his lifetime. He also had a passion for collecting. As a result, the interior of the home was decorated with countless pieces of fine art, primarily paintings and sculptures, but also gorgeous furniture and tapestries. The entryway alone contained a Rodin flanked on each wall by a Degas, all three of which Sir Allan had purchased directly from the artists themselves. Scarlet was sure that if his sister had one-third his appetite for art, this should be a very fruitful afternoon.

The maid had let her in and was now showing her to the conservatory where Dame Angelica was waiting.

"Comtesse d'Auvergne," the maid announced as they entered the room.

"Thank you for making the journey out to my humble home," said an older woman, perhaps in her early seventies.

"The pleasure is mine," Scarlet said with a smile.

The woman had long, greying hair that was pulled up into a bun. Around her head sat a black band with a green and gold feather rising out of the left side. She wore a fairly simple, loose-fitting black dress, with a black shawl draped over her shoulders. Her jewellery was fairly modest too, though Scarlet reckoned that her pearl necklace was deceptively valuable.

"Please, will you join me?" the woman said, pointing toward the other chair at the table.

Lunch was steak and kidney pie with carrots, parsnips, and potatoes. There were also a few different cheeses on a board beside a loaf of freshly baked bread. The conservatory was warm since it received the afternoon sun, which was peaking out from behind the clouds just enough to make the space feel like early spring instead of early winter.

"So, Comtesse," Dame Angelica began as she cut into the slice of pie that was on her plate, "this is a most curious proposal you have written about."

"You may call me Aurélie if you wish," Scarlet replied.

Dame Angelica offered no alternatives to 'Dame Angelica'. Scarlet had taken a bite of her food in the meantime and waited until she swallowed to respond. She took her time.

"We consider it a step forward."

"I can understand that," Dame Angelica replied. "So how

are you mixed up in this whole affair?" she continued in a somewhat condescending tone, "I would have expected a delegation
of grey-haired men in hats to be bumbling about this business."

"Have no fear," Scarlet replied, "there are plenty of grey-
haired men - and women - involved in this process." Dame Angelica sat up a bit straighter and adjusted her shawl, smoothing
the front of it with her hand. Scarlet didn't look up from her
food, pretending to be unaware of her own subtlety.

"After some discussion between the Louvre and the Société," she continued, "I volunteered my services to make the
process a little more personal and discreet. My family has been
a benefactor of the museum for some time now, as well as
friends of the current and previous directors. So there is already
a certain degree of trust and understanding."

"And how has Monsieur Homolle fared in the last decade? I
seem to recall he was forced to resign after the theft."

Scarlet looked up at her. She was looking back at Scarlet
with her head leaning a bit to the right as though she were very
curious indeed about the former director's fate.

"I - I'm very sorry, Dame Angelica," Scarlet replied, hesitating
a little. The older woman smiled as though she knew something
Scarlet didn't. She kept her head cocked to the side inquisitively as she awaited her response.

"I suppose you wouldn't have heard the news," Scarlet continued, "but I'm afraid the former director passed away last
June. It was very sad. But the service was beautiful."

Scarlet looked down at her food, not waiting for a sign of
Dame Angelica's disappointment. After some small talk about
the house and its extensive gardens, as well as a story or two
about her late brother, which Scarlet found genuinely interest-

ing, the woman returned rather suddenly to the topic at hand.

"Why the *Mona Lisa* though, I wonder?"

"Why do you wonder?"

"Well, why would a museum choose perhaps their most famous piece to put on the auction block, so to speak? There must be a few lesser works that could combine for an equal sum but that would not be missed by the general public."

Just then, the maid arrived to clear their plates and what remained of the pie and vegetables. She left the cheeseboard and added to it a selection of biscuits, a pot of tea, and a matching creamer and sugar bowl. Cups and saucers were set in front of each of the ladies along with smaller plates for the biscuits.

"Thank you, Jillian," said Dame Angelica. "Please, help yourself," she said to Scarlet, who felt that the old woman may have been warming up to her just a touch as the afternoon went on.

"I think it is hard to underestimate," Scarlet replied, picking up with the last question she had been asked, "the psychological impact that the theft had on the museum. Signor Peruggia was no cunning burglar. To think that such a man, unskilled and unaided, standing barely taller than my shoulder, should have been able to lift such a treasure from the wall and simply walk home with it wrapped up in his smock is something of a slight to the entire institution - from the director all the way down to the cleaners who paid him no attention."

Scarlet paused to have a biscuit while Dame Angelica reflected on these things, nodding her head and looking out the window thoughtfully.

"To this, one must also add the man's motivations," Scarlet

continued, "which appear to be more of that insidious nationalism that drove us to the Great War not much more than a decade ago. The museum's reputation as a bastion of culture and of all that is to be admired in the soul of man was called into question by an entire nation when this mercenary attempted to stir Italy against France."

Scarlet's natural disposition would never have allowed her to engage in spirited political rhetoric. But perhaps under pain of death she may have admitted to having fun playing the part.

Dame Angelica was listening closely. She was no longer looking out the window but instead kept her focus entirely on Scarlet.

"And so you see, Dame Angelica --" she tried to continue, but the old woman interrupted her.

"Angelica is fine."

Scarlet smiled. "And so you see, Angelica, selling this piece is about more than profit. It is about removing a stumbling-block, and clearing the way for a revitalised future."

As she finished, Scarlet looked down at her cup of tea, as though Angelica's response, whatever it may be, would have no bearing on the truth of her statements.

"I understand now why they sent you on this errand," the woman replied. "Discretion indeed. I think perhaps 'diffidence' may be more to the point. A bit too sheepish to admit these things themselves, I think."

Scarlet hadn't expected that line of reasoning, but it worked quite well and so she embraced it.

"I think you have a keen intuition, my lady," Scarlet replied, giving her a knowing look as if she were confirming something. Angelica looked mildly pleased with herself.

"So, let's say I were interested in this proposal," she replied, "what are the finer points of the arrangement?"

Scarlet set down her cup of tea after taking the last sip, then patted her mouth with the napkin that had been stretched across her lap.

"I will be perfectly blunt," she began. "As the sale of such a piece is unprecedented, the museum has taken its time attempting some kind of appraisal. The figure is somewhere in the neighbourhood of two million pounds."

Dame Angelica was clearly jarred by this number but also clearly trying to compose herself as though she weren't.

"Somewhere in the neighbourhood, you say? Where exactly in the neighbourhood?"

"Well, that is the thing," Scarlet replied, "the Société believes, and the museum has agreed, that the best plan is to leave the matter with the buyers."

"Ah, yes of course, I see," Angelica replied with a laugh. "A bidding war, eh?"

"Or a real-life valuation, one might call it. I may tell you that my ring is worth a million pounds, but if no one will buy it for that price, what good is my assertion?"

"But if someone will buy it for two million, or three, then you may have sold yourself short."

"Precisely why we are trusting to the collective wisdom of a group of astute aficionados," Scarlet replied, then added, "such as yourself."

"Indeed," Angelica said, squinting her eyes slightly, "I certainly do see why they sent you. Well, Comtesse," she continued, her eyes returning to normal, "I shall have to give this some thought of course."

"There is one more point I must inform you of," Scarlet said. "It is something of a condition."

"A condition?" the woman replied with a surprised tone, "I cannot imagine."

"It is not burdensome, I assure you," Scarlet replied. "Both the museum and the Société would like this arrangement to strengthen their relationship with the British Museum - their Sister across the Channel, as they like to think of it - and so also benefit the British people as a whole. Hence, along with the *Mona Lisa*, they plan to share two other masterpieces, a Raphael and a Correggio. The condition is that the da Vinci be loaned to the British Museum for a twelve-month exhibit, where it will hang beside the other two pieces before eventually finding its permanent home in the buyer's own collection."

Angelica didn't even flinch, responding straightaway with, "But of course, Comtesse. I would expect nothing less. I should have offered an exhibit myself were it not requested." She gestured widely with her hand toward the house, adding, "What is the point of all this if one cannot share it with humanity? My brother was the collector, but I hope to ensure his work is appreciated in the future."

Scarlet suddenly warmed to Dame Angelica, seeing something in this last statement that hadn't been obvious all along. She hadn't anticipated that the obscenely wealthy and reclusive spinster in the Surrey Hills was concerned about sharing anything with humanity at large. For a brief moment - but only a moment - she felt herself hoping that Angelica wouldn't end up being her only option for a buyer.

Before Scarlet left that afternoon, Angelica showed her around the house. It was a very pleasant tour and did nothing to help suppress the niggling feeling she had experienced at the end of their lunch. Scarlet wasn't a novice, however, and was able to keep her mind focused on the task at hand.

"That was a truly delightful afternoon," she said to the woman as they drew near to the front door. "Your devotion to your brother's legacy is inspiring."

"Thank you, Comtesse," Angelica said, appearing to have been touched by the fact that Scarlet had noticed. "I will contact you about this matter within the next few weeks. When will you be leaving Brown's?"

"After the New Year. Probably around the tenth or twelfth."

"Excellent. You shall have my answer before then."

"I look forward to hearing from you," Scarlet replied, "and if I am able also to help crown your brother's achievements with this greatest of masterpieces, then I will look forward to that too."

Dame Angelica only smiled and nodded. She offered Scarlet her driver to take her to the station, then bid her goodbye and wished her safe travels back to London.

Chapter 15

London
December 14, 1925

Scarlet dressed more casually that morning than she had for her meeting with Dame Angelica. Based on his letter, she believed she would find Mr. Milliner a less demanding lunch partner. And she wasn't wrong.

"That is the Comtesse now," she overheard the man at the desk say as she wandered into the lobby at about noon-ish. Before she had scanned the room for potential matches to her Mr. Milliner, she heard a voice crying out to her.

"What ho, Comtesse!"

A tallish, lanky sort of fellow was sauntering over to her, his right hand held up in greeting and his left at his side grasping the brass knob at the top of his black walking stick. He wore a blue suit with wider than average pinstripes, a white hat, and black shoes. Scarlet didn't want to underestimate him and guessed that despite its slightly ostentatious appearance, his suit was probably Saville Row.

"What ho!" he repeated as he drew closer, "That is to say, Bonjour! Greetings and salutations, Miss d'Auvergne!" As he spoke, he reached for her hand, which she offered in return and which he promptly pulled up to his mouth and kissed.

"A pleasure to meet you at last, Mr. Milliner," Scarlet replied, unsure exactly how to play the scene.

"Please, call me Milly, or Mill, whichever rolls off the tongue easier."

"Oh, uh, I think I shall stick with Mr. Milliner, if that's ok?"

"Quite alright, quite alright," Milly replied, "but you'll sound rather silly once we get to the club. You have been warned!"

"I'll take my chances," Scarlet replied, genuinely smiling as she was finding Mr. Millin - or rather, Milly - quite entertaining if nothing else.

"Right then," he said, stepping to her side and offering her his arm, "shall we sally forth and put on the nosebag?"

Milly led her through the city for about fifteen minutes before they arrived at their destination.

"Ah, here we are," he said, pulling the door open for her.

"Good afternoon, Mr. Milliner," said an older man, probably nearing eighty, who manned the entrance.

"Afternoon, Fitzy! And how's the wife these days?"

"Very well, sir," the man replied, smiling and nodding.

"Splendid!"

Scarlet wasn't exactly sure what this place was but she followed Milly past Fitzy, through a doorway and into a lounge. There were low tables scattered sparingly throughout the room, each with about three or four leather chairs around them. There was a bar at one end of the room and a piano at the other, with floor-to-ceiling bookcases lining one of the longer walls between them. Through another doorway, Scarlet could see a more proper dining area. There were about fifteen or twenty young men, probably spanning mid-twenties to mid-thirties, spread out across both rooms in little groups.

"Milly!" one of the groups called out. "Milly, ol' boy, come over here! Introduce us to your friend!"

"Now now, steady yourselves, chaps," he replied, "we're here for a feed and a civil tête-à-tête. The Comtesse has no time for some tedious imbroglio."

"Comtesse!" one of them said, "Since when does ol' Milly associate with the nobility?"

"Or when does the nobility associate with ol' Milly!" another added, to the great pleasure of his fellows.

"Haven't you heard?" Milly replied, "I'm up for a knighthood. The Comtesse here has come to pay homage on behalf of the French." He bowed as he finished, twirling his walking stick as he straightened up.

"Indeed I am," Scarlet jumped in, much to Milly's surprise and delight. "Monsieur Milliner is a friend of Europe and his honour is our honour."

The men at the table lost control of themselves with laughter. Milly took another bow as they all, mockingly, paid him various signs of respect.

They exchanged a few more words relating to the day's menu, an upcoming soirée at the club, and the Comtesse's decidedly French brand of beauty. One of them even proposed to her before she and Milly entered the dining room. She declined the offer.

The menu consisted of a typical roast dinner, including Yorkshire puddings, boiled potatoes, and carrots. Milly suggested the perfect wine to complement their 'cosmopolitan' fare and Scarlet agreed.

"I must say, Comtesse" he began, "your English is sans défaut."

"Thank you, Monsieur," Scarlet replied. "My parents hired tutors for me from a very young age. And we took many trips to England over the years, sometimes for several months at a time."

"Well, it certainly paid off, what?"

Their wine arrived and Milly sniffed, sipped, and swished, finally giving Scarlet leave to enjoy it without reservation. The waiter poured their glasses and then left the bottle on the table.

"Now, about the curious business of said painting," Milly started, resting his elbows on the table and folding his hands under his chin. "What's the posish?"

"As you may recall from my letter, the museum feels that --"

Milly cut her off, waving one of his hands as if at a fly.

"No no, Comtesse, I couldn't care less about their reasons. Some burglarious Italian made off with their cheddar - or brie, as the French may have it - and now, a few years down the road, the men at the top want to be done with the disgrace. Say no more."

Scarlet was trying not to laugh at his flippant, yet insightful summary of the situation. It was sufficient for her purposes, and more importantly it was sufficient for Milly, so she didn't worry about elaborating.

"It is what it is," he continued. "No, what I'm talking about is the almighty guinea. The oil of palm. Clams, as our rebellious cousins across the Pond might say."

Scarlet was trying not to lose a sense of her role in the midst of her amusement.

"After much consultation between the museum and the Société, we have decided to allow our buyers to make their best offers. However, I will say that anything under two million pounds may not be taken seriously."

"That certainly is a goodish pile, what!" Milly leaned back in his chair and looked out the window. He was quiet for a minute or two and then continued.

"I don't buy it though," he said.

"I'm sorry?"

"That little grin of hers. The lady doth feign mirth, I think."

"Perhaps."

"She has all the signs of being one of the deprecating and disapproving females of the species. Not the sort of bonhomous disposition a chap's normally on the lookout for."

"I suppose not."

"Still, there's no deprecating or disapproving of Signor da Vinci's skill. He is a master of the oil and canvas!"

"The *Mona Lisa* is painted on poplar."

"Exactly. I suspect she was far too ligneous to depict on anything pliable."

Their food arrived and the conversation changed to talk of British versus Continental cuisines. Milly fancied himself an expert in the field and praised the well-shaped puddings with their dry bottoms, but declared that he would chide the chef upon their next meeting as the boiled vegetables were far too al dente for the discerning customer.

Despite her enjoyment of the afternoon, under most circumstances Scarlet would have cut their lunch short so as not to waste her time. There was nothing about Mr. Milliner that suggested he was in the market for any piece of fine art or culture. But Scarlet knew he was a man of considerable means. Unlike Dame Angelica, Mr. Milliner had experienced the unusually good fortune of having not one but three separate estates entailed upon him, all of which had settled over the past two years. The raucous pack in the lounge were rich young men as well, but Milly was on a different level entirely.

As their lunch came to a close and their glasses emptied, Scarlet tried to pull the conversation back to the painting.

"So, Milly, have you a place in mind where you might hang her?" she asked.

"I think she'd go nicely just above Fitzy in the entryway. Would add a certain je ne sais quoi to the place, don't you think?"

Scarlet must have looked horrified because Milly quickly added, "I'm kidding, Comtesse! I understand the magnitude of the thing. Don't think me entirely devoid of the savoir-vivre!"

She smiled. "Of course not, Monsieur."

"No, I was actually thinking that if I were to procure said prize I would probably ship her off to the British Museum and let her fraternise with the other masterpieces. I'm sure she'd quickly find my company opprobrious anyway and be glad of the arrangement."

His answer surprised her but also reminded her that she hadn't yet specified the condition that the painting be exhibited at the museum in London for twelve months after the sale. She filled in the details and Milly made no objection, informing her that he would think carefully about the matter as a whole and get back to her before she returned to France.

When they had finished their meeting, Milly walked her back to the hotel, but not before she received two more proposals of marriage from his friends on her way out of the club. Each of them pledged their undying love to her and declared that they didn't even mind that she was French, as long as she didn't speak it much around the house.

"But look at this one!" said Dana, pulling another magazine out from under the one they were looking at and setting in on top with a 'slap'.

"What is that? Where is that?"

"It's called Schloss Neusch..." Dana stumbled over the pronunciation, then tried again. "Neuschstan--"

Gina cut her off, having read the name at the bottom of the page.

"Neuschwanstein."

"Yes, that's it! Can you imagine anything so grand? So romantic?!"

The two girls were sitting together at Dana's house, a small stack of magazines between them on the sofa and two empty cups of tea on the coffee table. The picture in front of them was a painting from the cover of that month's *Adventure* magazine, depicting a perfectly quintessential storybook castle, with whitewashed walls, turrets, and a bridge for an entrance, all towering above an equally storybook-looking forest.

"But do you suppose it actually looks like that?" Gina asked.

"Of course it does! Why shouldn't it?" Dana replied.

"It's just too perfect, isn't it?"

"How can anything be 'too perfect'?"

Gina didn't respond, she just shook her head a little as she kept staring at the picture. It was quite beautiful. She imagined herself walking across the bridge, or leaning out of the highest turret and taking a deep breath as she looked up at the sky and then down at the trees.

"It says inside that the king was a hopeless romantic," Dana said. "You'd have to be to build such a thing, right? Accountants don't build castles. It wouldn't make sense."

"And did you say where it is?"

"Bavaria."

"I'm not sure the BRT has trains that go there," Gina laughed.

"Nooo..." said Dana, shuffling through her magazines as she left Gina hanging for a few seconds. She pulled out a piece of paper and placed it down with another 'slap' on top of the Neuschwanstein picture.

"But look what I just got at work today!"

Gina picked up the paper and read the top: "Calling All Hello-Girls! General Pershing Needs You!"

"What's this about?" she asked.

"Apparently they need telephone operators on the front. I guess they've got their lines crossed or something and can't get through to each other, so they're looking for women who know the job to come sort it out."

"Really? So are you all packed already?"

"Not hardly," Dana replied with a frown. "You really think my dad is going to let me do this?"

"But he let you get the job in the first place, didn't he?"

"Yes, but you could practically throw a stone to his office from my switchboard. There's a war going on, Gina, remember?

133

I don't think he wants me more than a few blocks away."

"True."

They were quiet for half a minute before Dana continued.

"Buuut, I was thinking... maybe this would be perfect for you?"

"Me?" Gina said with a confused face.

"Sure, why not?"

"Why not? Are you kidding?" she laughed. "Uh, how about the fact that I'm not a telephone operator?"

"Maybe not," Dana said, "but you have been studying French, right?"

"A little."

"Come on, more than 'a little'! You're practically a native, aren't you?"

"Hardly."

"But look here," Dana said, pointing to the paper, "they want operators who know French, or at least who could learn it quickly."

She was right. The flyer said that they would prioritise ladies who were both trained operators and bilingual.

"Even if I were fluent," Gina replied, "I still don't know how to operate a switchboard, which seems kind of important, don't you think?"

"Oh, it's nothing," said Dana, waving her hand at Gina. "Plug in this, unplug that, say 'Hello!' in a friendly voice. You could do it in your sleep!"

"It took you months to learn the job, and more months to get good at it."

"I'm not very smart," said Dana, giving Gina a wink and a nudge with her elbow, "but you are!"

"Are you trying to get rid of me?" Gina asked. "You want me to fall into a trench and get lost in the mud somewhere in France?"

"Goodness no! You'd be in a comfortable tent or something, I'm sure. And no, I don't want to get rid of you. It's just that I think you're the only hope of one of us getting to see all these amazing things we've been reading about for so long now."

Dana and Gina had become close friends because Dana was the only person with whom Gina felt completely relaxed. She could be herself in pretty much every respect and Dana accepted her. And not only accepted her but genuinely cared about her happiness. When she suggested that Gina experience the wonders of Europe for them both, Gina knew that if she went, that's exactly what would happen. Somehow, Dana would gain as much joy from it as she would.

"I'll tell you what," said Dana, "how about I teach you?"

"Teach me what?"

"How to be an operator."

"You mean right now?"

"No! Don't be ridiculous!" Dana laughed. "It's almost dinner. I'll teach you tomorrow."

Despite her best efforts and unflinching optimism, Dana was not able to teach Gina everything there was to know about operating a switchboard the following day. Especially not in her bedroom with a cardboard box and yarn for props.

"How much time do I have before I need to sign up for this thing, or whatever it is I need to do?"

"The flyer said there's a special train leaving Grand Central for Maryland on November 1st. I think you just show up."

"Sounds kind of disorganised," Gina said. Having slept on it the previous night, she had actually been getting more interested in the idea. Unlike Dana, Gina didn't have a job. In fact, her life had been somewhat reclusive. However, recently she had been craving something new, something altogether different. Of course, she hadn't exactly imagined that it would be the Western Front! Oddly enough though, fear wasn't what made her hesitant.

"Aren't they calling girls from all over the country?" she asked.

"I think so."

"There could be thousands of them that show up. I doubt I'm going to be the pick of the litter, not once they see how incompetent I am at actually completing a call!"

"Just improvise," said Dana, shrugging her shoulders and gesturing toward the cardboard box.

"Right!" Gina scoffed, "And we both know how good I am at that!"

The two girls spent the rest of the afternoon and evening together, their conversation drifting back and forth between switchboard operations, all the wondrous things Gina would see in Europe on her grand adventure, and the serious difficulty Dana was having at work trying to decide which of her two managers, Frank or Fred, was the cutest.

"They don't seem quite as hungry today. Maybe someone already fed them."

Evelyn laid the bag of stale bread on the bench next to her

and watched the birds flitting about on the trees and shrubs. They whistled and chirped and made a beautifully unstructured symphony that complemented the sunny October afternoon.

"What's that one again? The white and tan one?"

"It's a sparrow."

"And the black ones?" Gina asked.

"They're starlings," answered Evelyn.

"Oh, that's right. I knew that."

"You know, when I was a little girl, there were no starlings in Central Park."

"What? Really?"

"Someone introduced them from Europe when I was a teenager."

Gina looked over at a few of them bouncing along the path in front of their bench and suddenly the little iridescent birds took on a whole new sense of mystery and romance. Or rather, a sense of mystery and romance. Apart from times like today when she and her mother would make the trip to Manhattan to enjoy the park, she really didn't think much about the limited wildlife around her in Brooklyn.

"I'd like to go to Europe someday," Gina said with a distant look as she watched one of the birds flutter up to the tree above them.

"I love the park in the Fall," her mom replied.

They were quiet for a while, then Gina continued.

"Mom, what if I told you I might have a chance to go to Europe?"

Evelyn didn't respond, she just looked up at the sky and smiled.

"Dana told me about this thing where the army is looking for girls to operate switchboards to help with the war effort. They especially want girls that can speak French. Mine's pretty good."

Evelyn picked up the bag of stale bread, reached inside, and pulled out a few pieces of crust.

"Maybe I wasn't making the pieces small enough," she said as she rubbed it between her fingers and dropped the crumbs on the ground in front of her. A couple of sparrows came close and pecked at it.

"Can I try?" Gina asked.

Her mom handed her the bag. She rubbed a few pieces together until they were very fine and then walked over to one of the trees where the starlings had been coming and going. She looked up and then reached down and spread the crumbs on the ground. She backed up a little bit and watched.

Despite the singing overhead, none of the birds came down for the food. But just then, from behind the tree, a little starling hopped across the ground and over to the bread. It pecked and ate and then hopped a little further, pecked and ate again. Gina smiled and her heart beat a little faster.

Then she noticed something. One of its wings seemed lower than the other, as though it were drooping and not tucked away neatly at the bird's side. Gina took a step closer and the starling responded by taking a couple of hops in the opposite direction. She decided to move more slowly, hoping very much that the little thing might let her touch its head.

She slowly got down on her knees and the bird seemed to be ok with it. Then she started to extend her hand as slowly as she could. She was still about a foot away when the starling made what Gina felt were several fairly perturbed little chirps. It attempted to use its wings to pull away from her but as it tried, it only got a few inches off the ground. She thought it looked not only scared now but also in pain as it kept making its disgruntled sounds while trying to flap its injured wing.

Gina got up quickly and backed away to the other side of the path, back to the bench where she and her mom had been sitting. She felt sick to her stomach and wasn't interested in feeding the birds anymore.

"Can we go now?" she asked her mom.

"In a little while," Evelyn replied, looking in the opposite direction.

Gina sat down and folded her arms tightly. She leaned forward and stared at the gravel path, then at the grass. Anywhere, except up at the birds.

When the day came, Dana hadn't been able to go with Gina to the station because of work. But the night before, they had stayed up late in that mix of well-wishing, reminiscing, and nervous chatter that usually attends the departure of loved ones setting out on a distant journey.

Gina had only been to Grand Central once, a very long time ago, when her father was still alive. Those memories felt like she was peering into the head of a completely different person. Scenes of the three of them smiling together, her dad buying a newspaper to read on the trip, her mom making sure she didn't get away from them in the crowd. Holding hands as they boarded the train for Connecticut to visit her mom's brother and sister. Leaning her head on her dad's shoulder as she fell asleep somewhere just outside of Manhattan.

ANDREW STOPYRA

She shook them off, much as she had been doing for the last six years. As far as she was concerned, that life had ended... if it ever really existed in the first place. She glanced back and forth quickly across the crowds at the station, trying to reset her mind and focus on the moment.

She eventually found the platform where the ladies were waiting to board the train to Maryland. Gina felt like she had underestimated. 'There must be a thousand just here in New York!' she thought.

In reality, there were only about two hundred, but it looked like far more because they were organised into a long line that snaked up and down the platform beside the train. Gina stood on her toes and craned her neck to see what they were waiting for. There were multiple cars, why weren't they all just boarding wherever there was room?

She could see four men with papers at the front of the line, talking with each woman for three or four seconds, then pointing some toward the train and waving others away. She decided to get in the back of the line and see if anyone around her knew what was going on.

The two girls in front of her were talking when she came up behind them so she decided to wait for a lull in the conversation to ask them about the men. After a few minutes with no lull, pause, hesitation, or slowing down, Gina decided to ask one of the girls who had gotten in line behind her.

"Um, hi," she started. Talking with strangers was not her specialty. In fact, she avoided it at all costs.

"Hi!" said the blonde-haired girl who was next in line. "This is so exciting, isn't it?"

"I guess so," Gina replied, then quickly added, "I mean, yes,

140

it really is!" not wanting the girl to feel like she was disagreeing with her.

They were quiet for a minute, during which time Gina chickened-out and decided not to ask her question about the men at the front. The line actually ended up moving faster than she expected, or maybe faster than she hoped since she was getting more and more nervous with each step forward.

When she was about five or six spaces from the front, she was finally able to see and hear exactly what the men were doing. They had lists of all the registered operators from all the offices in the New York area. Because so many women had volunteered, they were prescreening them to limit the actual number that got on the train.

Gina's palms started to sweat. She took off her jacket and draped it over her left arm. She was carrying her suitcase in her right hand, setting it down each time the line stopped. She started contemplating slipping away before she was embarrassed by the men with the lists.

But then it was her turn.

"Name?" the man asked, looking up from his list with an impersonal stare.

Before Gina could even think about his question, before she even realised what was coming out of her mouth, she heard herself answering him.

"Dana Greenley."

———————————

"Excellent work today, Dana. And thank you for helping explain the passé composé a bit more clearly."

"Of course," Gina replied, "I'm really enjoying the classes, and I think the girls are picking it up quickly."

"Let's hope so!" replied Gina's French teacher. "We've only got until March and then the first lot needs to be ready to ship out."

"Will you be coming with us?" Gina asked.

"I'm afraid not. I'm needed here to keep training the servicemen."

"I'll definitely miss you when the time comes."

"You're too kind," the woman said. "But it is nice to hear that sort of thing from a student. Before the war, most of my students were rich children whose parents wanted them to be more 'cultured'. So they hired tutors for all kinds of subjects - from languages to music to art. Most of the children hated it and just wanted to play outside. They were certainly never sorry to see me go!"

Gina's French teacher had actually come to America from France when she was a teenager. She had been in the country for twenty-seven years, and while she made her living teaching French, her English was impeccable.

"Besides," she continued, "if the girls have any trouble, you will be there to correct them!"

"Now who's being too kind!" Gina laughed.

"I'll see you tomorrow then," the woman said as she waved goodbye and started to walk away.

"Until tomorrow then, Miss d'Auvergne," Gina replied with a wave of her own as she headed off in the opposite direction.

That evening, Gina sat up looking over the books and papers they had given all the girls for their switchboard and communications training. She had been pleasantly surprised to find that things were simpler than she had thought they would be. Even though the girls were all supposed to be trained operators already, the military made sure to review everything with them just to be safe, which helped Gina immensely. It wasn't exactly easy, but at the same time she wasn't making a fool of herself in class. She was even feeling as though she might be able to do the job effectively once she got to Europe.

But even more than getting her head around the lessons, Gina felt that her confidence had skyrocketed since that awkward moment on the platform when she had adopted her new identity. In fact, she felt as though it had grown precisely because of that moment. Using Dana's name, assuming her identity to a certain extent, it had made her feel liberated.

After her father's death, her world had collapsed - not just figuratively but experientially too. She and her mom distanced themselves from friends who knew the old Hank because it was just too painful to live the lie. They started shopping at different stores and avoiding all the places where they had always gone to socialise. Jenny had moved to Manhattan and rarely visited, though they were still close and saw each other when they could. The Greenleys had been their only friends, their only family.

And Gina had learned to live with it. She had adapted to this cloistered lifestyle, and with the exception of that recently awakened, niggling feeling that had been nudging her towards change, she had become relatively content with it all.

But the moment she became Dana Greenley, it was as though barriers she hadn't even realised were there began to crumble. Behind them, the sun shone brighter, the sky more blue - or rather, there was a sun and a sky again. It even seemed as though her hair moved with the wind again... and she liked the way it felt.

She had wrestled with her decision since arriving at Camp Franklin, wondering if she had done the wrong thing by lying about her name. She had come to the conclusion that Dana wouldn't have cared at all. In fact, she thought it was exactly the kind of thing Dana might have suggested if she had been there with her! But even more than that, after finding a breach in the wall surrounding her old life, she simply couldn't entertain the idea of ever being Gina Parker again.

Just then, there was a knock at the door.

Gina opened it and was greeted by a brown-haired girl with a big smile on her face.

"Dana! I --" she stopped herself and lowered her eyebrows.

"Yes?" Gina replied.

"I'm so sorry!" the girl continued. "They told me this was Dana Greenley's room but I must have gotten the number wrong. We were old school friends but I haven't seen her in years. When I heard she was here I just had to say hi. Sorry to bother you!"

"It's no trouble," Gina answered. Of course, it was a massive load of trouble, but what was she to do?

The girl turned to leave but then turned back again.

"You wouldn't happen to know where Dana's room is, would you?"

Chapter 17

London
December 17, 1925

The offices of Sir Henry Culpepper were far enough away from Brown's Hotel that Scarlet would need to take a cab. She allowed herself to sleep in that morning but still got up with enough time to have breakfast before setting out. Though it certainly fortified one for the day ahead, she found that she could never handle a full English breakfast for more than a couple of days in a row. She had pared it down to two boiled eggs and toast with a cup of tea for the last week or so but she was longing for strong coffee and pastry. As a rule, she didn't trust English bakeries.

After as late a breakfast as time would allow, Scarlet got her cab over to Chelsea. Sir Henry was originally from the north of England, the son of a wealthy gentleman who owned several clothing factories. Henry had decided not to take up the family business but instead to study the law, becoming a very successful barrister while he was still a relatively young man. Eventually, he founded his own legal practice which now, thirty-three years later, had offices throughout the country.

His personal success coupled with his stake in the family business, now run by his brother, meant that Sir Henry had considerable resources. For the last decade or so, he had been making sizeable donations to both the British Museum and the

Victoria and Albert Museum, in addition to amassing a valuable collection of his own. Despite his philanthropy and appreciation for the finer things however, he retained a reputation for being a somewhat difficult person to deal with. Most would have said 'litigious', with no pun intended.

Scarlet's cab pulled up in front of the building and the doorman came out to help her from the car. He showed her into the foyer where a receptionist sat behind a massive wooden desk, her head barely visible from a distance.

"Hello, may I help you?" she asked.

"Yes, I have an appointment with Sir Henry Culpepper at eleven."

"Your name?"

"d'Auvergne."

The woman scanned the schedule in front of her.

"Oh, of course," she replied, "the Comtesse. Someone will be with you shortly."

"Thank you."

Scarlet sat in one of the two armchairs that was positioned just to the right of the entrance. It was about five or six minutes before she heard her name again.

"Comtesse d'Auvergne?" a man said.

"Yes," Scarlet replied, standing up to greet him.

"My name is Neville Penwell. I'm Sir Henry's attorney."

"You'll forgive my asking, but the owner of the practice needs a lawyer?"

"You're not the first to ask," Mr. Penwell laughed, "but yes, it's always wise for even the keenest of legal minds to have some objective counsel."

"Seems very prudent."

"Sir Henry is waiting for us upstairs. Shall we?"

Mr. Penwell led her past the receptionist's wooden bulwark and down the hall a few steps to a lift.

"His office is on the fourth floor," he said as he slid open the cage and pulled back the door for her. The lift clunked and whirled into motion as the two of them stood in silence until they had reached their destination.

Sir Henry's office could more accurately have been called Sir Henry's floor. He had taken over the entire fourth floor, opening it up as much as was structurally possible for the old building. There were large windows overlooking the street, sumptuous couches, and a variety of indoor plants, some of which were practically small trees. There were also several pieces of very fine furniture, including a large roll-top desk, a mahogany secretary packed with papers and small notebooks, and a massive coffee table in the main seating area. Scarlet later learned that the table had been custom-made for Sir Henry from a single piece of redwood he had purchased while on holiday in America.

"Ah, Comtesse d'Auvergne," Sir Henry said, entering the seating area from the right through one of the few doors in the space.

"Sir Henry," Scarlet said, extending her hand to him. He shook it firmly.

He was perhaps about six feet tall, or just under, Scarlet reckoned, based on her own height of five-seven. He was older but still had a strong appearance. In fact, Scarlet felt that he reminded her very much of Teddy Roosevelt in his later years, being slightly overweight but in a kind of sturdy, imposing sort of way. He even had a similar moustache and short hair, most of which was grey now, though a few streaks of its original brown were visible.

"Shall we sit?" He moved toward the only chair beside the redwood table and sat down. Either side of him, facing one another across the table, were two couches upon which Scarlet and Mr. Penwell sat.

"You're younger than I expected, Comtesse," Sir Henry began, not maintaining eye-contact with Scarlet but glancing back and forth between her and whatever else was catching his eye around the room.

"Is that a problem?" Scarlet replied.

"I'm not sure yet," he said, smiling at her and then briefly looking in Mr. Penwell's direction.

Scarlet had disciplined her mind and emotions over the years to handle insults or other derogatory remarks in the course of a con. She couldn't let comments like this throw her off and make her lose sight of her goal. Besides, if Sir Henry did end up being her buyer, she would more than repay his condescension.

"I believe I heard a story once," Scarlet said, "about a young man discontent with the clothing industry who eventually started his own legal practice at the age of twenty-seven. Perhaps I shall try to find this man. I'm sure he would be more open to the possibilities and potential of youth."

Sir Henry laughed and then reached into his jacket pocket and pulled out a cigar.

"Would you like one, Comtesse?"

"No, thank you."

He lit the cigar with several large puffs, then leaned back a bit in his chair and crossed his legs.

"So, the French can't afford to keep their own museums going and they've turned to the English for help, is that it?"

"If one is a cynic."

"Or a pragmatist," Sir Henry replied. He leaned his head back and slowly released a cloud of smoke into the air.

Scarlet was quickly finding him rather obnoxious. While this was certainly not the first time she had dealt with the rich and powerful, people who believed their wealth validated any and all of their opinions, Sir Henry was of the self-made sort, which usually included a generous helping of narcissism in the mix.

"Perhaps you are right, Monsieur," Scarlet said, changing her approach. She turned her head away from him slightly and tugged at the bottom of her dress a little to straighten it. "My father has said similar things."

"Has he now?"

"There is a reason he married an Englishwoman, Monsieur."

Sir Henry let out another laugh and puffed happily on his cigar.

"I think I would enjoy chatting with your father," he said.

"I'm sure he would find you most refreshing."

Sir Henry cleared his throat and then turned to specifics.

"So what is the museum hoping to earn from this deal?"

"At least two million pounds." Scarlet decided to skip the formalities and be as direct as possible.

"At least?"

"I mean no offence, but if you recall my letter, you are only one of a group of potential buyers," Scarlet replied. "Each of you will have the chance to make your offer."

Sir Henry stared at the ceiling for a moment, then at a plant across the room, then gave a quick look in Mr. Penwell's direction before looking at Scarlet again.

"And how is the buyer to take possession of the painting?"

"The museum will crate the piece as it would normally for the removal or storage of such an object. Four attendants will be assigned to it, a specialist and three security officers, who will then accompany the painting by train to London. It is expected that the buyer will send one or more attendants of their own to Paris to oversee the process."

"Absolutely," Sir Henry affirmed.

"It is also expected that the buyer will arrange for the transfer of funds by wire in advance of shipment, preferably one week prior to the day."

"Unacceptable," he said, no longer looking at her.

"I'm sorry?"

"Half would be wired in advance but the other half would be held until I hear from my man in Paris on the day, and he assures me that the item is safely aboard the train for Calais. There would be no negotiation on this point."

"I understand," Scarlet replied. "I am sure the museum would be willing to work with you on this."

"I'm sure they would be," he replied.

Scarlet coughed a few times and Sir Henry offered her a drink. There was a cart across the room with spirits of every sort in an array of bottles and fine crystal decanters.

"Just some water would be lovely," she replied.

"I'll get it," Mr. Penwell said.

"And a brandy for me, Neville," Sir Henry added.

"Of course."

Scarlet was beginning to see that Mr. Penwell was more than legal counsel. He seemed to be Sir Henry's right-hand man. As he returned with the drinks, he addressed him simply as "sir," much as an employee or servant would.

"Hold out your hand, Comtesse," Sir Henry said, shifting to the edge of his chair and leaning towards her. Scarlet obliged, sliding to the edge of the couch to reach him.

"Palm down, please."

When she turned it over, Sir Henry dipped his finger into the liquid in his glass and dabbed it on the back of her hand.

"Now, give that a minute or so, then take a big whiff and tell me what you get."

As the spot on her hand began to dry, Scarlet pulled it up to her nose and gave it a sniff.

"Figs?" she said.

"Yes. And?"

She smelled again but was unsure of any other distinct flavour. She took a guess.

"Dates?"

"Apricots, actually." He swirled the beverage in his glass a few times. "There are few things more satisfying than the smell of a perfectly aged Armagnac." After a few more swirls, he took a sip.

"You see, Miss d'Auvergne," he continued, "I am not cynical about all things French."

After a few minutes of listening to him pontificate about the only proper ways to distill, package, and enjoy brandy, Scarlet returned to the business of the painting.

"There is one other part of the arrangement which was not in my letter."

"And what is that?"

"The museum would like this sale to benefit not only itself and the buyer but the British people as a whole. They will include two more masterpieces, a Raphael and a Correggio, as loans to the British Museum. A condition of the sale is that the buyer allows the piece to be displayed alongside these two other works for a twelve-month period following the sale. At the end of this time, they may do as they please with it while the others will be returned to Paris."

Sir Henry made an audible "hmm" as he turned toward Mr. Penwell.

"Sounds like good publicity to me," he said to Sir Henry.

"It certainly does," he agreed. "'The Culpepper Exhibit' has a nice ring to it, don't you think?"

"And perhaps eventually 'The Culpepper Wing'," Mr. Penwell added.

"Now you're on to it, Neville!" Sir Henry laughed.

He set down his cigar on an ashtray at the edge of the redwood table and stood up with a deep breath.

"Well, Comtesse, I will think this over and get back to you in a few days."

"You may take a few weeks if you like. I will be at Brown's until the second week of January."

"No no. If I cannot decide in a few days, then the answer should be no regardless."

"Whatever you prefer," Scarlet replied.

"I do have one request for you, Miss d'Auvergne," Sir Henry said as he stepped away from the table and walked over to the large windows overlooking the street.

"Yes?"

"Inform me of the other offers as they come in. If I decide to purchase the painting, I want to purchase the painting. Do you understand?"

Scarlet thought about this for a moment and then stood up and walked over to the window, not too close to Sir Henry but near enough that she made her presence felt. She looked out at the tops of the surrounding buildings as she spoke.

"It may be easier than that, Monsieur."

She could tell Sir Henry had turned to look at her but she continued staring at the buildings and the sky.

"How so?" he asked with an eagerness that betrayed the first hint of vulnerability she had sensed in the course of their conversation.

"I am in a unique position to communicate all offers to the museum and the Société for consideration. One might say that what is written or told to *me* is another matter entirely."

Sir Henry looked back out the window and down at the street. He was quiet for a minute or so, taking in and letting out a few forced breaths and making a 'ticking' sound with his mouth. Finally he turned and faced Scarlet completely.

"Miss d'Auvergne," he said, holding out his hand, "it has been a pleasure."

Scarlet gave him her hand, which he shook with less vigour this time.

"Agreed," she said, nodding slowly and smiling at him.

"Mr. Penwell, would you be so kind as to show the Comtesse out and get her wherever she needs to go?"

"Of course, sir."

"You are too kind, Monsieur," Scarlet replied to Sir Henry. Then she walked towards the lift, accompanied by the attorney.

When she stepped inside, she turned around and looked back towards the windows just in time to catch a glimpse of Sir Henry as he vanished through the doorway where he had first entered the room. Then Mr. Penwell slid the cage shut, closed the door, and the lift descended to the foyer.

"And how long have you worked with him?"

"About twelve years."

Scarlet was trying to make small talk in the lobby with Mr. Penwell as they awaited Sir Henry's driver to take her back to the hotel.

"Are you often in London?" he asked her.

"Maybe twice a year, or less."

Just then a man came through the front door and went up to the receptionist's desk. Scarlet and Mr. Penwell were sitting together in the chairs off to the side, so she paid him little notice. That is, until she heard the receptionist's voice.

"Ah yes, a Mr. White, is it?"

"That's correct," the man said.

A shot of adrenaline ran through Scarlet like a jolt of electricity. She could feel her heart pounding in her chest. A wave of anxiety warmed her body.

Thomas White stood at the desk as the receptionist was going through some papers. He was preoccupied with her and whatever she was doing, and Scarlet could only hope he would stay that way until she was able to exit the building.

"Ah, here we are," said Mr. Penwell, standing up.

The car was parked outside and Thomas was still distracted as she got up. She was halfway to the door and facing away from him, toward the street, when Mr. Penwell decided to be cordial.

"Well, as Sir Henry said, it was a pleasure, Comtesse."

He couldn't see her face, but Scarlet winced as though she were in pain. Then she heard another voice from behind them.

"Comtesse?" Thomas said out loud. "A real-life Comtesse, eh?"

She knew they both expected her to turn around, Mr. Penwell as an act of politeness, Thomas because - well, just because. She hesitated only a few seconds but it felt like an eternity.

Then she turned around.

Chapter 18

Camp Franklin
December 1917

In the days after she had first assumed the name Dana Greenley, Gina had figured there was a chance that someone from Dana's office might be part of the group and expose her as a fraud. Thankfully, this hadn't been the case. After a few weeks of anonymity around the camp, she had thought that she was clear of any danger.

But now the girl was staring at her, waiting for an answer. Gina hesitated only a few seconds but it felt like an eternity.

Then she thought of something.

"May I ask your name, please?" she said.

"Harriet McMillan."

"I don't recall having met you so far as part of the group. Did you just arrive at the camp?"

"Sort of," she said. "My sister is here and I've come to visit for a few days."

"Ah, I see," Gina said. "I'm sorry for the interrogation but they've been teaching us to be cautious around here, as you can imagine."

"Of course!" the girl said with a smile.

"I think there's been some confusion. I am in fact Dana Greenley."

"From Brooklyn?" the girl asked with a confused face.

"Only recently. My family moved down from Queens about six months ago."

"Ahh, ok."

Despite the fact that this had been sufficient to clarify the situation for the girl, Gina found herself getting oddly caught up in the moment.

"I hesitate to share this with you, for security reasons, as I alluded to before," she said, "but my name isn't technically Dana Greenley."

"Oh, I --" the girl started but Gina interrupted her to continue.

"You see, it's actually Blanche Greenley. Dana is my middle name."

"I see," the girl replied. "But why use your middle name?"

"Blanche? Really? Wouldn't you?"

The girl laughed. "I suppose so!" she agreed.

"If you wouldn't mind, please keep this to yourself?" Gina asked with a pathetic tone.

"Oh, of course! Hush hush!" she said with a silly, sneaky face, putting her finger up to her mouth and bending over slightly.

"Thank you so much!" Gina replied.

Harriet eventually left Camp Franklin three days later, but not before she and Gina had shared a few subtle winks and taps of the nose as they bonded from afar over their shared 'secret'.

Gina's switchboard training continued, as did her French lessons under Miss d'Auvergne. The French teacher had sort of taken Gina under her wing, not simply in the finer points of grammar and syntax but also as an older woman imparting wisdom to a younger woman whenever she could. She also introduced Gina to the virtues of a very strong cup of coffee, but lamented that there were no quality pastries that side of the Atlantic to accompany it.

"You must promise me something, Gina."

"What's that?"

"When you make it to France," her teacher said, "you must visit a little place called Ladurée in the Rue Royale."

"What is that?" Gina asked.

"Just a bakery. But you will understand when you go there. Only make sure you order at least three macarons, regardless of whatever else you get. Two is never enough."

"What's a macaron?"

"Surely they have macarons in Brooklyn?"

"Probably, but my family didn't really try exotic things. We were pretty simple."

"Exotic! Well, you will find out soon enough," Miss d'Auvergne said with a smile, "and you will wonder how you ever lived without them."

Gina laughed. "Ok, I'll write it down somewhere so I don't forget!"

"You may find it's the most important thing you've learned during your stay at Camp Franklin!"

The two of them were sitting in a corner of the mess hall in the late afternoon. No one was around except for a handful of kitchen staff behind the service counters who were beginning to chop vegetables and tenderise meat in preparation for dinner.

Miss d'Auvergne was quiet for a while and then asked Gina a question in a different tone.

"Are you nervous?"

"Nervous? About what?"

"About eventually being shipped off to the war."

"Not really," Gina replied in all honesty. She had been surprised by it herself but it was the truth.

"That's good. There's no need to borrow trouble. You might as well enjoy the time you have here."

"What is it like?" Gina asked, "France, I mean."

"I haven't been back in over ten years," Miss d'Auvergne replied with a sigh. "I imagine some things will be different now, though some things never change, I'm sure."

"Will I see castles, do you think?"

Her teacher laughed. "I'm sure you shall! Let's hope they are still standing after all the artillery shells have been fired."

"Have you ever visited Paris?"

"Where do you think Ladurée and the Rue Royale are?" she replied with a note of surprise in her voice.

"Oh, I didn't --"

"I'm only teasing you, dear. How would you know! But yes, of course I have been to Paris. Many times, in fact. I am from a place just outside of Paris, called Montreuil."

"Is it a romantic place?"

"I don't really believe that a place can be romantic," Miss d'Auvergne replied, pursing her lips as she appeared to be thinking about her own statement.

"Are you still teasing me?" Gina replied with a confused look. "Have you never seen pictures of Castle Neuschwanstein?"

"I certainly have, and it is a very beautiful place. But I wouldn't necessarily say that the building is romantic."

159

"What?" Gina said, at a loss for what more to add.

"I think when you see a picture like that," her teacher answered her, "you find it romantic because you immediately begin to imagine what might be happening there. Let me guess, you saw a picture of the castle and imagined yourself in a gown, crossing the bridge with an army of white horses and gilded chariots?"

"No, of course n--"

"Or leaning out of a turret and looking down on the trees, your hair blowing in the wind, perhaps?"

Gina didn't know how to hide embarrassment well. She squirmed a little in her seat and her cheeks reddened.

"Ok, maybe," she replied with a sheepish smile.

"Listen carefully to me, my dear," her teacher said, leaning in towards the table where they were seated. "Romance - real romance - is about people, not places. Where it happens is secondary. It is always secondary. The highest turret of the tallest castle... or the busy lobby of the drabbest office building. It makes no difference. It is about what happens in here," she said, tapping on her chest.

Gina was skeptical but Miss d'Auvergne's solemn expression and quiet, steady tone gave her pause. She would have to think about this a bit more.

Eventually it was time for both of them to go. Gina needed to finish some classwork before dinner while her teacher had some more preparation to do for the following day's lessons.

As they were parting ways outside the mess hall, Miss d'Auvergne called out one last time.

"Gina, dear," she said, "promise me you won't forget?"

"Yes, I know... romance is what happens in here, not out

there."

"No no no," the teacher said, shaking her head. "Ladurée, Rue Royale. And three macarons - no less!"

"I've never had the pleasure of meet--" Thomas started as he walked over to her from the desk, stopping abruptly as soon as their eyes met. His eyes widened and a smile came across his face.

"Miss Greenley!"

"Mr. White," she said politely, but only just.

Mr. Penwell glanced back and forth between them a few times and was about to say something when Scarlet anticipated him.

"Mr. Penwell, I wonder if you would give me a few minutes with Mr. White? If the driver cannot wait, I'm happy to take a cab."

"Certainly," Mr. Penwell replied, obviously a little confused but willing to accommodate her. "I'll let the driver know and I'll wait for you just over here," he added, pointing back to the chairs where they had been sitting.

"You're too kind."

Scarlet walked to the opposite side of the foyer with Mr. White.

"Comtesse?" he asked, his smile turning half skeptical, half curious.

"Can I help you, Mr. White?"

"Well, I must say I never thought I'd see you again," he replied, "though I must also confess that I had hoped I was wrong."

'Why did he have to be here?' Scarlet thought angrily. She looked over at Mr. Penwell, who was staring at them rather intently from across the room. Then she looked at Thomas, whose stare was decidedly softer.

"I'm afraid this is terribly awkward," she said.

"Or terribly exciting!" Thomas replied. "Please, tell me you're some long lost French countess that was travelling in secret when we met? I've always kind of hoped I'd meet one of those - one of you, perhaps!" He laughed as he finished speaking.

Scarlet just stared at him in wonder for a moment, her mouth slightly open, eyes slightly narrowed. 'How does he... how did...?' She couldn't finish the thought, or didn't want to. Either way, she needed to wrap this situation up quickly.

"I must beg you to be discreet, Mr. White," she said. "I am going to speak with Mr. Penwell before I leave but I must ask you not to question him about me. Please, will you promise?"

Thomas frowned and glanced over at Mr. Penwell. Then he turned back to Scarlet and his look changed from confusion to something more familiar.

"Of course, you can trust me, Miss... is it Greenley or...?"

He hesitated, waiting for her to answer, but she was distracted by the look in his eyes. It was the same warmth with which he had sought to console Dana over the loss of her mother that evening on the train. It was a look that made her feel...

Scarlet felt the moment slipping away from her. She forgot about Mr. Penwell. She forgot about Sir Henry and their meeting. She forgot about Dame Angelica, and Milly, and the *Mona Lisa*. The sounds from the street outside the door faded to nothing. The clip-clop of clients and their counsel passing through the foyer dissipated into the air, and all was still and silent.

Then, from somewhere inside herself, she heard herself speaking.

"It's Haslewood."

"Miss Haslewood," Thomas repeated, nodding his head as though they were meeting for the first time. As he said her name, the sound rippled through her head and chest like waves across a pond when a stone has broken the surface.

Then all the other sounds around them came rushing back in upon her and she recalled herself. She remembered the *Mona Lisa* too, and Sir Henry, and Mr. Penwell watching them from across the room.

"Call on me at Brown's Hotel tonight at six o'clock," she said.

"Brown's at six," Thomas replied, "I can do that."

"Thank you, Mr. White," she said, smiling and holding his gaze just a second longer than was necessary.

As she turned to rejoin Mr. Penwell, she remembered something and turned back.

"Ask at the desk for Comtesse Aurélie d'Auvergne," she added. "Will you remember it?"

"Aurélie d'Auvergne?" Thomas repeated, raising one eyebrow and giving her a considerably puzzled look.

"Yes," Scarlet insisted, now very aware of how much time every word was taking. "Will you remember it?"

"Um, yes, I think so," Thomas said, shaking off his puzzled look in order to bid her goodbye. "I will be looking forward to it, Miss --"

Scarlet cut him off with a finger to her lips and a smile. Thomas smiled back and then kept his word. He returned to the receptionist's desk and went about his business without concern for Mr. Penwell.

"Are you ready, Comtesse?" the attorney asked as she drew near to him.

"Yes," she said with a sigh and a roll of her eyes. "I'm very sorry for the confusion."

"You will forgive my impertinence, but may I ask what that was about?"

"Of course!" she said with a friendly tone. "I met that man on the train to London. For obvious reasons, I like to maintain a certain level of anonymity when I travel alone. However, despite my best efforts at putting him off, he was rather insistent about enquiring into my personal life. Americans, yes?" rolling her eyes once again as she said it.

Mr. Penwell met her with a knowing look that encapsulated all the derision she had intended to heap upon Mr. White. It was a look the British have perfected over many centuries.

"So I gave him a fake name and imagined I would never see him again. Apparently, my luck failed me."

"Well, I hope you were successful this time."

"I think so," Scarlet said with confidence, waving her hand as though it were nothing.

Mr. Penwell escorted her out to the car and opened the door for her himself.

"Shall we try this again?" he said with a laugh. "It was a pleasure meeting you, Comtesse. And Sir Henry will be in touch soon. He is a man of his word."

"Thank you, Monsieur. I look forward to hearing from him. Good afternoon."

"Stupid! What on earth was that?"

Scarlet paced back and forth in her room, occasionally looking in the mirror and talking to herself out loud.

She eventually positioned the desk chair by the window and pulled back the curtains as far as she could. She sat down and put her feet up on the window sill as she stared at the buildings outside.

'Why did I feel compelled to give him my name?' she thought to herself.

She attempted to get back into the moment and retrace her steps. What had actually happened? And why? She had never lost control in the middle of a con like that. It was like her mouth had moved before she even knew what she was saying.

And Mr. Penwell! Had he believed her cover story? Surely he had... right? She revisited in her mind his every facial expression and syllable spoken for the last two minutes of their time together, scanning and searching for any hint of doubt. It all seemed genuine enough.

"But he is a lawyer!"

Then she turned her thoughts to Thomas, wincing once again as though she were in pain. She recalled his look of surprise, and then his outburst - "Miss Greenley!"

'Ugh!' she thought, crossing her arms, 'Why must he always be so ill-mannered and careless?'

But then there was that look. And that... that... whatever that was that happened to her after it. She let her head fall backward as she breathed out a growl and stared up at the ceiling.

"You're really quite stupid, you know that?" she said out loud.

Scarlet had stayed in her room all that afternoon. She read for a while, took a nap, and spent some time thinking over the next steps in her grand design. She also contemplated packing up and changing hotels before six o'clock.

When it was around four-thirty, she felt she should start getting ready for the evening. She went to her closet and pulled out a green dress and a red dress and laid them next to each other on her bed. She stared at them for several minutes, trying to decide which was the right one.

In reality, it was only a question of colour as the two dresses were identical. Both were very plain, no patterns or embellishments of any kind, just simple, sleeveless, close-fitting, three-quarter length dresses with a high neckline and a flare in the skirt. Neither were amongst her favourites but she didn't dislike them either. She brought them along more for utility than for making a particular impression. They were usually for those quieter days, when she was just killing time or running errands.

Eventually she decided on the green one. After she had put it on, she went into the bathroom to do her make-up and fix her hair. She determined not to put much effort into either, having convinced herself that this was just a quick meeting with a casual acquaintance whom she would likely never see again after that evening. She was just being polite, really. And making sure she covered her tracks well enough so that Mr. White wouldn't be a liability in the future.

As she was applying her eye-liner, she glanced down at her dress. She set down the brush and leaned her head back a little, tilting it to the right and then to the left as she examined the dress further. Then she stood up and fussed with it, tugging it this way and that. Finally she went back to the bed and held up the red one, at which point she decided to put both back in the closet and keep looking.

'What a silly thing!' she thought. 'Why did I even invite him here in the first place? It's all such a nuisance.'

At last she decided on her full-length grey dress. It was quite nearly the antithesis to the other two, replete with beadwork cascading down from the high waistline in a pattern that was something akin to waves on the sea. It had short sleeves in a delicate chiffon that continued across the v-shaped neckline on both the front and back. There were also a few silver streaks that fell from the shoulders in gentle curves, and which sparkled in the evening light.

"I suppose this will do," she said out loud with a sigh. "Such a nuisance."

Once she had slipped on the dress, she returned to the bathroom to finish her make-up. She applied her mascara, eye-liner, and eye-shadow modestly, adding just a touch of lavender powder to the blue of the eye-shadow for a richer tone. She applied some rouge even more sparingly, only enough to give her a hint of colour. Then she moved on to her lipstick.

She was about halfway through applying the deep red colour to her lips when she stopped and frowned at herself. Then she picked up a washcloth, wiped it off entirely, and started over again. She came to the same point, attempting to get that perfect dip in the top of the bow on her upper lip, when she dropped her hand to the table in front of her and let out a frustrated sigh.

"Just be patient," she told herself, "the ordeal will soon be over."

On the third try she managed to get her lipstick just as she wanted it. All that remained was her hair but by that point she was running out of time. She decided to leave it long and flowing, rather than attempting some kind of complicated arrangement. She thought it looked a bit wild, to be honest, but then she kind of liked it like that. And besides, she certainly had no vested interest in Mr. White's opinion anyway. Why shouldn't she just enjoy leaving her hair fall where it will for once?

Before she got up she put on a pair of simple but elegant ruby earrings, each with two small diamonds set on either side of the centre stone. To this she added a white gold necklace that split into three separate strands in the front, each set from end to end with more small diamonds. Lastly, she slipped on two rings, both on her right hand, one on her ring finger, the other on her index finger. They each looked like two rings that someone had twisted around one another, creating an interlocking pattern like links in a chain. In the open spaces were set emeralds on one and sapphires on the other, with the tiniest of diamonds at each point where the pattern overlapped itself. Scarlet adored these rings, which was why she had stolen both of them several years ago in Vienna.

She picked up her handbag and was about to leave the room when she caught sight of herself in the mirror that hung on the outside of the wardrobe. She opened the door and pulled out her white scarf, then put it back and pulled out a black one. She closed the door and looked at herself in the mirror as she quickly put up her hair in a very loose bun and then tied the scarf around her head, adjusting each strand of hair that hung down from the sides until she was satisfied that they were acceptable enough for a silly evening out.

It was now two minutes to six and she was ready to go downstairs.

Scarlet positioned herself in a small seating area within the lobby, where she would be able to see Mr. White when he arrived but not appear to be on the lookout for anyone in particular.

She waited there for two hours that evening, until eventually she grew tired and returned to her room.

Chapter 20

London
January 10-12, 1926

The last of the three responses had arrived that morning. Scarlet collected the envelope at the front desk and then sat down in the dining room with a cup of tea while she opened it.

It was from Dame Angelica and it read as follows:

Dear Aurélie,

I would like to offer three for the object in question.

Please reply with further details of the arrangement should this be acceptable.

Sincerely,
Angelica

The previous week she had received Milly's letter, which read:

Dear Comtesse,

Enjoyed our lunch immensely. Will have to pass on the lady, I'm afraid. Break the news gently to her for me, will you?

Do get in touch when you're next in London.

All the best,
Mill.

P.S. Biffy is still interested in matrimony if you change your mind. He was the short one with freckles.

Scarlet laughed to herself as she read it a second time. She could very well foresee having lunch with Milly again at some point in the future, should the opportunity arise.

She sipped her tea and then pulled out Sir Henry's letter, which had arrived only three days after their meeting, just as he promised. It was even shorter than the previous two, containing only the following:

2 + 250

Scarlet smiled the first time she read it, and then the second, and now again the third time. It had been her intention to suggest something similar to all three of her marks but once she was in the moment with the other two, it just didn't seem like the right play. But Sir Henry had been ripe for the picking.

Though her plan was still to sell the *Mona Lisa* in full, a 250,000 pound bribe upfront, a little over 1.2 million dollars, ensured that even if her plan fell apart completely, she would still be walking away with the largest single score of her career. She folded his note up and slipped it back into her bag, where it had been since she received it.

When she had finished her tea, Scarlet went back up to her room and dropped her bag on the small desk that sat beneath one of the two windows overlooking the street. On the desk were two other envelopes that had arrived for her over the past three weeks but as yet remained unopened. The first had been mailed from London while the second was from an address in

America, Baltimore specifically. Both were from T. White.

The first letter had arrived two days after the day they had met in the lobby of Sir Henry's building. When she read the name, she had nearly thrown it directly into the rubbish bin. She wasn't interested in whatever Mr. White had to say. But by the time she had walked up to her room, the urge to destroy the letter had lessened to a sort of aggravated indifference, and thus it sat on her desk for the last few weeks, unopened and ignored. When the second had arrived shortly after the New Year, it was met with a vacant expression and tossed on top of the other without ceremony.

———————————

Scarlet was due to depart on the Simplon Orient the following afternoon. But today she had one last errand to run before returning to Paris

At around ten to one that afternoon, she set out from Brown's to walk the quarter-mile over to Berkeley Square. There was a bench near the south side of the park where she sat down and waited.

Within two or three minutes, a man walked up with a large envelope and sat down beside her.

"The Comtesse, I presume?"

"That's correct."

"Sir Henry sends his regards and best wishes for a safe trip back to Paris," the man said, handing her the envelope and then getting up and walking away in the same direction from which he had come.

Scarlet waited five or ten minutes, enjoying the cold but clear afternoon, and the largely empty park due to it being the middle of winter. Eventually she got up and walked back to Brown's.

When she arrived at her room, she opened the envelope and fanned through the handful of bearer bonds inside. Sir Henry was indeed a man of his word.

A car pulled up outside for her as she checked out of the hotel that morning. The bellhops brought down her luggage as she waited in the lobby. She sat in the same place she had sat nearly four weeks ago when Mr. White had failed to meet her. She watched as the two young men hauled her bags through the doorway and out to the car. Then she got up and started to follow them, hesitating as she passed the front desk.

"Ah yes, Miss d'Auvergne. Can I help you?" the manager asked.

"Yes, I was wondering something," Scarlet began, halting a little as she spoke. "I, well, I know I have received a number of letters during my stay."

"You certainly have!" the manager said with a smile, "But I am not surprised that you are a popular guest."

"Yes, well, I was wondering whether I might impose upon you to forward any letters that may arrive after I have left? I am not expecting anything in particular but, perhaps... I mean, possibly there may be..."

"Of course, Comtesse. That would be no trouble at all," the manager said, reaching below the desk and grabbing a notepad and pen. He slid them across the counter to her.

"Just jot down your details here and I shall make sure anything that arrives for you is forwarded to the appropriate address."

"Oh, you're too kind Monsieur."

Her forwarding address was once again the Ritz in Paris, where she would be returning for the next two months. She wrote it down slowly, including the name 'Davenport'. When she had finished, she slid the pad and pen back over to the manager.

"Excellent. Ah yes, the Ritz. And what is 'Davenport'?"

"My business in Paris requires discretion," Scarlet said, smiling and giving the manager a particular look.

"That will be no trouble at all. And we look forward to hosting you again sometime soon, Comtesse."

"I look forward to the same. It was lovely, as usual."

The manager nodded and bid her goodbye, then Scarlet joined the bellhops as they finished securing her bags. One of them opened the car door for her and she got inside. By two o'clock that afternoon, she was once again aboard the Simplon Orient, on her way to the ferry and then back to Paris.

Later that evening, somewhere outside Paris, when most of the other passengers had retired to their compartments, Scarlet decided to slip out into the dining-car and open the two letters from Mr. White.

---

18 December

Dear Miss Haslewood,

I cannot begin to say how sorry I am to have missed our meeting yesterday. I was called away on a serious and urgent matter. Please believe me when I say that it was one of the few

ANDREW STOPYRA

things that could have diverted me from what I know would have been a lovely evening with you.

And now I'm afraid that I must compound this first apology with a second, namely that I will not be able to make it up to you anytime soon - that is, if you're still willing to speak to me after this! The matter in question has forced me to return to America. I will be leaving before Christmas. Unfortunately, I will not be able to extract myself from the situation to call on you before then.

I know it may be too much to ask at this point, but if you were willing to come visit me, I would very much like to see you again. I am staying at the Savoy, which is barely over a mile from Brown's. Again, I must apologise that despite the short distance I will be unable to leave until I depart for America. I will be here until the 23rd if you decide to call... but please don't feel pressured.

Sincerely,
Thomas

———————————————————

26 December

Dear Miss Haslewood,

I have been unable to sleep tonight so I thought that perhaps I would write you a note. You don't happen to have another Poe tale handy, do you?

I have no idea if you'll still be at the hotel by the time this letter arrives but I hope it finds you one way or another. Although, I'm not really sure whether or not you're interested in hearing from me? Perhaps it will only be a nuisance.

Well, either way, I hope you're keeping well.

If I am successful at introducing 'Buffet Class', would you be willing to come to America for the inaugural journey?

I suppose now I'm just rambling on. I should probably return to my cabin - I'm fairly certain the ship's night crew wants me out of the dining room.

Goodnight, Miss Haslewood. Sleep well.

Sincerely,
Thomas

Chapter 21

Paris
January 15, 1926

Scarlet awoke to find the city blanketed in a thin layer of snow. It had fallen during the night so there hadn't been enough time yet for it to turn grey from the wear and tear of normal life. She opened her window and breathed in the cold, crisp air, savouring the quiet stillness that accompanies the morning after a snowfall. Below in the Place Vendôme was a small fleet of black taxis parked in a perfect line, each with a patch of white on the roof. She thought it looked like pads of butter on pieces of toast. She was getting hungry.

Preparations for the day were accomplished fairly quickly. She didn't worry about too many details despite the fact that she was headed back to the Louvre for another meeting with the director. Scarlet had found that after making a solid impression on a mark, especially when that mark believed you were in a position to bestow large sums of money on them, one didn't need to go overboard with appearance on subsequent engagements. In fact, it was usually more productive to tone things down a notch or two. An overly officious appearance or a very business-like demeanour, while communicating the proper significance of the moment, had the tendency to spook the mark. They already believed themselves the object of tremendously good fortune while being asked to perform some difficult or awkward errands in return - it was best to avoid emphasising their obligations and to cultivate camaraderie at this point instead. One needed a soft touch.

Scarlet came down to the lobby wearing her basic green dress, the one she had fussed with and ultimately rejected the night... well, that other night. She typically enjoyed colder weather and had a fairly high tolerance for it, but after the snow the temperature had dropped low enough that she felt the need to wear her fur coat for the first time that winter. It wasn't an ostentatious fur, as much as that's possible to avoid while still being fur. It was three-quarter length and mostly consisted of dark browns with a few streaks of lighter browns and black. She had seen it in a shop window while on a trip to Sarajevo one winter and decided she must have it. Two days, two dinners, and a late night walk through the city with the shopkeeper later, and she was wearing it home on the train without having spent a single dollar... or dinar, as the case may be.

She skipped breakfast at the Ritz in favour of an indulgent brunch at Ladurée. She felt she deserved it after her stay in England. It did not disappoint.

When she had finished, she made her way over to the Louvre.

"Ah, Miss Davenport, yes?" the receptionist said as she approached.

"Yes. I'm supposed to meet with the director today."

"He is expecting you but he is currently on the north side of the museum in one of the galleries. I am sure he wouldn't mind if you'd like to join him there, or you are welcome to wait here."

"If it wouldn't be any inconvenience, it would be lovely to meet him amongst the galleries."

"Certainly," the woman said. She unfolded a map and placed it on the counter in front of her. Then she showed Scarlet where they were, where the director was, and the fastest route through the maze of pavilions. Scarlet didn't want to betray her intimate knowledge of the collection, so she asked one or two questions and then asked if she could take the map with her, just in case. The receptionist was more than happy to oblige, asking only that she return it when she was finished.

As she passed through the adjoining gallery, Scarlet began hearing voices, one of which was the director's. Instead of announcing her presence, she walked softly and stood beside the doorway, trying to see what was happening before she entered the room.

"And why Rubens, Luc? Did you ever ask them?"

"They felt like it was fitting to apply their ground-breaking techniques on a German artist first."

"But Rubens is Flemish, is he not?"

"But he was born in Siegen, sir," replied the curator. "They are claiming him as their own, I think."

The director laughed. "And what shall they claim next, eh?"

The two men stood beside a group of four workers in white coats who were lifting the painting from the wall, wrapping it in cloth, and placing it on a cart.

"I'll have it crated for protection in the meantime," the curator said. "They are still undecided if they will analyse it here or transport it back to their labs. They're supposed to tell us soon."

"That's fine," the director said, nodding his head. He put his hands in his pockets and started to walk in Scarlet's direction as the other men accompanied the Rubens out through the opposite doorway.

Scarlet breathed in and let it out quickly, adjusted her black cloche, and turned to face the nearest painting to where she was standing. As the director's footsteps signalled his entrance to the gallery, she turned and greeted him.

"Miss Davenport!" he said with a surprised but friendly voice. "I did not know you had arrived. I assume Charlotte told you where I was?"

"And lent me this map too. She is very helpful," Scarlet replied. "I could tell you were occupied so I figured I would enjoy some of the collection while I waited."

The director moved beside her to look at the work she had been staring at when he came into the room.

"Ah yes, Poussin's *Eliezer and Rebecca*, one of my favourites," he said. He was quiet for a minute and Scarlet could tell that despite being an easy mark with fairly loose morals, he genuinely appreciated the art he was charged with conserving. He tilted his head a little this way and that, took a step closer, even sighed once or twice.

"I cannot decide what I think of this story," he said at last.

"What do you mean?"

"Eliezer has travelled many hundreds, if not over a thousand kilometres to find someone specific but he does not know who she will be. He does not even know her name! Then he prays and all is revealed in a single moment, through one unexpected and generous act of service."

Scarlet was trying to follow what he was getting at. She decided to leave him space to continue rather than ask a question or attempt to add to what he was saying. After another half-minute or so, he focused his musings a bit more for her.

"Can it really be that easy? Is it not a little too perfect, as they say?"

"Can anything be too perfect?" Scarlet replied, half in character, half because she wanted to know his answer.

"Don't misunderstand, Mademoiselle, I think it is a beautiful story. I would not change it. On the best of days, I think I can almost believe it too. I could not do what I do if I did not have some kind of faith that things can be so! What is there to appreciate in all of this," he said, extending both arms as if to point to the entire museum at once, "if we have no such hope?"

"And what hope is that?" Scarlet asked.

"Order, meaning, purpose," the director said, trailing off as he continued looking at the painting.

Scarlet had been staring at the director as he spoke. She now looked at the painting again herself. She focused on Rebecca, her hand to her chest in what she felt was a certain degree of astonishment. 'Can it be?' she must be thinking. Then her eyes drifted to the right, to the woman in the green skirt, leaning against the well, her left hand on her hip. 'Can it be?' she seemed to scoff.

"But you have not travelled all this way for philosophical reflection, have you?" the director said, laughing and placing his hand gently on her back. "Shall we take a walk past the pieces that shall soon be on display closer to home for you?"

"Yes, of course," Scarlet replied, but she was having trouble shaking off the moment. The director made the odd comment here and there along the way about the various works they passed but Scarlet was only barely engaged with him, just enough to give a one or two syllable acknowledgment as he spoke. It was sufficient though and they arrived at the Grand Gallery with the director none the wiser.

They stopped first at Correggio's *Marriage of St. Catherine* and the director pointed out some of the finer points of the artist's style that were most likely influenced by da Vinci.

"I assume this is the Virgin here holding the Child, and Catherine receiving the ring here," Scarlet pointed, "but who is this behind her?"

"That is Saint Sebastian," the director replied. "You will notice the arrows he is holding. He was to be martyred under Diocletian I believe it was, but when they shot him through with the arrows, he did not die. Another saint saved him, but I cannot recall the name now. Eventually, however, he pressed his luck a bit too far, as you say, and was finally beaten to death."

"Oh dear," Scarlet said, pulling back a bit as she continued staring at the jovial face on the man who was condemned to death.

They moved on and came to Raphael's *St. George Fighting the Dragon*, which happened to hang just to the left of the *Mona Lisa*. Their conversation about Raphael was brief as their attention turned quickly to da Vinci's work.

The director waxed eloquent about various aspects of the style, the beauty of the sitter, and the skill of the man himself, but Scarlet was preoccupied with what she was about to accomplish. 'Besides, the fame of the painting was due almost entirely to its theft!' she mused. The director may extol its virtues but ultimately it was Peruggia who had drawn the world's attention to what was otherwise a rather uninteresting portrait of a rather un-attractive woman. Oh, of course the director praised her beauty now - fame and popularity have a way of bestowing qualities that are not obvious to the casual observer, much like the Emperor's new clothes. But the truth was, without Peruggia, the *Mona Lisa* would be one of those masterpieces that the average person would neither recognise nor remember.

"Yes indeed," Scarlet replied to his discourse, "quite breathtaking."

"So, when would your supporters like to put things in motion?" the director asked, changing gears to the business at hand.

"Let us plan for one month's time. We have been discussing the matter since I last saw you and the middle of February seems to be an ideal time for everyone, if that suits the museum?"

"Certainly. It is not as though the lady has any prior engagements!"

They both laughed and the director turned to face the painting once again, adding an epilogue of sorts to his previous narrative, at which Scarlet stifled a yawn and smiled in agreement.

"If you have no other plans, Miss Davenport, may I suggest we have lunch together to discuss the practical details and celebrate this historic moment?"

"That sounds lovely."

The director turned to walk away but she paused for a moment alone with the painting. She couldn't help mimicking "that little grin of hers," as Milly had put it.

'If Peruggia has made you a star, Miss Lisa del Giocondo,' she thought, 'then I am about to make you a legend.'

184

Chapter 22

Paris
January 16, 1926

After her meeting with the director, that same night Scarlet sat down to write a letter to Sir Henry to provide him with the details they had worked out over lunch. The letter was as follows:

15 January

Dear Sir Henry,

The dates of the transaction have been set for the 17th and 18th of February. The items will be crated and moved to a secure storage room in the museum on the 17th, then transported by car to the train station early on the 18th. The train departs Paris at 0946 that morning. As we discussed, I expect you shall send at least one liaison to ensure safe handling of the item.

I shall inform the British Museum of the logistics and tell them to expect the arrival of the pieces at their facilities late in the evening on the 18th. I assume you will be able to arrange suitable transportation for the object from Victoria Station to the museum? The Louvre's agents will obviously assist with this part of the process as well, as needed.

I shall ring your office between now and the 17th to provide account details for both the initial and final wires, as per our agreement.

Should any part of this arrangement meet with your disapproval, please contact me immediately.

Sincerely,
A. d'Auvergne
Hôtel Ritz, Paris

Scarlet had saved several pieces of paper with the director's letterhead on them from the incident with the Maltese last October, so she used them once again for her correspondence with Sir Henry. She had waited until morning to seal the letter in an envelope in order to give her a chance to reread it and make any changes if necessary. She was satisfied with what she had written, so she sealed and addressed the envelope, slipped it into her bag, and went downstairs for breakfast.

As she passed the reception area, she overheard a conversation that stopped her dead in her tracks.

"I assure you, Monsieur," the man at the desk said emphatically, "there is no guest here by the name of d'Auvergne, least of all a Comtesse."

"But I know she checked in here," another voice said with equal force. It was a familiar voice that sent a chill down her spine.

She just wanted to keep walking but she knew it would only complicate things even more if she didn't address the situation straightaway.

"I believe I can sort this out!" she called out to the men, walking over to the desk rather quickly. Both men looked over at her, the one confused, the other relieved. But before Sir Henry could speak a word, she continued.

"Please, Sir Henry, come join me for breakfast or a cup of coffee!" she said, smiling widely and gesturing towards the dining room. "But first, give me a moment with the manager, will you?"

Sir Henry's double relief at having located her and being liberated from the terribly frustrating conversation with the "incompetent little Frenchman" at the desk, as he would later describe him, allowed Scarlet a certain dispensation in which to clarify things for both men. Sir Henry was more than willing to leave the reception area and wait for her by the dining room while she lingered behind for a moment to speak with the manager.

The reality was, Scarlet was already planning to prepare the front desk for the possibility of receiving letters, or even a phone call, under the name 'd'Auvergne'. She was about to mail her letter to Sir Henry later that morning and needed to be ready should he contact her at the hotel. But given the complicated nature of the situation at hand, she was going to have to take a different tack than she had originally intended.

"I'm so sorry for the confusion, Monsieur," she began, "but this man is an uncle of mine and has been suffering from a touch of dementia for several years now. It has been getting worse of late and I'm afraid he has now confused me, his only niece, with a Comtesse he once met as a young man!"

"Mon dieu!" the manager exclaimed in a low voice, glancing to the right just in time to receive a look of utter reproach from the "brutish Englishman," as he would later describe him.

"Yes, Monsieur," Scarlet continued, adopting a heavily burdened and deeply grieved expression on her face, "apparently he had a romantic liaison with the young woman and was very attached to her, but she broke his heart and he never saw her again."

"Mon dieu," the manager repeated softly.

"As you can imagine, it has been very difficult for our family, especially out in society, as you have now seen firsthand."

"Of course, Mademoiselle," the man agreed, sympathising with her despite shooting Sir Henry a sideways glance replete with its own uniquely French brand of disdain.

"If you would be so kind as to avoid pressing the issue with him, I should be very grateful. If he asks for me under this name again, or if anyone else with whom he has spoken should call asking for me under this name, would you be so kind as not to complicate an already painful situation and simply refer to me as the Comtesse? I know it is excessively silly but it would be a tremendous service to me, as well as to a very sick old man."

As she spoke these last words, she gestured with her head towards Sir Henry. The manager, perhaps feeling that he now had the upper-hand, relaxed his gaze and looked with pity upon him.

"You have my deepest sympathies, Mademoiselle," he said to Scarlet, "and anything we can do for you to help alleviate your suffering, we are happy to do it."

Scarlet reached across the counter and squeezed his hand and then pulled out her handkerchief to dry her eyes. She was quite pleased with herself that she had managed to drum up a few tears at the very end.

———————————————

"I'm so sorry for the frustration and confusion!" Scarlet said with a note of exasperation as she sat down opposite Sir Henry. The waiter arrived at their table as soon as she was seated.

"And what would Mademoiselle Davenport like this morning?" he asked, completely unaware of what had just taken place in the lobby.

Sir Henry gave her a stern look but Scarlet shook her head, closing her eyes for a moment and waving her hand as if to say, "Don't worry, it's not what you think." He seemed unconvinced.

"Have you eaten yet, Sir Henry?" she asked him.

"It's nearly ten o'clock, Miss Davenport," he said gruffly, "of course I've eaten already."

"That's a shame," Scarlet replied, not missing a beat, "the Ritz has a wonderful breakfast selection." She and the waiter exchanged a knowing look and smile, leaving Sir Henry the odd one out.

"I'll have a croissant and a cup of fruit, please. And coffee, of course."

"Of course," the waiter said. "And can I bring you some coffee as well, Monsieur?" he asked Sir Henry.

"I suppose I'll have some coffee," he answered somewhat reluctantly.

"Parfait."

When the waiter had left, Scarlet continued with her apology and explanation.

"Again, I'm very sorry for this confusion. You see, the manager was only being protective of me. When I stay here, I usually don't want people to know who I am. The management understands this. So when someone arrives that I have not informed them about in advance, they will not acknowledge that

I am a guest."

"And why would a young woman such as yourself require protection, Comtesse? Who are your enemies?"

Scarlet felt that she knew how to connect with Sir Henry on this point.

"They are not my enemies, Monsieur," she replied, giving him a sincere and innocent look. "They are my father's."

Sir Henry crossed his arms and leaned back, giving her a look that said, "Continue."

"Despite having a title, we were not a very wealthy family. Well, compared to many I suppose we were, but not what you would expect if you moved in our kinds of circles. My father was determined to change this. To gain respect, even power, based on his own accomplishments instead of the mediocre living which accompanied his title."

Sir Henry gave her a single, slow nod, and she continued.

"He has invested throughout Paris. As you may know, when one is investing in land and businesses, one cannot afford the luxury of sentimentality or compassion. If one does not wish to be left behind, one must eventually leave others behind them. I am sure you understand what I'm saying, yes?"

The waiter arrived with their coffees and Sir Henry uncrossed his arms to add some sugar and milk to his. Scarlet took hers black.

"Of course I understand you, Miss... what is it?" he replied as he looked down at his coffee.

"Davenport is the name we have decided upon when I stay here alone."

"I see."

Scarlet sipped her coffee and tried to remain confident and

composed as she waited to see how her story would settle with Sir Henry.

"Well, Miss Davenport," he said, picking up his coffee cup and clearing his throat, "as I said before, I think I would enjoy having a chat with your father."

"I think you would, Monsieur."

"Perhaps you could set it up for sometime in the near future?"

"I would be more than happy to," Scarlet replied. "He is currently in America on business but he will be returning in the middle of February. I usually write him once or twice when he is out of the country. I will mention it in my next letter. He is in London two or three times in the year as well, if that ends up being more convenient."

"Excellent."

Scarlet's pastry and fruit arrived a few minutes later and she apologised to Sir Henry for eating in front of him. He wasn't bothered.

"So, may I ask what has brought you to Paris?"

"I was here on business and I thought it would be worth calling on you to follow up on a little painting I'm about to spend two million pounds on. Well, two million and two hundred fifty thousand, I suppose."

"And may I ask how you found me at the Ritz? I don't recall having given you my address in Paris."

"Miss Davenport," Sir Henry said with a flat expression on his face, "I have not gotten to where I am today by trusting others to do as they say without... oversight, shall we say."

"I see," Scarlet replied. She did not want to concede the advantage to Sir Henry but she also knew that the best course of action was to make him feel that he was in control more than he really was.

"So what do you propose, Monsieur?"

"At the moment," he replied, "nothing. But I will keep a careful eye on the proceedings. If there is anything I don't like, I will act accordingly."

"I would expect nothing less," Scarlet said, sipping her coffee and finishing the last two pieces of fruit in her bowl.

"As it happens, Sir Henry," she continued, "I have a letter here in my bag that I was about to post to you this very morning. It contains the practical details of the arrangement." She reached into her bag and pulled out the envelope, sliding it across the table to him.

He opened the letter and read it in front of her.

"And what do you think?" she asked after it had been long enough for him to have read it twice at least.

"This looks fine," he said, in the same reluctant tone with which he had ordered his coffee. It was as though he had hoped for some glaring hole in her plan that would have allowed him to exert his authority, but having found none he was almost disappointed with its transparency and efficiency.

"Excellent!" she replied.

They each finished a second cup of coffee before eventually Sir Henry said that he needed to be going.

"Well, Miss Davenport," he said, "I am glad we had this meeting. I will be in touch with you here in the coming weeks about the man I shall be sending along to oversee the removal of the painting."

"Perfect," Scarlet replied with a smile. "Would you like to have a look at it while you're in town? Just for the pleasure of it?"

"No, that's not necessary," Sir Henry replied, shaking his head. "I have a full schedule and am headed back to London early in the morning, the day after tomorrow."

Scarlet had a sense that Sir Henry was likely to decline the offer, which was precisely why she had made it. It would have been a risk to navigate the Louvre with him at her side. But by simply making the offer, she was able to emphasise that same transparency without having to act upon it.

She escorted him to the lobby of the hotel and they said their goodbyes.

"And so you know, I have informed the manager about our relationship in general terms, so he will acknowledge any enquiries from you under my real name in the future."

"Very good," Sir Henry said as he buttoned his overcoat.

"Oh, and if you have never been there, Monsieur, you must try Ladurée on the Rue Royale while you are in town."

"And what is that?" he asked.

"Perhaps the most delightful bakery on the Continent," she replied with wide eyes and a youthful excitement.

"That's ok. I'm not much for patissieries," he replied with a wave of his hand.

His pronunciation, or rather mispronunciation, made Scarlet's toes curl. She didn't typically trust anyone who was averse to pastry. But then, she didn't need to trust Sir Henry. She only needed him to keep trusting her.

Chapter 23

Chaumont
November 14-25, 1918

By the time the first of the telephone operators had arrived in Europe, there were only eight months remaining to the war. Of course, no one knew that at the time. Gina had been assigned to the American Expeditionary Forces headquarters in Chaumont, along the Marne in eastern France, about one hundred and seventy miles southeast of Paris. She had served with passion and precision, garnering the praises and recognition of her superiors as well as the respect of her colleagues on the switchboards. She had enjoyed the work far more than she had expected. In fact, there were many days where she had lost herself in it, and almost forgotten about her grand designs to have adventures abroad once the war was over. But now that the armistice had been signed three days ago in Compiègne, she was setting her sights once again on castles, exploration, and romance.

The latter had begun to blossom only a month after Gina arrived in Chaumont. A certain officer in the headquarters where she worked had been paying her a fair bit of attention for several weeks before eventually asking her to dinner one evening. Of course, there weren't many options at the time, so their first 'date' had been a tasty but simple coq au vin that was made for them by the little French grandmother who lived a few houses down from the headquarters. The officer, a Mr. Frank Watkins of Wichita, Kansas, had gotten to know the old woman over the past year, occasionally bringing her gifts like fresh fruit or a nice piece of red meat. So when he informed her of his interest in Gina, she was only too happy to prepare the meal for their special night, which they enjoyed in the AEF mess hall after hours so they could have the place to themselves.

Gina had embraced Miss d'Auvergne's exhortations regarding romance and the date had been one of the most perfect evenings she could remember. The metal trays and dishes might well have been the finest Spode dinnerware, and the table and benches the dining room furniture at Versailles. They spent the evening getting to know one another and forgetting that only weeks before they had been strangers, thrown together by a world war that was raging somewhere off over the horizon.

Their relationship was a little over five months old when the war came to an end and plans were being made to begin shipping home many of the staff in Chaumont. Of course, Gina hadn't planned to go home anytime soon. Now was her chance to break away and explore Europe... and she was hoping that Mr. Watkins would accompany her. She was hoping they could walk across the bridge at Neuschwanstein together, or spend an evening watching the sunset from beneath the Eiffel Tower. Miss d'Auvergne may have been right about where real romance takes place, but a beautiful backdrop certainly couldn't hurt.

"And how was your day today?"

"Busy. It almost seems like there are even more calls coming in now that the war has ended. You'd think there would be less to talk about!"

"People are happy," Frank replied, "and some people tend to overtalk when they're happy."

"Hey! Is that a not-so-subtle hint?" Gina asked with a playfully offended look on her face.

"All I said was 'some people'," Frank responded with his hands up as though he were under arrest.

They both laughed as Gina got up from her seat at the switchboard and they gave each other a long hug.

"Well, if you didn't make me so happy, then I guess I wouldn't talk so much."

"I suppose I could work on that."

"I'm not sure you can," Gina replied, giving him a kiss on the lips. Then they turned to leave the office, holding hands as they went and chatting about their day until they reached the hall just in time for dinner.

"Dana! Dana!" a woman called from across the room.

"Will you excuse me?" Gina asked Frank.

"Of course. I need to catch up with the Captain anyway. Have fun," he replied, giving her a peck on the cheek.

Gina made her way to a long table on the far side of the room and sat down with three other girls who were all operators like her.

"So did you hear about the schedule today?" one of them asked.

"No. What is it?"

"We're all leaving - well, all us girls - we're all leaving in two weeks. Isn't it so exciting!"

"Oh, of course it is! That's great news!" Gina replied convincingly despite not sharing the girl's sentiments.

"The officers will linger behind a bit longer though," the girl added, "so I'm afraid you and Watky will have to be apart for a while." The girls liked to call him that when they were teasing Gina, which they enjoyed doing fairly often. Gina didn't mind.

"I think I'll survive," she said with a smile.

The girls spent the rest of dinner discussing all the things they were looking forward to back in America, all the people, places, and food they had missed. But Gina's mind was preoccupied with the fact that the clock was now ticking. She had to figure out how to slip away in the next two weeks before they were packed up and shipped home. And how to convince Frank to slip away with her.

———————————

"Can you believe we've been in France for eight months and have never even been to Paris?"

"Well, it's not exactly like we've been on holiday."

"Oh, I know. But aren't you curious what it's like?"

"I suppose, a little I guess."

Gina was leaning on Frank's shoulder as they sat on a bench in a small park a few blocks from the headquarters. It was evening and they were looking at the stars and sipping coffee from their metal government-issue cups.

"Do you know yet when you'll get to go home?" Gina asked.

"Nope."

"I'm sure you're looking forward to being back in America though, right?"

"Of course."

"You know, you're awfully chatty tonight," Gina said, turning her face up towards his and giving him a cheeky smile. "If you don't calm down, I'm going to have to say goodnight."

"Oh, I'm sorry," Frank replied, seeming to snap out of whatever had been occupying his thoughts. "I guess it's just the end, you know."

"The end?"

"Of the war. Of everything my life has been for the past year or so."

Frank had arrived in Europe in late 1917, about five months before Gina. She had turned twenty while in Chaumont, and he had celebrated his twenty-seventh birthday there. Prior to the war, he had been an accountant at a large office in New York. He was on track to have a very good career, and still was. The war was really only a hiatus in many ways. But before meeting Gina, Frank had spent time at the front. He didn't talk about it much and Gina didn't press him for information. As with most young men who had spent time in the trenches, it had a profound impact on him in ways he would be processing for many years to come.

"But isn't it a good end? You wouldn't want to stay here forever, would you?"

Frank was quiet for a while and Gina waited patiently.

"No, obviously I don't want the war to continue. I wouldn't wish that on anybody. I guess I'm just..."

He trailed off as Gina waited for what came next, expecting him to finish the thought any second. It was a few minutes before she eventually asked him what he was going to say.

"I don't even know," he replied.

Then he sort of came back to himself and wrapped his arm around her, pulling her in close and kissing her on the head. Gina closed her eyes as he did and smiled, though he couldn't see it. They sat there another half-hour, saying very little apart from pointing out stars and talking about how nice it was going to be to drink coffee in real coffee mugs again.

Shortly before they got up, Gina tried again to see if she couldn't stir up a little adventure in him. She was still hopeful that he would decide to stay in Europe with her. And she wasn't ready to face the idea of going back to America if he didn't.

"I bet the stars are stunning from the Alps, don't you think?"

"I'm sure they are."

"Could you imagine drinking coffee under the stars on a snow-covered mountain?"

"Seems like it might be a bit cold, though I'm sure it would certainly keep you awake!"

Gina laughed, feeling as though she may have chipped away at him just a little. Of course, she was still a novice at the more subtle aspects of communication.

"I've heard that in Scotland they eat this thing that's made from sheep stomach!"

"C'mon Dana, we're eating!"

"Oh, I'm sorry!" she said, not actually stopping however. "But aren't you just a little curious what it tastes like?"

"No, not really," one of the girl's replied.

Frank laughed and added, "I think that's an experience I can go without and still die happy."

After lunch, Gina and Frank were walking back to the headquarters for work as she tried to salvage her earlier disaster.

"You know, there's more than sheep stomach in Scotland. Maybe we could see the highlands when the heather is in

199

bloom!"

"I'm on to you, Dana Greenley," Frank replied, nudging her with his elbow and looking over at her out of the corner of his eye.

"What are you talking about?" Gina replied as innocently as she could. Perhaps too innocently.

"You're hoping I'll say, 'Oh boy, let's go travel Europe together and forget about America!'"

Gina blushed a little.

"Oh, don't be silly," she replied, "how could we possibly do that? I mean, you've got to go finish being an accountant, right? You don't have time for castles and highlands and sheep stomach."

"Exactly," he replied, giving her another nudge.

Gina had tried but she couldn't be patient anymore.

"Oh c'mon! Why not? Don't you want to see these things?"

"There it is!" Frank laughed as he stopped walking and turned to face Gina.

"There what is?" she asked.

"What you've been trying to say for quite a few days now."

"Maybe."

Frank's expression changed to a more even one, not smiling but not rude or condescending either.

"It just can't happen, Dana. I'm sorry."

"But why not?"

"It just can't."

"That's not a reason."

"It's going to have to be."

Gina was flustered. She wasn't very good at saying one thing while feeling or thinking another, especially when there was something she wanted badly. But she had been trying so hard for the last week or so, and now to realise that all her 'hints' and 'suggestions' hadn't been getting her anywhere, she was feeling exasperated.

"Ok, so what happens when we leave?" she asked.

"What do you mean?"

"What do I mean? Us, of course."

"Us what?" Frank asked, seeming genuinely confused by her question.

"Us what? Us what? Do I have to explain it to you?" She was moving from exasperation to irritation now.

"What did you think was going to happen?"

Gina couldn't answer him. She just stared at him, then down at the ground. 'Is this really happening?' she thought to herself.

"Wait, did you think --" Frank started, but Gina cut him off.

"Don't say it!" she yelled. Then she felt her eyes starting to fill with tears and she turned away from him. He reached for her shoulder but she pulled back. She was ready to walk away and took her first step, but then something started welling up inside her. It quickly grew from a wave to a flood of emotion.

She spun around and slapped Frank across the face as hard as she could. He gave her a look of shock as he stumbled a bit from the surprise.

Then she slapped him again.

As she raised her hand for the third time, he grabbed her wrist.

"Dana, what's gotten into you? Calm down!" he said.

She wrenched her hand free and turned around, walking away as quickly as she could. He called out to her one last time as she hurried away.

"Dana, please!"

Still walking away, she yelled back at the top of her voice.

"It was never real! None of it! Hateful man!"

Late that night, probably around midnight, Gina packed her kit bag with two changes of clothing, a few of her toiletries, her pillow, and a box of chocolates a few of the operators had given her for her birthday back in August. She had been trying to savour it since they didn't often get such things, so there was still half the box left.

"Dana?" one of the girls said quietly as she awoke to the rustling sounds of packing.

"Shh," Gina replied, putting her finger to her mouth. "Just sleep, everything's fine."

The girl frowned but then rolled over and quickly fell back asleep.

Gina slipped out the front door of the bunkhouse and started walking down the road.

She had no idea where she was going.

But she was going.

Chapter 24

Reims
April 14-15, 1919 &
January 21-22, 1920

"Heavens, girl, whatever is the matter?"

"I'm so sorry! Ple - Please forgive me!" the girl said, hurrying out of the bedroom and shutting the door behind her.

A few seconds later, an older man came through the same door from the hallway and entered the room, looking back and forth between the girl who had just passed him in tears and his wife standing beside the armoire.

"What on earth was that about?" he asked.

"I'm not sure," the woman replied. "I walked in and the maid was making the bed. I said hello to her then took off my rings and set them on the nightstand. She looked down at them and burst into tears! I haven't the faintest idea why."

"I think we'll be seeing a lot of strange behaviour in the coming months, my dear," the man said as he went about the business of changing his coat and shoes. "The war has taken a terrible toll on everyone, some of the worst being the ways we cannot see with our eyes."

"I'm afraid you're too right," the woman replied, removing her earrings and taking off her shoes.

The two of them lingered in the room for half an hour or so, then made their way downstairs for dinner around six o'clock. When they entered the dining room at Le Fil Écarlate, they were shown to their table by the host, who seated them in the front window.

There wasn't much to see in the immediate foreground as Reims had suffered badly at the hands of German shelling. The buildings directly opposite them were missing walls, pieces of which were lying in ruins that cascaded down to the edge of the street below. One could see through some of the open spaces to the next block, where the situation was much the same. A few shops and apartments remained intact between the rubble and life poked its head out of the most unlikely of places, like grass or flowers through a broken sidewalk. Beyond the foreground, Notre-Dame de Reims, itself badly damaged, still stood tall enough to shine forth as a beacon of hope and order amidst the chaos.

"Do you know what you're having, dear?" the woman asked her husband. They were an older, English couple, probably in their seventies, and fairly wealthy if appearances are anything to go by. They had travelled to France to visit family who had been living there when the war broke out. They spent the last few weeks with them in Troyes and were now on their way home to England.

"Probably the boeuf bourguignon," the man replied.

"But you had that last night."

"Have they run out?"

The woman rolled her eyes and looked down at her menu.

"I know what I like," the man replied, closing his and looking across the room for their waiter.

"Dear, I think it's that girl again," he said to his wife in a half

204

whisper.

She looked up and confirmed his suspicions. Their waitress, who was crossing the dining room towards them, was the same girl as the misty-eyed maid that had fled their room for some unknown reason.

"May I take your orders?" she asked as she arrived at the table, not realising who they were for a second or two. Then it seemed to click and she began apologising for her earlier behaviour.

"It's nothing dear, don't trouble yourself," the woman said. "But if you don't mind my asking, what affected you so?"

"Oh, it's nothing, really."

"You'll pardon my persistence, but it didn't seem like nothing. Did we do something to offend you?"

"Oh no! Not at all! I'm very sorry if I gave you that impression!"

"I'll have the boeuf bourguignon," the man interjected. "And some of that crusty bread, if you've got any."

His wife shot him a very crooked glare, to which he initially responded with a look that said "What? I'm hungry!" but then softened to "I'm sorry, go ahead and console the girl."

"You know, my dear," the woman continued, "everyone has suffered so much. You're not alone. You can talk to us if you want."

The girl was quiet at first, appearing to struggle with the offer but clearly wanting to take it. Then she teared up again and sat down beside the man on the right side of the table, facing the woman on the other. The man shuffled a little to his right, as though her tears might be contagious and he wasn't taking any chances.

The older woman extended her hand and the girl took it, squeezing it for a moment and then relaxing her grip.

"My fiancée was at Passchendaele," she began, to which the woman responded with a deeply sorrowful look. Even her husband turned from looking out the window and started paying attention. Unless you had spent the entire war in a cave, you knew that name. And you knew that any story that began with it was going to end in suffering and tragedy.

The girl began telling them about how they had met and eventually gotten engaged in 1916 but were waiting until the war had ended to have their wedding.

"It was a nightmare waiting to find out what had happened after the battle. Days went by, even weeks, before eventually I received a letter saying that he had actually survived."

"That must have been quite a relief," the woman said, giving her a very faint smile.

"Oh, it was!" the girl said, but then she began tearing up again.

"But the worst of it was when he got home. He was like a completely different person. I tried to interact with him, to console him, to comfort him, but nothing got through!"

She started sobbing too much to continue.

"I'm so sorry!"

"It's ok dear, take your time," the woman said.

It took about two or three minutes but eventually she was able to proceed.

"He demanded I give him back the ring he had given me on our engagement. And the earrings he had bought me just before he left for the war. He said he was no longer interested in love. He said that for him, love had died with the war! I'm sorry,

I'm so sorry!" she said as she broke out into even heavier sobbing.

The man took out his handkerchief and offered it to her. The woman lifted her other hand and held the girl's hand with both of hers now, squeezing it tighter and even rubbing the back of it gently.

"Oh, my dear," she said, "I cannot imagine. I'm so sorry, my dear." She knew there was nothing she could say to make it better, nothing she could do to remove the hurt. But she wanted the girl to know that she was there for her.

"Thank you," the girl managed to whisper in her overwhelmed state, squeezing the woman's hand in response.

It took about five or six minutes but the girl eventually regained her composure. She sat with them for a few minutes after that before things finally got back to where they had started and she took their orders for dinner. Then she left the table and delivered them to the kitchen.

After their meal, the English couple had gone for a walk through the neighbourhood, taking in the sights of destruction mingled with the rebuilding that had already begun. They were out for about an hour before they returned to their room for the evening. When they got there, they found their bed made and a note lying on one of their pillows.

"What's it say?" the man asked his wife.

"It's from that girl. She just wanted to thank us for listening to her and apologise again for imposing on us at dinner. Poor thing."

"Terrible, absolutely terrible," her husband replied as he

went about settling in for the night. He took off his shoes and socks, grabbed his robe and a towel, and went into the bathroom, saying once again as he disappeared through the doorway, "Just terrible, all of it."

The woman sat on the edge of the bed for a moment, removing her earrings and rings again and setting them on the nightstand. She stared at them for a little while, picking up one of the rings and turning it this way and that. Then she held it in her hand and looked out the window for a few minutes.

"Dear?" she called out to her husband through the bathroom door.

"Yes?"

"I'll be back in a few minutes. I need to speak with someone."

"Ok."

She left the room and went downstairs to the front desk.

"May I help you, Madame?" the manager asked.

"Yes. Where is the girl who made up our room and served us at dinner tonight?"

"Is there a problem?" he asked in a concerned voice.

"No no, not at all," the woman assured him, "I just want to speak with her about something."

"I'm afraid she has left for the night," he said, "but she will be back tomorrow afternoon. I can pass a message to her if you wish."

"Oh, ok. Unfortunately, we're leaving in the morning."

She thought about it for a moment then continued.

"Do you have an envelope I might borrow? And a piece of notepaper?"

"Of course," he said, reaching below the desk and pulling

out an envelope that was pre-stamped with the hotel's name and address, as well as a sheet of paper with the hotel's letterhead. "Is this ok?"

"Yes, that's fine."

The woman grabbed the pen that was lying on the desk and wrote a short note on the paper, then she slipped it, a ring, and a pair of earrings into the envelope and sealed it.

"Would you see that the girl gets this envelope, Monsieur?"

"Of course, Madame. No trouble at all."

"Merci."

"I'm so glad you decided to introduce yourself at the bar."

"Me too."

"I've really had a lovely evening," the young man said, smiling at the girl opposite him and taking the last sip of his wine.

"Me too," the girl replied with a smile of her own.

"So did your father buy this restaurant or start it himself?"

"My grandfather started it actually, then my father inherited it."

"So will you be the next restauranteur in the family?" the man asked with a laugh.

"Possibly, I haven't decided yet. I am an only child so there is a lot of pressure," she said, rolling her eyes to the side.

"I can imagine."

They talked a bit longer, mostly about where the young man was headed the next day. He was only passing through Reims for the night, on his way back to Brussels from Paris.

"Will you excuse me, please?" the girl asked. "I'll go let my father know that we're leaving. He may want to meet you, if you don't mind?"

"No, of course not," the young man said.

"I'll be back in a moment."

The girl got up and disappeared through a door at the back corner of the restaurant. The young man leaned back in his chair and breathed out a sigh of delight and satisfaction. He really had enjoyed the evening thoroughly. He had never dined in such a fine restaurant before, and rarely with a young woman who was quite so charming.

Just then, the host and the bus boy came out of the kitchen and walked straight towards the man's table.

"Monsieur, what are you trying to do?" the host asked.

"Pardon?" the man replied, unsure what they were asking him.

"It's over, Monsieur. Time for you to leave."

"Uh, well, Mademoiselle d'Auvergne said that she was just going to speak with her father before we left. May I wait for her? I'm not sure what this is all about."

"The young lady explained the situation to us, Monsieur. We will not have any of that kind of thing in our restaurant. You will pay for the meal at once and never return," the host said with a stern voice and an even sterner expression.

"What?" the man replied, more as an exclamation than an interrogative.

"You heard me, Monsieur."

"But I am here with the owner's daughter! Speak with him, or her if you wish. They will explain everything."

"The owner has no daughter, Monsieur. And the owner is not even here tonight. He is away visiting family in Paris."

"But --"

"Now, you will pay and leave, Monsieur."

"Where is the young woman I was here with then?" he asked with a tone that had quickly changed to one of desperation.

"We have sent her on her way. She told us what you were trying to do. Inviting her to a nice restaurant and then threatening to follow her and do her harm if she would not pay. You are an animal, Monsieur, and you must go now."

"What?" the man replied, this time nearly shouting the word. "This is preposterous! I have done nothing of the sort! She is lying to you!"

"If you saw the state she was in when she came into the kitchen, you would not expect us to believe you," the host said. "Now, it is time Monsieur, get up."

The two men approached his chair as if they were about to eject him from the restaurant by force, at which point the man got up and went with them to the front door. They argued for some time over the fact that he did not have nearly enough money on him to pay for their dinner and still make it home to Brussels. The host eventually agreed to accept half the cost in cash and half in the form of the man's gold watch, which he reluctantly handed over in order to prevent them calling the police.

"Good morning, Aurélie," the manager said as Gina entered the hotel.

"Good morning, Jacques. And how are you today?"

"Very well, thank you. There is something here for you," he said, reaching below the desk and pulling out an envelope. "A guest left it for you last night. A Madame Haslewood, I believe it was."

"Oh, really? Thank you," Gina replied.

"Did you have a pleasant evening?"

"Yes, very pleasant. I even had a lovely meal compliments of a nice young man I met at a club."

"It's wonderful to see that the war has not doused the fires of love!" the host said with a laugh.

"It certainly is!" Gina replied with a nod and a smile.

Then she took the envelope from the desk and headed back to the laundry room to fetch linens and cleaning supplies for the start of her shift.

———————————————

Gina took the long way home that evening, walking by the cathedral and then back down the hill to her room, which was only a few blocks from the hotel where she had been working for the past three months. Jacques at Le Fil Écarlate had been very generous to her when she first showed up enquiring about a job back in January. He started her cleaning rooms and making beds, which she was still doing, but after a month he allowed her to serve in the dining room as well, increasing her pay accordingly. He even found her the room she was currently renting and had ensured that she got it for a reduced rate. If she continued to do a good job at the hotel, he was contemplating allowing her to run the front desk a few days a week.

She pushed open the heavy door to her building and let it slam shut behind her. Then she climbed the four flights of stairs to her room and went inside. She dropped her bag and jacket on the one chair she had that sat beside her very small table. Her whole room, which included a small kitchenette, was hardly

212

bigger than a prison cell. The only window was little more than a slat just above eye-level on one wall. Occasionally she would stand on her chair to look out through it.

But despite the limited space, it was her space, and Gina was happy. The life she was living was her life now, and hers alone.

She opened the envelope from Mrs. Haslewood. She could feel it contained a few small items, so she tilted it up and dumped them into her hand. Then she slid out the note and read it:

My dear girl,

I know this can never replace what you've lost but I hope it helps you know that someone cares about you. All is not lost, my dear. There is still love in the world.

Sincerely,
Evelyn Haslewood

Gina read it twice, including the woman's name. She felt a flicker of something inside her but quickly shook it off, not allowing it to take shape. She crumpled up the note and tossed it in the rubbish bin along with the envelope.

Then she looked down at the jewellery in her left hand. There was a beautiful white gold band with five sapphires, and a pair of matching sapphire earrings set with a few very small diamonds around each gemstone.

She smiled as she slipped the ring onto her finger and then put the earrings on. She picked up the tiny mirror she had on her nightstand and looked at herself, turning her head side to side to see if the earrings glinted in the dim light of her bedroom.

Gina had never intended to stay very long in Reims, it just kind of happened. Paris had been her goal from the moment she walked out of Chaumont, and it still was. She had spent her year here setting aside as much money, and other objects of value, as she could so that when she eventually arrived there it wouldn't be as a pauper. She wouldn't be rich, of course, but at least she would be able to rent a slightly nicer place, and maybe even pay for her own meal at a fancy restaurant from time to time... if she felt like it.

"I cannot believe you are leaving us, ma chère!" Jacques said with a genuinely sad expression, not intended to induce guilt but only to ensure that Gina knew how much he would miss her.

"I cannot believe it either, Jacques! One year. It has gone by so fast! But I have enjoyed every minute of it. I have learned so much too, and I cannot thank you enough for the opportunities you gave me."

"Oh, it was nothing, ma chère. I would help you a dozen times over if I could. You are a special girl, Aurélie. Please come back and visit us here, eh?"

"Of course! I couldn't imagine not seeing you or Le Fil Écarlate again! This is like home to me now."

The manager got a little misty-eyed but tried to wipe it away quickly before it formed into something more obvious. He stepped forward and gave Gina one of the biggest hugs she had ever received. She hugged him back and closed her eyes for a moment. Then she opened them as wide as she could, fluttering her eyelids to prevent anything coming out.

"And are you sure you would not like help getting to the station in the morning?" he asked her.

"No, really, I'll be just fine," Gina replied, smiling and waving off his suggestion with her hand. "In fact, I would like to take a little walk by myself to say goodbye to Reims on my way."

"That sounds lovely. I wish you all the best, my dear!"

Gina walked up to the cathedral in the early hours of the morning, when most of the city was still asleep. It was barely light outside but what light there was shone in rays from the horizon, creating a mix of bright spots and shadows along what was left of the southeastern facade.

She wandered around the outside for a little while and then peered in through the front doors. She looked across the pieces of rubble and columns lying on the floor, then up at the sky through the vast opening where the roof used to be. The rising sun was turning everything a deep pink, creating an ethereal juxtaposition between dawn and debris.

After ten or fifteen minutes more, Gina made her way down the hill towards the train station. She only had a single bag and a small pack she carried on her back. She had thrown away her kit bag shortly after getting the job at the hotel. She wasn't interested in remembering those days.

In fact, she decided that she needed to distance herself even further and mark this new chapter in her life with something more than a change of luggage. When she had enquired after the job at Le Fil Écarlate, she had used the name of her old French teacher for two reasons: it was a French name and it wasn't the name that rang in her ears the night she left Chaumont. But she didn't want to continue borrowing Miss d'Auvergne's name indefinitely. She needed something that was hers. Something that was significant to her, and her alone.

The hotel had been the place where she had determined to define her life going forward without respect to anyone else. She certainly appreciated Jacques. If she allowed herself to think in such terms, she may have said that he had become something of a father-figure to her during that time. But she wasn't going to allow herself to go down that path again. He had served his purpose and the hotel had been something of a sandbox for her, a place where she could experiment and begin to set the course for her new life to come.

And the Haslewoods. The poor, sentimental Haslewoods. 'How easy it all was! They lapped up every word, every tear!' she had thought to herself in the days that followed. She had gotten plenty of meals out of lovestruck young men before that, and lifted the occasional scarf or hat from shops around town. She had even convinced another couple that Jacques hadn't paid her for several weeks and managed to double her earnings that month as a result of their generosity. But 'The Haslewood Arrangement', as she liked to refer to it, had netted her her first truly valuable prize. And she had determined that it wouldn't be the last, or greatest.

"Ticket please, Mademoiselle."

"Here you are," Gina said.

The conductor inspected it and then returned her portion. Then he gestured toward the train with a smile.

"Welcome aboard, Mademoiselle Haslewood," he said with a nod of his head. "Have a pleasant journey!"

"Thank you," Scarlet replied, "I believe I shall."

Chapter 25

Paris & London
February 16-18, 1926

The only major variable that remained was the identity of the man, or men, that Sir Henry would send to oversee the removal of the painting. If Mr. Penwell were in attendance, it could complicate her personal involvement on the day. If, on the other hand, they were men she had never met, things should be fairly smooth.

As Scarlet was on her way down to breakfast, the desk manager stopped her.

"Miss Davenport, I have a telegram for you."

"Excellent," she said as she stopped and took the paper from him.

It was from Sir Henry's office and it read:

MR. FOSTER WILL ARRIVE AT PARIS AT 2117 ON 16TH. WILL MEET YOU AT LOUVRE AT 9AM FOLLOWING MORNING.

Scarlet was relieved that at least the situation wouldn't be more difficult than it needed to be. All she needed to do now was ensure that the director would be ready for them tomorrow morning at nine o'clock.

"Miss Davenport, how are you today?"

"Very well, thank you. And you?"

"I am excited," the director said, "this is a tremendous moment for both museums. Indeed, for both countries!"

"I agree," Scarlet replied with a smile.

They had arranged for a brief meeting at a café about halfway between the hotel and the museum, just to review and confirm the details for the following day.

"So when will your contacts be arriving tomorrow?"

"It will be one man, a Mr. Foster. He arrives later tonight and is planning to meet us at the Louvre at nine o'clock, if that is ok with you?"

"Of course, of course. We are all at work by eight anyway, so anytime after that is just fine."

"Perfect," Scarlet said, taking a sip of her coffee. Then she continued with a more delicate matter.

"I feel very silly sharing this now but I must make you aware of something in order to avoid any confusion when Mr. Foster arrives."

"Certainly. What is it?" the director asked.

"My full name is actually Countess Rosalind Davenport of Carlisle."

The director was sipping his coffee as she said this. His eyes widened and he swallowed with a little more effort than normal.

"A Comtesse?" he said in a surprised but intrigued voice.

"Well, there you have it," Scarlet said, "you've anticipated me! You see, as I mentioned at our first meeting, several of our supporters are quite the Francophiles. In fact, it has become something of a joke for them to refer to me simply as 'The Comtesse'!" As she said this last part, she covered her eyes with her hand for a moment and then removed it, giving the director a shy glance with a timid smile.

"You must think me very silly indeed!" she added.

"No no, of course not!" the director replied.

"You're too kind, Monsieur."

"Not at all! In fact, this is very exciting," he said with a big smile. "Why shouldn't such a historic moment be marked by the presence of nobility!"

They both laughed as Scarlet slowly shifted back from shy and in need of comfort, to her easy but confident demeanour.

Eventually they finished their lunch and Scarlet walked part of the way back to the Louvre with the director.

"Well then, until tomorrow, Comtesse!" the director said with a wink as he took her hand and kissed it. "It has been a pleasure, as always."

"Until tomorrow, Monsieur."

The following morning, Scarlet got up early to make sure she wouldn't be late to the museum for any reason. As much as she had laid some groundwork that would hopefully prevent any question regarding her identity, she still wanted to make sure that she was there with Mr. Foster and the director from the moment they met until the day was over.

She wore her deep red dress, embroidered on the front and embellished with tasteful beadwork, and cinched tight around the waist with a red belt. Her shoes were black, as were her gloves, which covered the two rings she was wearing. The one on her left hand was white gold with a row of five sapphires, the other, which was on her right hand, was a single ruby surrounded with smaller diamonds. Her earrings tied both together as they each had one ruby and one sapphire set within a figure-eight of white gold. Her hair was curled and then folded into a chignon at the base of her neck, with a few strands hanging down on both sides along her temples. She wrapped herself in her white woollen shawl since it was still late winter outside. And lastly she put on her red beret, which sloped gently to her left.

After breakfast, she walked to the Louvre, taking her time through the Tuileries and eventually arriving at the director's office around quarter to nine.

"Good morning, Miss Davenport," he said.

"Good morning."

"This is all very exciting, isn't it?"

"It is indeed!"

"Well, shall we join Mr. Foster?" he asked.

"Oh, yes, of course," Scarlet stumbled over her words for a moment. 'Really?' she thought with a mental groan.

"He arrived a little earlier this morning, about fifteen minutes ago. I had instructed Charlotte to direct him to the gallery if he arrived before you. I haven't met him yet myself."

Scarlet's mind sighed with relief.

"That sounds perfect," she smiled. "Shall we then?"

The two of them made their way to the north side of the museum, to the Grand Gallery where the three paintings were. Several museum staff were there in white smocks with linen cloths, sacks of wood wool, and three wooden crates, each about triple the depth of their respective paintings. They were in conversation with a tall man in a grey suit.

"Mr. Foster, I presume?" the director said as they approached the group.

"That's correct," the man said in a rather business-like tone, extending his hand to the director.

"It is very nice to meet you, sir," the director said, shaking his hand vigorously.

"And you must be the Comtesse I have heard about," the man said as he turned toward Scarlet.

"Pleasure to meet you, Mr. Foster," she said as she shook his hand.

"Sir Henry speaks very highly of you," he added, though he tempered the compliment with a faintly critical look in his eyes.

"I'm sure he was being too kind," Scarlet replied.

"You know him well enough to know that an excess of kindness isn't something he's usually accused of," the man said, softening his gaze and stifling a laugh.

Scarlet only smiled and gave him a look that established the first threads of rapport between them. She didn't want to be curt but she also didn't want to encourage extraneous conversation.

"Ah, and here she is!" the director said, stepping in front of the *Mona Lisa*. Scarlet could feel another monologue coming.

"I will direct your attention to the background," he began, and did not stop for a solid six or seven minutes. In fact, he only stopped when Mr. Foster interrupted with the 'suggestion' that they get a move on and see to the packing, though he managed to do so with a tactfulness Scarlet hadn't expected from him.

"Of course, of course," the director replied. Then he motioned to the staff in the white smocks and they got to work.

Despite its diminutive size, the *Mona Lisa* is quite heavy due to its poplar 'canvas' and ornate but solid frame. Though it could have been a one-man job, two men lifted it slowly and carefully while a third man stood at the front in case either side should slip or the painting should topple forward.

"Your staff are very skilled," Scarlet commented.

"Indeed they are. We offer extensive training in handling all of the various works of art in the museum."

"Oh, is that right?" Scarlet replied with an artificial but convincing curiosity.

"Oh yes. We also make it a point to hire only the most responsible and conscientious workers. We can train them but we want them to feel a sense of ownership over the works they are charged with keeping."

Scarlet glanced at Mr. Foster, feeling that a wry comment about Signor Peruggia's 'sense of ownership' may be percolating to the surface. Thankfully her feeling was wrong this time.

"And now, thanks to your generous contribution," the director continued, looking towards Mr. Foster, "we will not only be able to continue hiring the best workers but we can also expand on our facilities and collection as well."

"We all benefit then," Mr. Foster replied drily, not looking away from the men who were handling the painting.

Scarlet had been a little concerned about having to manage the conversation, so to speak, in order to keep the two men from stumbling onto each other's differing perspectives on the situation. However, she was relieved to find that Mr. Foster's aloofness was containing the discussion quite nicely for her. Not to mention his obvious irritation at the director's overall personality.

Nevertheless, Scarlet thought it best not to allow too much

space. She didn't want the director especially to feel compelled to fill it without her direction.

"Monsieur, I wonder if you could comment on the style in Raphael's *St. George Fighting the Dragon*. The last time I was here, you discussed the Correggio a bit but I never got to hear about the Raphael."

Scarlet was certain Mr. Foster had rolled his eyes.

"Funny you should ask, Comtesse," the director said, giving her a little wink as he used the title, "I was just thinking about this piece on my way to work this morning."

"Really? How fortunate!" Scarlet replied.

The two of them moved closer to the Raphael but Mr. Foster stayed at a distance, watching the museum staff like a hawk. The director pontificated for quite some time, and Scarlet certainly didn't discourage it. She asked several more questions and also pretended not to understand some of the finer points of the director's discourse, forcing him to clarify them at great length.

By the time they were finished talking, the workers had finished crating the *Mona Lisa*. Once they had lifted it from the wall, they had wrapped it in several layers of linen cloth, then set it down upon a bed of wood wool, roughly six inches deep, in the middle of the crate. They carefully packed more of the material around and above it, but not before they had set a board across the face of the frame to prevent the wood wool pressing against the painting through the cloth. When they had finished, they placed the remaining side of the crate in position and secured it with nails around the edges.

Since the director was standing in front of the Raphael, he told them to pack that one next.

As they were gathering around it to start the same job over again, Mr. Foster let out a deep breath and clapped his hands together once before putting them in his pockets.

"Well, I think that's all I needed to see," he said. "Comtesse," he continued, nodding towards Scarlet, "and Monsieur," he said, giving another nod to the director, "I shall see you both tomorrow morning. Say, half past eight?"

"Perfect," Scarlet replied before the director could speak. "We will be looking forward to it."

"And I shall contact Sir Henry's office to ensure that the funds are ready for transfer as soon as the train leaves the station, around quarter to ten tomorrow."

"Again, perfect!" Scarlet said with a smile.

Mr. Foster turned and walked out of the gallery. The director had a confused look on his face.

"He is not interested in the rest of the pieces?"

"Mr. Foster is only a liaison, an employee of sorts. And I'm afraid not every institution has the benefit of conscientious employees," Scarlet said, touching his shoulder with her hand. "You are very fortunate to be surrounded by such men here that you forget that most workers are satisfied with the bare minimum!"

"I suppose you are correct, Miss Davenport."

"Well, as long as we are here, why don't you tell me more about the collection while we are waiting for the Correggio?"

The director looked like a child in a candy store as he led Scarlet around for the next twenty minutes or so. She endured it willingly however, as she was now less than thirty-six hours from her prize.

"Well then, I shall see you here in the morning?" the director asked when they were finished.

"Definitely. And the paintings will be stored beneath the gallery, yes?"

"Yes, locked away in one of our research rooms, as we discussed earlier."

"Excellent," Scarlet replied, "then I shall sleep well knowing they are safe!"

The two of them exited the gallery as the men in white wheeled the three crates away on two large carts in the opposite direction.

"Good morning, Miss Davenport!"

"Good morning," Scarlet replied as she tried to hold back a yawn. "Oh, excuse me. I didn't sleep very well last night."

"All of the excitement has caught up with you, eh?" the director laughed.

"I think you must be right!"

Two cars were parked outside one of the service doors behind the north side of the museum when Scarlet arrived around quarter past eight that morning. She had gotten there before Mr. Foster this time and she and the director waited for him before they had the paintings removed from the building. He showed up right on time.

The conversation was kept to a minimum. The director appeared to have taken Scarlet's words to heart about Mr. Foster being a mere employee, and a rather heartless one at that, and did not engage him much beyond pleasantries. Scarlet couldn't have been more pleased.

The paintings were quickly loaded into the cars. Two of

them were placed in one car and the other in the second, and all of them were secured with ropes in order to prevent jostling during the drive to the station. Mr. Foster rode along in the second car, which contained the *Mona Lisa*.

"Are you sure you would not like to join them at the station?" the director asked Scarlet.

"No, I think there is little I could contribute at this point," she said.

"Sir Henry asked me to pass along his thanks for your tireless work in negotiating this deal, Comtesse," Mr. Foster said from the car before it pulled away. "And as I said, you should expect the funds anytime after quarter to ten."

"Thank you very much, Mr. Foster. It has been a pleasure," Scarlet replied.

As the car pulled away, the director shook his head and muttered under his breath.

"'This deal' he calls it, huh! Philistine."

"Well, as soon as the funds clear in our French accounts, I shall forward them to the museum. You should expect the full amount in the next 2-3 days, I would think," Scarlet said.

"Excellent!"

"I cannot thank you enough for your willingness to... how shall I say it? Do the unprecedented!"

"Speaking of that," the director said, "Would you be so kind as to meet me sometime in the next few days? It would be for about an hour or so. A local reporter would like to do a story for the newspaper. I thought it best to hold the news until after the exchange had gone through. We know many people will not be happy with the arrangement and we didn't want any interference."

"Very wise," Scarlet replied. "Shall we say three days from now?"

"I will let the reporter know."

Sir Henry arrived at the British Museum around quarter past six that evening and was greeted by five eager and excited members of its staff.

"Have they arrived yet?" he asked.

"Not yet. We expect them any minute."

The men stood around in relative silence for ten minutes or so, most of them taking the chance to have another cigarette, until two cars pulled up outside the service entrance.

"Ah, here we are!" said Sir Henry as Mr. Foster and the Louvre staff got out and greeted them.

"Good to see you, Sir Henry."

"And you too, Sam. Was it a smooth journey?"

"Very."

"Excellent. Well then, let's get these treasures inside and have a look, eh?"

The paintings were carried in through the large double doors of the service entrance and straight to one of the research rooms in the basement. The British Museum staff had the privilege of removing the nails and cracking open the crates.

The Raphael was first.

"Jolly good!" one of the museum employees said with patriotic enthusiasm as they lifted the painting from the crate and set it on a stand that had been prepared in advance.

"Feels like he's come home, doesn't it?" another one laughed. The men from the Louvre remained quiet.

228

The Correggio was next.

"Interesting," one of them remarked. They paused, staring at it on its stand. While it didn't evoke the same energetic response, they all seemed to pay it equal respect with a few minutes of careful observation.

And finally, the da Vinci.

The top of the crate popped open and the wood wool was thrown aside. The protective board lying over the front was laid against the wall and the painting, wrapped in linen cloth, was placed on the table beside them. Three men carefully unravelled the protective layers. Then one of them folded up the cloth while the other two carried the painting to the third stand and set it on display for all to see.

A woman with a faint smile stared back at the men. They observed her in silence for what was really only several seconds but what felt like an eternity. Her blonde hair and wide eyes held their gaze until the younger men of the group were the first to look away and check the responses of their colleagues.

"Tell me there's another crate in your vehicles," Sir Henry said, still looking intently at the young woman on the red background.

"No, Monsieur," one of the men from the Louvre replied.

"Then where is my painting?!" he shouted.

Mr. Foster's heart was pounding in his chest, his collar suddenly feeling far too tight.

"I cannot imagine what happened, Sir Henry," he said, his voice shaking slightly. "I watched every step of the process, I assure you."

"Then you watched them pack this... this... what is this?!"

"I think it's a Rubens, sir," one of the younger men chimed in.

229

"Yeah, definitely a Rubens," another confirmed, happy to be of service to the group.

"I did not pay two million pounds for a Rubens! Where is my painting?!"

"I'm sorry, Sir Henry," one of the curators from the British Museum interrupted, "but what do you mean, 'my painting'?"

Chapter 26

Paris
February 16-18, 1926

"It was very nice of you to meet me. You really didn't have to come out so late this evening."

"It's nothing, Mademoiselle. I thought you could use help getting to your hotel."

"That's very nice of you."

He picked up her two cases, one in each hand, and they walked together from the platform to where the taxis were parked outside.

"Were there not a few more of your colleagues from the Staatliche Museen coming to help with the painting?"

"Oh, they are here. We travelled in different cars and are staying in different hotels. It's a bit of a story," she said, rolling her eyes.

The man loaded her cases into the taxi and they got inside together.

"The Ritz, please."

"The Ritz?" said the man who had met her on the platform, "I would not think that a humble researcher would take a room at the Ritz!"

"Well, it is a little embarrassing," said the woman, "but my father insisted. He is a businessman, a very successful one too. He does not like me travelling alone, or even with a few colleagues, and often gives me a little extra, shall we say, to stay in very nice places. It makes him feel more comfortable knowing I'm being looked after, though I do feel a bit self-conscious around the others. This is why we are staying in different places."

"I think that is a very lovely thing he does for you," replied the man, "and I would not give your colleagues a second thought!"

"You're too kind, Monsieur."

The car pulled up in front of the hotel and the man leapt from his seat to attend to her luggage before the bellhops had a chance. The woman got out and paid the driver, then met the man by the entrance where he had set her cases.

"Shall we get you checked in?" he asked rather eagerly.

"I appreciate your help very much, but I think I will have to say goodnight here I'm afraid."

The man's face fell a little but he did not want to displease her.

"That's no problem at all. I will see you tomorrow, yes?"

"Yes, of course!" the woman smiled. "I cannot wait to look around the museum."

"And I have been looking forward to giving you a tour!"

"Tomorrow then? Say, three o'clock? I'd like a little time to rest in the morning and maybe visit a few shops, if you don't mind?"

"No, not at all. Three o'clock then. I'll meet you at the main entrance."

"Excellent," the woman said, gesturing for one of the bellhops to come take her cases inside, "and again, danke schön for meeting me at the station, Monsieur Durand."

232

"You are very welcome, Mademoiselle Wolf. And please, it's Luc."

"Well, danke schön, Luc," the woman said with a smile, "and you may call me Dagmar."

"Until tomorrow then, Dagmar!" Luc said, giving her a silly bow and a wave goodbye.

"And this is the Grand Gallery," Luc said as they entered the large room at the north side of the museum.

"Beautiful!" Dagmar said with a breathless voice. "Absolutely stunning!"

Luc smiled with pride.

"And what are these spaces for?" she asked, pointing towards a section of wall that was oddly bare. "The lights make me think you are awaiting some new acquisitions to hang there."

"Actually, we are in the process of loaning out three pieces for exhibi--." He stopped himself, realising what he was about to say. "I'm very sorry, I'm not supposed to say yet, not until the loan has taken place."

"Oh, that sounds very exciting!" the woman said, widening her eyes and moving a bit closer to Luc. She nudged his shoulder and jokingly put her finger to her mouth, making a "shhh" sound as she did.

"Yes, it's all very clandestine, I suppose. Honestly, I'm not even really involved in it anyway. The director has been handling everything personally."

Luc shared several of his favourite pieces with her from the Grand Gallery before walking her through several rooms that led to where the works she was most interested in were displayed.

"And you'll notice this space here," he said, pointing to a gap on the wall. "That is where your piece hung until shortly after you contacted us. We have moved it below into one of our research rooms. Shall we go down and have a look? It is packaged for transport but you may inspect it before shipment if you like."

"Yes, please, that would be lovely. Not that I don't trust the museum but it would actually be quite interesting to see the inner workings of the Louvre at the same time, if you don't mind?"

They walked back through the pavilions until they came to the Grand Gallery again. Before they entered the room, there was a service door on the right that Luc stopped and opened, using a set of keys that he had in his left jacket pocket.

"Right this way, Mademoiselle," he said, holding the door for her.

"Danke schön."

He locked the door behind them and then led her down a set of stairs and along several wide corridors littered with various museum pieces, mostly fragments of sculptures or bronze statues, some of which were partially covered in heavy drop cloths. She could see tags on several of the objects, with what she assumed were dates and accession numbers scribbled on them.

"Here we are," he said, opening a door into a dark room and entering before her. He flicked on a light and Dagmar saw several tables with lamps on them and a few chairs scattered around the large room. There were magnifying glasses and microscopes, as well as various instruments for taking measurements of size and weight. Standing up against one of the walls was a large crate.

"I had the painting packed shortly after your second letter in January. Until your telegram a few days ago, I did not know whether you would be analysing it here or taking it back to your lab in Berlin."

"Yes, well, I'm afraid none of us knew," she said with a sigh. "There was a lot of discussion and no one could make up their minds! I'm sure you know how it can be."

"I certainly do!" he laughed. "Shall we continue the tour? I can show you where we do some of our restoration work if you like?"

By the time Luc had finished giving Dagmar the grand tour of the basement beneath the Grand Gallery, including a wink and a silly smile as he pointed toward the room where the mysterious missing pieces were being held, it was nearly six o'clock.

"I think I'm getting a bit hungry," she said, "how about you?"

"Oh, uh, yes, I am quite hungry actually."

"Then perhaps we should go find something to eat?" she said with a smile as she slipped her arm through his and gave him a little nudge with her elbow.

Luc stumbled over a few more words before agreeing to her idea and locking up the last of the doors as quickly as possible. Then he led her back through the corridors and out a different passage than the one they had entered through, one that led directly to the outside. He locked that door behind them and dropped the keys back into his jacket pocket.

"So where shall we go?" she asked him.

"If you are up for a short journey, we could go over to Le Dôme Café. It is very popular."

"Only if you promise to keep me warm," she said, squeezing his arm just a little and making a shivering sound with her mouth.

"Oh, uh, yes, I can do that," he replied with a smile. Then he pulled her as close as he could and led her out to the road to find a taxi.

"Are you ever in Berlin?" she asked him as they danced. After a lovely meal at Le Dôme, they had made their way over to a nearby club for a drink.

"I have never been there, I'm sorry to say."

"Oh, you must visit sometime! I would love to take you on a tour of the Gemäldegalerie especially."

"I'm sure I would like that very much."

They danced another song, and another after that, and eventually left the club around midnight. They hired a fiacre and Luc offered to accompany her back to her hotel, to make sure she got home safely.

The ride was pleasant, if a bit cold, so they sat close to one another and Luc kept his arm around Dagmar. They didn't say much along the way until they got close to the Ritz.

"I have walked by it many times," Luc said, looking up at the hotel. "You know, I should spend a night here sometime, just to experience it."

"Can we tell the driver to keep driving a little longer?" she asked, resting her head on his shoulder.

The fiacre made a large loop, ambling slowly and peacefully through the streets surrounding the Place Vendôme, before it finally returned to the Ritz.

"I've had a lovely evening," Luc said, helping her down from the carriage.

"Me too," Dagmar replied with another smile that warmed him more than all his layers of clothing.

"It is a pity you are only in Paris this one night."

"Yes, I feel the same way. But I don't think it will be the last time."

"I hope not."

"And besides, now you must come to Berlin, yes?"

"Of course!"

It was about two o'clock in the morning when they exchanged a few more awkward sentiments as they stood in the cold outside the hotel. Luc's 'hints' and 'suggestions' fell on deaf ears as Dagmar seemed completely oblivious, despite the fact that he believed them to be supremely subtle and clever.

"My train departs tomorrow at half past seven in the evening. My colleagues will meet us at the train station, if that is ok?"

"That's fine."

"And you are ok with arranging your staff to transport the painting to the train for us?"

"It's no problem at all."

"I cannot thank you enough for your hospitality. And for such a wonderful evening." She paused for a moment and then continued, "Well, goodnight, Monsieur," giving him a quick peck on the cheek.

"Goodnight," he replied, taking her hand and kissing the back of it softly.

The station was a little quieter than usual. The train for Berlin left at an odd hour between several other departures and arrivals, leaving the platform relatively clear. It was the perfect time to board with a crate containing a work by a Flemish Master.

After her colleagues had gotten the painting situated in a secure location, Dagmar went back out onto the platform to thank Luc.

"We will be looking forward to the results of your analysis," he said. "I cannot wait to hear from you."

"I cannot wait to write," she said with another one of those warm smiles. "Will you... oh, never mind."

"Will I what?"

"Well, I wondered if perhaps you might... if it's not too silly... write to me sometime?"

"You may count on it, Mademoiselle."

She gave him a hug and then squeezed his hand as they pulled away from each other. As she boarded the car, she looked back and they waved to one another. Then she disappeared inside. Luc hesitated for a few minutes, let out a deep sigh, and then turned and walked away.

"Thank you, Claude. Really, thank you very much. Here is what I promised, with a little extra just for you."

"It's all good fun," Claude replied with a laugh. "And we can always use a little extra money."

"Remember, when the conductor sounds the final boarding call, each of you leaves the train through a different car and exits the station in a different direction, ok?"

"Got it."

"Thank you again, and I'll see you back at the hotel, yes?"

"I'll be carrying bags again tomorrow morning, bright and early!"

"Excellent. Well, goodnight. And don't spend all of that on a woman, eh?"

"I'll try not to!"

—————————————

Scarlet waited until Luc was out of sight and then pulled off her auburn wig, stuffed it into a rubbish bin on the train, and shook her head side to side to release her hair. She took off her blue overcoat, revealing a thin red jacket she had been wearing underneath it. She rolled up the coat into a ball, tossed it into an empty sleeping compartment, and shut the door quickly. Then she reached into her bag and pulled out a pair of flat white shoes, kicking off her black heels at the same time. She buttoned her jacket from top to bottom, then slipped her red beret from the pocket and put it on quickly but carefully. As she exited the train, she glanced side to side, then threw her black heels under the car behind her as she walked away across the platform.

—————————————

"Here, these are yours," Luc said, handing a set of keys to one of the men that had helped him transport the painting to the station.

"And you really can't recall where you left them?" the man asked him.

"I haven't the faintest idea. But please, do me a favour.

239

Don't tell the director. Give me a day or two to look around, will you?"

Chapter 27

Paris & Reims
February 18-22, 1926

By the time the phone began ringing at the Louvre that evening, no one was around to answer it. It wasn't until a little past eight the following morning that Charlotte received the first call.

"Yes, just a moment please, I'll get -- yes, I understand that it -- just a mome-- I will get him, please hold!" she finally blurted out in a raised voice.

"Will someone fetch the director? And do it quickly."

Within a minute, the director was at Charlotte's desk.

"Bonjour, how can I --"

"But that is impossible! We packaged and oversaw the removal ourselves. Your man was here!"

"I understand that but --"

"No, I will not!"

"I have been very patient with you, Monsieur, but I have not even received your donation yet! How can I return what you have not given?"

"Well then what was it?"

The director's eyes widened. He breathed in sharply and released it through even more animated conversation.

"That is utterly and completely preposterous! The museum would never agree to such a thing! I would never agree to such a thing! You are gravely mistaken sir!"

"Pardon me?"

"And I will expect that our paintings are returned at once!"

"How dare you, sir!" And with that, he slammed the phone down, missing the catch initially and hitting the base, then slamming it down again in the correct position.

The staff behind Charlotte's desk were silent, as was she, all of them staring at the irate director pacing back and forth and breathing heavily.

"May I ask what that was about, Monsieur?" Charlotte asked.

"You may not!" he shouted, then turned and walked back through the door that led to his office, slamming it shut behind him.

It was about three minutes later when the phone rang again. Charlotte was a little hesitant to answer it this time but did her job regardless.

"I'm sorry, where are you calling from?"

"Ok, please hold."

She turned and asked the same staff member to fetch the director again. When he refused, the man next to him volunteered.

"Hello. Who is this?" the director asked rather forcefully.

"Oh, please forgive me. It's nothing. How may I help you?"

"Yes..."

"Yes..."

"The what?"

"You're joking."

"And what time did it arrive?"

"Is that when you were expecting the Rubens?"

"The Rubens."

"For analysis? In your lab?"

"I cannot believe this."

"Ok, thank you, I will be in touch." And with that, he set the phone down gently this time. Charlotte wondered if her question might be better received if she tried it again, now that the director seemed calmer.

"May I --"

"You may not!" he shouted, then turned and walked back through the door that led to his office, slamming it shut behind

243

him.

"We are truly sorry to be losing your business, Miss d'Auvergne. Is there nothing we can do to keep you?"

"No, Monsieur, I'm afraid there is not. You see, I'm leaving Paris. And if I return, it will only be for the occasional visit. So there is no need for a bank account here."

"Well, I wish you all the best for your new life ahead. But you will miss Paris, I think?"

"I will," Scarlet replied, "especially French pâtisserie!"

"I understand! I don't know what I would do without my morning stop by Ladurée," the manager said, shaking his head as though expressing some grave sentiment.

"A man after my own heart, Monsieur!"

"Now, I have the details for the transfer here... Credit Suisse, is that correct?"

"Yes, that's right."

"And the balance of the account is currently in pounds. Two million. Is that correct?"

"Yes."

"Ok, I will put that request through immediately. We have a close relationship with Credit Suisse, so the funds should arrive very quickly."

"Excellent."

Scarlet and the bank manager stood up and shook hands. Then she left the bank and went back to her hotel room to pack.

By quarter to six that evening, she was boarding her train at the Gare de l'Est. About ten minutes later, she was sipping a cup of coffee as she passed through the outer arrondissements.

"Aurélie? Is it really you?"

"It is indeed, Jacques!"

"It has been... how long now?"

"Too long."

He gave her a hug almost as tight as the evening before she left Reims six years ago. Then he had the bellhop take her things to her room as he accompanied her to the dining room.

"When you wrote to say that you would be visiting again soon, I could hardly believe it."

"Yes, well, I felt like it was the right time. I wanted to see you again. To see Reims again."

"It certainly is much improved from your first stay all those years ago, eh?" the man laughed, pointing out the window into the night where lights could now be seen in windows that hadn't existed after the war.

"It's beautiful," she said as she looked up at the silhouette of the cathedral against the moonlit sky.

"Now, what will you have? I'm sure you're hungry after your trip."

"What have you got?"

"Anything you wish, my dear!" he said, extending his arms as if to offer her his kingdom if she so desired.

"I have always trusted your chefs, Monsieur. Tell whoever is back there to surprise me!"

The manager leaned over her and gave her a half hug as she sat at the table.

"I have missed you, my girl."

On the third morning after she arrived at Le Fil Écarlate, Scarlet went out for an early walk before breakfast. She stopped by a shop and purchased a newspaper, then headed up to the cathedral.

The structure was still undergoing repairs and probably would be for decades to come. Walls were still crumbling in places, the roof still largely missing. But the purples and yellows of the morning sky cast warm tones over the facade, blanketing it in a layer of peace amidst the painstaking work of restoration.

She found a bench that gave her a view of the city and she sat down for a while. She breathed in the cold, crisp air and closed her eyes for a minute or two. Eventually she leaned back, crossed her legs, and opened her newspaper.

The front page headline read:

MASTERPIECES ON HOLIDAY ABROAD!
La Joconde visits Berlin in monumental mix-up!

The article continued with as many details as the Louvre appeared willing to share. There was no mention of a sale or donation, only that there had been confusion over a possible exhibition in London, and so on. Of course, the article also announced the resignation of the current director, which Scarlet had expected from the beginning.

When she finished the story, she folded up the paper and laid it on the bench next to her. After another half an hour or so enjoying the sunshine and the view, she got up and walked back to the hotel for breakfast.

She spent the evening catching up with Jacques and a few of the other hotel staff that she knew. They had a very late dinner together after all the guests had retired for the night. Scarlet enjoyed it so much, the five of them sitting around the table, the dining room all to themselves, that for an hour or two she almost completely forgot about what she had just accomplished.

"Have you thought about how long you'll stay with us?" Jacques asked her as they were all getting up and saying goodnight.

"I'm not sure yet. Is that ok? I don't want to inconvenience you if you need the room."

"Are you kidding, my dear? You may stay as long as you like. I would rather turn guests away than see you leave for another six years!"

They both laughed and she thanked him for his hospitality and kindness, not only now but for the first time as well.

"How could I have turned you away?"

"Did it ever bother you that I said my parents had thrown me out of the house? Did you ever wonder what I had done?"

Jacques smiled and shook his head a few times before he answered.

"My girl, I never believed that story for a second!" he said, still smiling and without a hint of suspicion or accusation in his voice.

Scarlet didn't know how to respond at first, but she didn't frown or pretend to be offended.

"What did you think about me?" she asked.

"You were like an injured bird. Like a little starling with a broken wing."

Scarlet felt her eyes begin to fill. She didn't want to cry in the dining room, in front of everyone. She quickly gave Jacques a hug, hiding her face over his shoulder and saying in his ear, "Thank you." Then she pulled away without looking at him and went up to her room.

As she was getting ready for bed, she glanced over at the small desk in the room and saw an unopened envelope. When she checked out of the Ritz, the manager had given her one last letter that had arrived for her. It was from Thomas and she had ignored it until now.

She picked it up and stared at it for a few seconds. Then she took it with her as she got into bed and pulled the covers over herself. She still hesitated for a minute or two but finally slid her finger along the flap and opened it.

The letter read as follows:

1 February

Dear Miss Haslewood,

I really have no idea if this letter will find you but I am hoping it does. I had also hoped that I would be able to say many of these things in person but I'm afraid that the time for that may have passed. At the very least, I feel like I owe you more of an explanation for abandoning you last December.

My father and I were in London on business and he took ill very suddenly. In fact, he lost consciousness shortly before I was supposed to meet you that evening. Doctors were summoned and did everything they could. He came to after a little while but when he did, he no longer had the use of his legs.

The doctors insisted that he be taken to the hospital and kept under observation but he refused. Instead, he insisted that we leave London at once and return to America. He said that if it was his time, he wanted to go at home and not in some foreign country. Remarkably, he made the voyage home, confined to his cabin of course but nonetheless he endured the journey.

We had two weeks with him before he lost consciousness again suddenly one evening in mid January, and didn't wake up again after that. The funeral was a few days later and he was eventually interred in our family cemetery, just a stone's throw from my grandparents, his mother and father.

I cannot forgive myself for missing our engagement that evening but I hope you can understand how desperate the situation was. I was in a strait betwixt two, as they say, and could not get away to see you.

Scarlet stopped reading as she remembered the note he sent her the day after their failed meeting. The note she had tossed aside and hadn't opened until she was back in France. How he had asked her to come visit him if she could. He had been "barely over a mile" away...

She continued reading:

I know this is a long shot but I will be back in London soon to conclude some business affairs from last December. If you are still in the city, would you like to try meeting for an evening? I will be staying at the Savoy again, from the 16th of February to the 7th of March. I would still very much like to see you again. Of course, I understand if you don't feel the same way.

I'll make this my last letter. Partly because I don't even know if you'll receive it... but also because I don't want to be a perpetual nuisance!

I wish you all the best, Miss Haslewood.

Yours sincerely,
Thomas

She folded up the letter and set it on the nightstand.

She lay awake after that, staring at the ceiling for nearly an hour, unable to fall asleep but trying not to think. Eventually she got up and went over to one of her cases and slipped her hand down inside and underneath a few pieces of clothing. She pulled out two folded-up pieces of paper and took them back to the bed with her.

When she had gotten comfortable again, she opened the first and read it. Then she opened the second and read it. Then she reread each once or twice more, then reread the one on the nightstand. After about ten minutes, she dozed off with the last letter still in her hand.

Chapter 28

Reims
February 24, 1926

Scarlet wasn't sure that a trip to London was the safest thing for her right now. It was a very big city, of course, but perhaps not big enough to ensure that she didn't see someone she didn't want to see. She recalled bumping into Daphne Faucheux, Dr. Dufour's maid, at the Gare de Lyon. She also recalled how Thomas had shown up just in time.

She went for a long walk that afternoon. She walked toward the south end of the city, through neighbourhoods in various states of repair. Some homes had miraculously survived the war and were just as they had always been, while some were missing entirely from the rows where they once stood, the rubble having been cleared away to make room for future growth.

As she neared the edge of town, she looked out over the first fields she came across. She saw a farmer riding through one of them on a large wagon pulled by two horses. The back was filled with sacks of what she imagined was grain or oats, but she really had no idea.

The scene brought back vivid memories. She remembered sleeping in barns and spare rooms, wherever anyone was willing to house and feed her for a few nights. Then a bumpy journey in the back of a wagon to the next village or town before she had overstayed her welcome. She remembered the last farmer that got her all the way to Reims, and how he had given her a few francs for food. It was really very little but it was probably everything he had at the time.

Just then, as she leaned on the fence that surrounded the nearest field, a bird flitted down and landed two posts to her left. Then it hopped along the top rail and up onto the next post closest to her. She didn't have any bread or crumbs to share, so she just watched. Much to her surprise, it continued along the next rail and hopped right up to the post that stood beside where she was leaning.

Scarlet stayed perfectly still as the little bird alternated between pecking gently at the wood with its lemony beak and looking this way and that, twittering and whistling a few times in the process. Its purplish-black feathers were iridescent, speckled with flecks of white that sparkled in the waning light of the late afternoon.

Then it slowed down and became almost entirely still. Her arms were folded as she leaned on the fence, so she carefully and slowly pulled her left hand free and started to move it towards the bird. She tried to move as slowly but as steadily as she could, so it would get comfortable with the presence of her hand.

When she was only inches away, the little bird did something she did not expect. It made a short half-hop closer to her hand and nudged her finger with its head. Scarlet could hardly believe it. She could feel her heart beating in her chest. And she couldn't stop herself from smiling.

She left her finger where it was a bit longer before the little bird chattered and whistled and flew away. She watched it flit across the field until she lost sight of it in a stand of trees far off to her right.

She waited a few minutes, then started back towards the hotel, smiling the entire way and arriving just in time for dinner.

Later that night, after another long evening enjoying the company at the hotel, Scarlet sat down to write the following letter to Mr. White:

24 February

Dear Mr. White,

I am very sorry to hear of your father's passing. I am also sorry that I could not see you before you left London in December. And I am afraid that I must now apologise in advance, that I will not be able to see you there on this visit either.

I am currently in France. I will be returning to Italy on the 8th of March aboard our favourite train.

I wonder, Mr. White, have you ever been to Venice in the springtime? I know a lovely place where you can get a perfect pain au chocolat.

Sincerely,
S. H.

"You are leaving us already?"

"It is time, Jacques. I'm so sorry. But I will make every effort to see you again before another six years has passed!"

"Oh, well, how generous of you!" the manager said. "Of course I'm only kidding my dear! All I want for you is to be happy. The world needs that smile of yours!"

"I'm sure I could be very happy here," Scarlet replied, "but there are some things that I need to do. To say, actually. It is a long story."

"The ones that are worth hearing always are," he said rather solemnly, "and the people that will listen are the ones worth your time."

She looked up at him the way a daughter might look up at a father she loves. Then she hugged him tightly and thanked him again for his grace and generosity. The bellhop placed her bags in the car and Jacques told him to accompany her to the station to help get them loaded onto the train.

By about six o'clock she was on her way back to Paris, unsure of what awaited her there.

———————————

Rather than stay a night in Paris before catching the Simplon Orient for Venice, Scarlet decided to arrive as close to the departure time as she could. She wanted to spend as little time in the city as possible and limit her chances of an infelicitous encounter. Unfortunately, however, that meant she had a little over three hours to kill in the uncomfortable train station.

She found a bench where she could sit with her bags not far from the platform where she would need to be later. She was wearing her blue and white hat, the one from Scaletta's shop. She had worn it precisely because of its large brim, which she kept tilted down a little lower than normal in front. Not awkwardly so, but enough to prevent the casual notice of her facial features by anyone that might be passing by.

She read for a while, which helped keep her face pointed down without appearing strange. Then she spent some time people-watching, glancing around the large open space and taking in the variety of passengers coming and going. She noticed the assortment of shoes, hats, jackets, scarves... she also noticed the pain in her lower back from the unforgiving bench and thought to herself, 'If I get a faulty banquette again...'

Eventually and by no means too soon, the train pulled up to the platform. Once the passengers from Calais had exited she would be able to board. In the meantime, she found the attendants and had them load her bags into the fourgon.

She watched carefully as a few passengers got out and collected their things. A few others obviously stepped onto the platform just to stretch their legs during the longer than average stop.

"Mademoiselle Haslewood, welcome aboard!" the conductor said as she showed him her ticket and he checked the details against his list.

"Merci," she replied as she stepped up and onto the train.

As she entered the corridor inside, she looked behind her and then through each open door as she made her way to her compartment. A couple of the doors were closed but she was able to see that there was an older couple in the room next to hers and a young-ish single woman in the one before that.

She brought her medium case aboard with her again this time and had it delivered to her compartment. She entered and shut the door behind her, then sat down and put her feet up on the suitcase. She took a deep breath and let it out slowly, folded her arms, closed her eyes, and leaned her head back against the banquette.

About five minutes later, there was a knock on her door.

"Mademoiselle," the conductor said, "I am informing all of the guests that our departure time has been delayed."

"By how long?"

"Roughly half an hour, maybe a little more."

"Ok," Scarlet replied, feeling the throbbing again in her lower back.

"I'm very sorry," the conductor continued.

"It's fine, I'm sure there's nothing that can be done."

"You are right, ma chère. However, by way of an apology, we will be offering a light supper in the dining-car once we have departed."

"Excellent!" Scarlet replied, genuinely happy to hear it as she hadn't been able to have a proper meal before boarding.

She went back to sitting quietly, comforting herself that she had just gone three hours on a train station bench, surely she could handle another thirty minutes or so.

It ended up being a little over an hour before the train was ready to leave the Gare de Lyon. The conductor apologised more than once and invited passengers to the dining-car for the promised supper while attendants prepared their compartments for the night. After a small but sufficient snack, Scarlet went back to her room and got ready for bed quickly. She was happy at last to be able to lie down and get some sleep.

Shortly after she had gotten into bed, however, she heard a great deal of thumping and footsteps in the corridor. She heard several voices as well, and then a compartment door open sharply and slam shut again a few seconds later.

'What on earth...?' she thought to herself.

Then she began to imagine the worst.

'Could it be...?'

'But that's not possible! How could they know where I am?'

'He did use the word 'oversight'... perhaps he has been watching me?'

'But then why not stop me sooner? Why not in Reims?'

'Maybe he only found you when you returned to Paris?'

'In the three hours I sat on the bench? Surely I would have seen or noticed something, right?'

As she argued silently with herself, the thumping stopped and the footsteps and voices slowly faded away, and everything was quiet again. A few minutes later, the train lurched forward and they were on their way out of Paris.

Scarlet tried to get some sleep but the adrenaline rush of imagined danger had put her into that terrible purgatory of excited exhaustion. She really did want to sleep, and really did feel as though she should be able to, but her body resisted. She tossed and turned, covered, uncovered, then covered herself again. She fluffed her pillow, folded her pillow, even punched her pillow, then removed it entirely only to put it back in its original position shortly thereafter.

'How dumb is he anyway?' she thought to herself. 'Did he not understand my letter? I was quite clear, wasn't I?'

'Perhaps he simply couldn't extend his stay?'

'Perhaps.'

She lay flat on her back, staring up at the ceiling for a while before she looked at the clock. It was a little after one o'clock in the morning, and she realised that an hour and a half had passed since she had first attempted to sleep.

"Just stupid!" she muttered out loud.

She got up and put on her long red jacket over her nightgown and slipped on a pair of shoes. She quietly opened the door to her compartment and glanced both ways down the corridor. She felt a little bit like a child sneaking out to steal cookies during the night.

Scarlet paced up and down the hall a couple of times, then stood and looked out the window for a while, trying to make out any stars in the sky. She recalled Mr. White and his bag of dates, and laughed to herself.

Eventually she made her way to the dining-car. She opened the door and turned around to shut it carefully, not wanting to attract any attention. As she turned back around to choose a table, she nearly lost her balance from fright.

"Miss Haslewood!"

She just stood there, like the proverbial deer in the headlights.

"Faulty banquette?"

She recovered herself quickly and was able to respond.

"No, it's quite serviceable this time. In fact, I was sound asleep until just a few moments ago. Really quite comfortable, these sleeping-cars."

"I see," said Thomas, squinting his eyes slightly and nodding his head. He clearly didn't believe her but, oddly enough, she was glad he didn't.

"Well, I don't want to interrupt your peaceful repose, but perhaps you'd like to join me?" he said, motioning toward the chair opposite him.

"I suppose a few minutes wouldn't hurt."

There were two chairs on the opposite side of the table, so she pushed them together and over a little bit to enable her to sit crosswise.

"You don't happen to have any dried fruit on you, eh?" she asked, her eyes closed as she rested her head against the vibrating wall of the train car. "I could murder a fig right now."

"No, I'm afraid not," Thomas said with a frown.

"That's too bad," she replied, eyes still closed.

"You wouldn't happen to have a good story to hand, eh?"

"No, I'm afraid not."

"That's too bad," he replied.

They were quiet for a while before Thomas continued with a question.

"So, Comtesse Aurélie d'Auvergne, huh?" he began, "That's an interesting name."

"Is it?" she asked.

"Where'd you come up with that?"

"I can't recall. Probably a story or something."

"Hmm, interesting," Thomas replied, sounding unconvinced.

"Can I take an absolutely wild guess about you, Miss Haslewood?" he asked.

Scarlet thought about his question for a second before responding. 'What could he possibly think he knows?'

"If you must," she replied.

"I'm going to shimmy out onto the farthest limb here and guess that you first came to Europe as a Hello Girl during the war. Am I right?"

Scarlet still had her head back and eyes closed. She tried to keep her reaction under control but her throat betrayed her and produced a couple of shallow coughs.

"Excuse me," she said, opening her eyes and adjusting her position. She added another cough and a throat clear, as though some legitimate physical irritation were troubling her. Thomas didn't stare her down, however. He just imitated her, leaning his head back and closing his eyes. But she was sure she detected the faintest traces of a cheeky little grin.

Despite the extreme awkwardness, Scarlet was still practised enough at improvisation that she was ready with a response. But then she hesitated, unsure if she wanted to improvise. As she considered the alternative, Thomas asked another question.

"Can I get you some water?"

"Yes, please. That would be lovely." She punctuated her reply with another fake throat clear.

Thomas got up and walked to the end of the car, then disappeared through the doorway. Scarlet stared up at the ceiling, then down at her hands folded in her lap. She didn't formulate any ideas or hold any kind of mental conversation with herself while he was gone. She just... waited.

He returned a few minutes later with a tray that held two glasses of water and a pitcher filled with what she assumed was more water. There were also two plates with a croissant on each.

"This was all I could find," he said as he set the tray down on the table and took his seat.

"Perfect," she said, reaching for one of the glasses. She drank about half of it without coming up for air, then set it down and picked at the croissant a little.

"So, what makes you so confident, Mr. White?"

"When I was a child, maybe eight or nine, my parents hired a French tutor for me. I hated it but it was the done thing, so I had to do it. That poor teacher. She was so nice and I was so hideous."

He sipped his water and tore off the end of his croissant.

"Is that right?" Scarlet replied. "Sounds like a lovely person."

"She certainly was. In fact, I heard that when General Pershing put out the call for operators to be sent to Europe, she volunteered her services as a French teacher at Camp Franklin."

"A patriot too! What a woman."

They were quiet for a while, enjoying their croissants and water. Scarlet was already on her second glass.

"So," she continued, "a private French tutor? Doesn't sound like something the average child would have."

"I suppose not. I suppose we were fairly well off."

"What business brought you back to London this time?" Scarlet asked, changing the subject.

"Well, before my father passed, he had made an arrangement with a certain colleague of ours there. I returned to finalise the deal."

"I see."

"Unfortunately, however, things didn't really go as planned."

"Is that right?"

"Yes, that's right," Thomas said, raising his eyebrows and looking down at what remained of his croissant.

"You see," he continued, "my father had paid our colleague a rather large sum of money, as a sort of down payment on a forthcoming acquisition."

Scarlet nodded and listened carefully, but not too carefully.

"I returned to London to confirm receipt of the item and to transfer the remaining funds. However, the whole arrangement ran into a bit of a snag."

"A snag?"

"A snag."

"What kind of snag?" Scarlet asked, a little too eagerly. She pulled back a bit and said, "I'm sorry, I don't mean to pry. You know, I just love a suspenseful story." She cringed inside as she heard herself.

"The item didn't arrive as planned."

"Oh dear."

"Yes. Apparently it caught the wrong train and ended up in... Berlin." As he said this last word, Thomas took a drink of his water and stared directly at Scarlet over the rim of the glass.

She feigned surprise and curiosity, but not convincingly.

"Berlin? Sounds like a monumental mix-up!"

"It certainly does, doesn't it."

Scarlet's whole body suddenly became a little too warm. She would have taken off her jacket, were she not in her nightgown.

"May I --," she began, but she stopped herself, unsure if she should continue. Then she decided that she needed to know the answer, so she finished her question.

"May I ask how much money your father paid? And did you recover it?"

"About ten million dollars, American. Roughly two million pounds. And no, I have not recovered it. Our colleague forwarded the funds to the intermediary who had negotiated the deal from the beginning. Where they are now is... well, anyone's guess."

Thomas continued staring at her and she looked back at him as best she could. She wanted to look away. She felt that she really should look away. But she couldn't.

"You said the money was a down payment. How much had your father agreed to pay in total?"

"Twice that amount. Another ten million, US."

Scarlet's heart jumped. Shame was overshadowed by shock and disgust at the thought that Sir Henry had been playing her. 'He was going to double his money on my work! That lying scoundrel!' She wanted to explain it all to Thomas then and there, how Sir Henry was the real criminal in all of this.

"I assume you didn't give him the remaining funds?"

"That's correct."

Thomas kept his gaze fixed on Scarlet. Her eyes had wavered once or twice but they kept returning to his. The outrage and frustration she had felt slowly began to dissipate as guilt and shame returned to the fore.

Then it happened again. The rhythm of the train car clanking along the tracks started to fade away. The gentle jostling of the train suddenly became undetectable. The car grew silent and still, and all she could feel was the tide of emotions inside her.

Rising and crashing, then receding for a moment before washing over her again. Her eyes began filling with tears as she heard herself speaking from somewhere inside herself.

"It's Scarlet, by the way."

Thomas smiled and reached out with his right hand across the table. She extended her left hand very slowly to meet his, her fingers shaking as she touched his palm.

"Scarlet Haslewood. It's a pleasure to meet you. For the first time, of course," he said with his warm smile as he gave her hand a gentle squeeze to steady the shaking.

Then all the sounds of the train car came rushing back in on her. The car suddenly began jostling again and the clanking of the train on the tracks resumed its rhythm in perfect time.

They spent the night together at the table, her hand in his, and Scarlet thought about how handsome Thomas was. His perfect brown hair and soft brown eyes. They talked for a long time about many different things, from train travel on the Continent to the state of baking in England, never once touching on paintings, museums, or lawyers.

Chapter 30

Venice
March 9-10, 1926

They arrived in Venice around four o'clock in the afternoon. Neither of them had slept and they were both feeling the exhaustion in full force.

"I believe you promised me some pain au chocolat, Miss Haslewood," Thomas said as they were walking out of the train station. "I haven't made this journey for nothing, you know."

"Perhaps we could postpone until tomorrow? I think I would fall out of my chair if I tried to sit at a café right now! Besides, I think there is still much to talk about. We should probably have a good night's rest."

As they loaded their bags into two separate taxis, Thomas asked her where she was going. She had been rather preoccupied on the train and then so incredibly tired when they arrived that she had completely forgotten that she no longer had accommodation in Venice. Where was she going?

"I suppose I'll find a hotel somewhere near the Piazza San Marco," she said.

"I thought you lived here?"

"Well, I did but I don't actually have a home at the moment. It's a little embarrassing, I suppose."

"That's ok," Thomas said, waving his hand as if it were a trivial thing not to have a home. "I know a good place. I'll get you your own room, it'll be my treat."

The taxis travelled in caravan as far as they could until they offloaded Thomas and Scarlet, and their bags, onto a water taxi. The boat took them the rest of the way, looping around the city to the south and pulling in along the Riva degli Schiavoni, just east of the Piazza San Marco. As their bags were carried up to the hotel, Scarlet glanced to her left, at the spot where she used to meet Signor Luzzatto when she had something worth selling.

The Hotel Danieli was Venice's finest. It was over five hundred years old but restored to the height of luxury. Scarlet had walked past it many times but had never stayed there.

"Are you sure about this?" she asked Thomas as they walked inside the foyer.

"Why?"

"No reason, I guess."

He secured two rooms for them, both suites overlooking the water. They had an early dinner before they turned in, both of them barely holding on by the end of the night, which was the very late hour of seven o'clock. Scarlet got ready for bed quickly and fell asleep within seconds of hitting the pillow.

───────────────

In the morning light, she was able to appreciate her room far more than the previous night. She pulled back the sumptuous green curtains that hung in deep folds, revealing the bustling lagoon below and the crowds of people enjoying the beautiful weather, the first they had seen in weeks. It is a strange thing to see a place one knows so well but from a completely new vantage point. It was a homey scene, yet altogether fresh and new at the same time.

Her bathroom was a magnificent display of marble and porcelain, combined with that dusty pink that seems to capture eighteenth and nineteenth-century Venice so well. She took her time getting ready for the day, enjoying every detail and fixture in the process. They had agreed to meet downstairs for breakfast around eight o'clock, a time that Scarlet would typically have scoffed at, but given their early bedtime she figured it was more than reasonable.

Thomas was already waiting for her when she got to the lobby.

"Good morning! You slept well, I hope? No faulty bedding or anything like that?"

"No, quite serviceable," Scarlet laughed.

"Well, shall we?" he asked, gesturing toward the dining room.

"Oh, no no no. We must go to the place I told you about. Please?"

"Of course, how could I forget!"

"Twelve hours of sleep can make your mind a little groggy."

"I think you're right," Thomas said, rubbing his eye and yawning as if on cue.

The Café Riparo was less than ten minutes' walk from the hotel, across the Piazza San Marco. They paused for a few minutes to enjoy the square in the morning and observe the gondolas and other boats coming and going along the lagoon.

"So you have been to Venice before, Mr. White?"

"Twice, but neither visit was very long. And it was a number of years ago. I was a teenager at the time, actually!"

"Ah, ok," Scarlet replied. "So were you wide-eyed and inquisitive, or unimpressed with everything and everyone you met?"

"Probably a bit more of the latter than the former, I'm sorry to say. My parents had a lot of expectations of me and I think it made me shut off to things that I would normally have found quite interesting."

"Well, perhaps we can make up for previous visits this time round," Scarlet said with a smile. "Let's start off with that pastry I promised you. It's right down this alley."

As they walked up to the café, they were barely within the outdoor seating area when they heard a voice yelling from inside.

"Scarlet! Are you really here?"

Maria came out to meet them, walking at a brisk pace. She went straight up to Scarlet and gave her a hug, squeezing her so tightly, Scarlet felt like she could barely breathe.

"It's lovely to see you, Maria!" she said with the limited breath she had left.

Then Maria pulled back from their embrace and gave her a crooked glare.

"Why don't you write? Why don't you call? I have been worried sick about you!"

"I'm very sorry, truly I am. And I will explain everything to you soon, I promise. It is a very long story but I will tell it to you. All of it."

"I certainly hope so," Maria said, still giving her a hard look. Then she softened her gaze and smiled again, and moved closer for another hug.

When she was finished greeting and rebuking Scarlet, Maria turned toward Thomas. She hesitated a moment, looking back and forth between them and giving Scarlet a surprised and curious look.

"Maria, this is Mr. White. This is Maria. She owns the Café Riparo."

"A pleasure!" Thomas said, giving her a nod and extending his hand. Maria didn't take his hand, opting instead to give him a hug the way only an Italian woman can. She was a few inches shorter than him, so she pulled him down with her embrace and then, before he knew what was happening, she planted a kiss on each cheek.

"Signor White, it is lovely to meet you!"

"Please, call me Thomas."

Maria glanced at Scarlet with a raised eyebrow and then invited them both to sit down and allow her to get them some breakfast.

"I forgot to mention that I knew the owner, didn't I?"

"Maybe," Thomas laughed.

A few minutes later, Maria returned with two cappuccinos and two plates, a warm sfogliatella on each.

"I haven't forgotten you, you see?" Maria said with a wink, nudging Scarlet in the shoulder.

"I'm so thankful you haven't," Scarlet said, looking up at her with another apologetic face.

"Brighten up, my dear! Smile, you're in my café!"

They both laughed and she leaned down and gave Scarlet another hug, whispering in her ear, "I have missed you, mia stellina. I'm glad you are safe and sound." Scarlet whispered back, "Thank you."

She left them alone and Thomas stared down at his plate.

"This doesn't look like pain au chocolat."

"Who said anything about pain au chocolat?"

"You did."

"I don't remember anything about that. But this is a sfogli-atella. The most delightful thing you'll ever eat!" As she finished speaking, she picked up the flaky little triangle of flour and butter and took a bite, the chocolate filling oozing out and overcoming her senses.

"It really doesn't get any better," she said with her mouth full and her eyes closed.

Thomas laughed, watching her slightly silly face as she tried to control the chocolate and the falling flakes of pastry. Then he picked up his and followed her lead.

"Wow, you're right! That is very good."

"See? You can trust me," she said with a wink.

They lingered around Maria's café for quite a while that morning, chatting with one another and with Maria whenever she wasn't taking care of customers. After a couple of hours, they left, promising again and again to return the following morning.

Scarlet led Thomas on a long walk around various neighbour-hoods of the city, through tight back alleys, over picturesque bridges, and along some of the more bustling thoroughfares. Eventually, as they were walking down one of the quieter streets they had been on, they passed an old church.

"Can we stop for a little while?" Thomas asked.

"Of course."

"Shall we see what's inside here?" he said, pointing toward the church.

"Sure, let's have a look."

As they went inside, she noticed the inscription on the wall and the tired wooden beams holding up the ceiling, and she remembered that she knew this place.

"Oh, I've been here before," she said. "Just once, on a rainy night."

There was no one there this time and they were able to wander freely around the room, touching the stone walls and inspecting the altarpiece more closely. Then Thomas walked toward the back of the church and sat down on one of the pews. Scarlet joined him in the same row.

They were quiet for a little while. The abandon Scarlet had felt since the morning started to fade, and she knew she needed to share things with Thomas. As many things as he would hear.

"I'm from Brooklyn," she started, staring straight ahead toward the altar as she spoke.

"Baltimore," Thomas replied.

"I know. It was on your letters."

"Oh, of course."

There was silence for another half a minute, then she continued.

"I was an only child. My father and I were very close. My mother too, actually. We were a very happy family."

She took her time and Thomas didn't rush her.

"He was the one that encouraged my love of stories. Especially fairy tales. He would read them to me when I was little.

Then one day, the day after my thirteenth birthday, as it happens... We were told to come quickly to the grocery store where he worked. He was the manager. He was very successful, for a man with little education that started by delivering vegetables.

His employees came to work that morning and found him dead on the floor of his office."

Thomas shifted his position and faced her as fully as he could along the same pew. He didn't reach out to her though, giving her the space she needed to think and remember.

"As if that weren't enough, we found out two days later that he... hadn't exactly been the man we thought he was.

My mother met his mistress when she went to clear his things out of his office."

Thomas frowned and sighed deeply, but he still didn't speak or touch her. Scarlet pulled out her handkerchief and dabbed around her eyes.

"The funeral was a joke!" she said, laughing and smiling a little through the tears.

"It's ironic, really. All of these people, thinking he was a pillar of the neighbourhood... when behind him was a mound of ruins."

She wiped her eyes again, apologising as she did.

"My mother was strong at first. I think the anger propped her up, you know. But then after a year or so, she had started to... erode, I guess you could say. She didn't go crazy or anything like that. She was always a smart woman and still was. But she just sort of withdrew. We interacted about everyday things but nothing of substance. And I didn't feel like I should push her. I didn't really know what to do.

The one bright spot was a family that knew the truth. They never let us down and probably could have done more, if my mother hadn't shut them out after a while. I still spent time with them though. It was the only time I felt normal. Like my life was like everyone else's.

Their name was Greenley," she said, looking over at Thomas out of the corner of her eye and smiling a little. He gave her a smile in return.

"It was their daughter, Dana, that suggested I sign up for the war as an operator. That was her job. I wasn't an actual operator, of course, but she seemed to think that wouldn't matter!" Scarlet laughed.

"Believe it or not, I wasn't accustomed to passing myself off as something I wasn't! But when the time came, I just kind of... did it. It wasn't that it was thrilling or even a little exciting... it was just survival, I think. At least, at first.

So I became Dana Greenley and I was happy for a while.

I served in Chaumont for several months in 1918, right up until the armistice. It was an incredible experience and I wouldn't trade it for anything. Well, the service part."

She stopped for a minute or so and looked around the room, but not at Thomas. Finally she looked forward again, toward the inscription. She analysed every contour of the letters and the stones on which they were engraved as she continued telling her story.

"There was a man there. A Mr. Frank Watkins of Wichita, Kansas. What a stupid name, don't you think?

Anyway, Mr. Watkins professed all kinds of wonderful sentiments to me and showed me a great deal of attention," she said with a satirical lilt in her voice. "But when the war was over... well, so were we."

Scarlet reached up to dab her eyes again and let out a mixture of coughing and laughter.

"I was very silly back then, as you can see! What a stupid little girl."

She shook her head at herself, then she focused again and continued.

"So I walked out of Chaumont one evening and never looked back. Hmm, I guess I can confirm that the Simplon Orient is faster than walking!"

Thomas laughed and she glanced over for a second, just in time to catch that warm smile of his.

"I ended up in Reims in January of 1919 and lived there for about a year. Actually, almost exactly a year. That was when and where I decided that allowing people access to me, so to speak, wasn't worth the pain. But it wasn't about survival anymore. I think it became more about... control?"

She made a curious face as she looked up at the ceiling, as if she were thinking about a question for the first time and was unsure of the answer.

"It didn't start out big. Mostly dinners with gullible men I met in clubs. The odd piece of clothing here and there. Then jewellery. Cheap stuff at first. But then that's where it started to escalate. I realised the expensive stuff was just about as easy to take as the cheap pieces. So why not, right?"

She looked over at Thomas and made the face that often accompanies a "Why not?" He made the same face in return.

"My first big triumph was an older couple. They were English, visiting family in France after the war. Upper-class type... I mean, you had to be, to be travelling and staying in nice places after the war. But they were friendly enough. At least, the wife was... the husband was fairly oblivious to anything but his dinner and his tobacco I think! But that sort of made my play even easier, actually. He wasn't interested enough to balance the emotions I was able to stir up in his wife. Or if he was, she had become accustomed to ignoring his input anyway, so it didn't matter.

Anyway, I fed them a story about love and loss, trenches and tribulation... all the juicy stuff... put on some tears and sobbing. It was horrible of me, really. But I did what I did. Eventually the wife felt compelled to 'comfort' me with a gift. You've seen the ring before. A beautiful sapphire piece... quite exquisite, really."

She reached into her handbag and pulled out a folded-up piece of paper. It was full of creases, as though it had once been crumpled up and discarded, then recovered. It was fragile and yellow with age. She handed it to Thomas without looking at him.

"That was the note she gave me. Read it."

Thomas unfolded it and read the message that Evelyn Haslewood had left for her at Le Fil Écarlate seven years earlier.

"Hasle--" he started to say out loud as he got to the end of it, but he cut himself off.

"And Écarlate?" she asked, gesturing with her head for him to look at the top of the note, at the letterhead.

"Oh yes, of course," he said. "Scarlet."

"I kept that note with me all these years because it reminded me. It reminded me that I didn't need to wait for people to care about me anymore," she said, raising her voice as she continued. "And I didn't need to hope that they meant it when they finally did."

She paused for a minute, frowning and staring down at the back of the pew in front of her. She couldn't see it but Thomas had a pained look on his face for her. And she didn't know it, but all he wanted to do was hold her hand. But he waited.

"I could get what I wanted... anything I wanted, anytime I

wanted it... fine things or emotional attachment! And it didn't cost me anything. There was no risk anymore... at least, not the truly painful kind."

Fresh tears filled her eyes and she held the handkerchief over them for a while this time, letting herself cry more freely than she had from the start. Thomas looked down at the floor and closed his eyes for a minute as he took in everything.

"And I didn't feel anything anymore," she added in the midst of her sobbing, "and I didn't care that I didn't feel anything anymore. It was easier not to feel."

Then she raised her voice a little again as she continued.

"But then you had to come along!

With your stupid bag of dates...

Why didn't you just go to bed? Why on earth would you sit in the dining-car all night?"

She gave him a confused look, as if she wanted an explanation. But Thomas knew she didn't.

"And for some bizarre reason, I hated lying to you!"

She wiped her eyes again with the handkerchief as her crying slowed.

"And then seeing you in Sir Henry's building! That was the topper! I mean, you've got to be joking, right?

And giving you my name!

But it was... it was like I couldn't stop myself."

She turned to face him.

"What's the matter with you anyway?" she asked, as though they had been in an argument this whole time. Then she laughed at herself and turned back, facing the front.

"But it wasn't just that I couldn't stop myself. What bothered me was that I didn't want to stop myself. I wanted to say so much more, in fact. And I probably would have, if you had shown up that night..."

Scarlet indulged in her emotions from that night for a second before she caught herself and remembered why Thomas hadn't shown up.

"Oh, I'm so sorry!" she said quickly, "Please, I mean no disrespect. I just got carried away for a moment."

"It's fine," he said quietly. And she knew it was.

She kept staring at him this time, and he held her gaze as long as she was willing.

"I just..." she started, looking for the words to continue. "I just feel so... safe with you. I can't explain it but I feel like I know it's all ok... I know I can rest."

They kept looking at one another for a minute in total silence. Then Thomas felt like it was time to respond.

"I've never approached a woman before, out of the blue like that," he said looking down at the floor, a little embarrassed. "I mean, I'm sure you're utterly surprised by that since I exude such charm and wit, huh?" he laughed.

Scarlet laughed with him but didn't say anything.

"But I just had to know who you were," he said, looking up at her. "I can't explain it either but there was something about you. Something that told me that there was even more about you, if that makes sense? And I wanted to know the whole story."

He took a breath but paused for a second before he continued.

"There's more about me you should know too. I don't really work with trains," he said.

Scarlet frowned but not out of fear. It was a peace that surpassed her reason, and she wasn't afraid of anything Thomas might say. She trusted him now.

"I actually sort of... own them."

"Is that right?" Scarlet said with a funny smile.

"Yes, it is. You see, my father built something of an empire around trains and transportation in America. And I was sent to Europe to represent the company when we purchased forty percent of Wagons-Lits."

"Oh, ok."

"So, two nights ago in Paris. You remember that little delay at the station?"

"Yes?"

"I sort of held the train for myself," he said with a sheepish smile.

"I see," Scarlet replied, squinting her eyes a little as if she were ready to reproach him, but smiling at the same time.

"Yes, well, why spend millions of dollars to invest in a train company if you can't change the schedule for your own purposes every now and then, eh? Besides, I knew that if I didn't catch that train..." he trailed off for a few seconds, then finished, "I knew I would probably never see you again."

He reached out with his right hand and she took it with her left, not shaking this time but firm and sure. She squeezed his hand as tightly as she could and he leaned towards her and kissed her as perfectly as he could.

They sat together for a few minutes more, holding hands and taking in the moment. Eventually they got up together and left the church. It had started raining while they were inside, but they couldn't have cared less. They held hands and took their time, enjoying every second of their walk back to the hotel.

After an early dinner that evening, they went back out and sat by the lagoon for a while. Even though it was no longer raining, it had gone on long enough to scare off most other pedestrians. It felt like the waterfront was their own private balcony.

"I'm very sorry that I won't be able to stay longer right now," Thomas said as they stared off towards the islands opposite the city.

"I understand, don't worry," Scarlet said, taking his hand in both of hers.

"You know I want to."

"I know."

"Like I said at dinner, I would love it if you would come with me."

"I would love it too. But I think I need to be here for a little while. I need to talk with Maria and a few others. And I should really take another trip back to Reims."

"You know they're going to be looking for you now, right?" Thomas said, turning towards her with a more serious face.

"But Sir Henry didn't lose anything on the deal, right? It was your money. And of course I'll give that back to --" she cut herself off as she remembered something.

"Oh dear."

"What is it?" Thomas asked.

"Your father gave him two million, right?"

"Pounds, yes."

"He gave me two hundred fifty thousand as a bribe, to make sure he was the buyer."

"I see."

"He must have figured he would make so much on the sale to your father, it wouldn't matter. I still have it. I never deposited it. It's in bearer bonds. Do you think if I returned it to him? Discreetly of course... I wouldn't exactly walk into his office or anything!"

"Oh no, Scarlet. It's not about the money."

Scarlet took a deep breath and let it out slowly.

"I'm sure you got a sense for Sir Henry in your dealings with him?" Thomas said.

She nodded.

"Trust me, my dear... he's far more underhanded than you think."

"Then why was your father doing business with him?"

"Our relationship with Sir Henry began as a matter of convenience. My father needed legal counsel in England for some business deals and Sir Henry was the obvious choice. We realised in time that he didn't always do things 'above board', shall we say. But to be honest, that didn't worry my father too much, as long as they got done."

"Were you concerned?" Scarlet asked.

"Very much, believe me. The day you saw me at his office was the first time I had ever met with him alone. I only went because my father was feeling unwell that morning."

"So, he's a dishonest lawyer and businessman. I mean, that's it, right?"

"If all you had done was steal from him, I might say yes. But you humiliated him."

Scarlet didn't respond. She turned and looked off across the water. Lights were starting to shine from windows as the sun had nearly finished setting.

"Don't get me wrong," Thomas continued with a little laugh, "seeing Sir Henry humiliated is something many people would be happy about. There are plenty of innocent victims in his wake that would make you their national hero!"

Scarlet didn't laugh with him.

"Unfortunately, however, I think that finding you is now going to sit at the top of his agenda. Perhaps for a long time to come."

"Do you think you could talk to him?" she asked, knowing how pathetic it sounded.

"I can delay a train in Paris but I'm afraid I can't mend Sir Henry's wounded pride."

Thomas looked at her for a minute as she continued looking out over the water. He could see the pain in her face, the stress and anxiety. He wished he could lift it off with one act or word.

"But I will be in this with you," he said. "You're not alone."

She leaned over and let her head rest on his shoulder. He put his arm around her and pulled her close.

"When will you be back?" she asked.

"About seven weeks. But I'm going to make sure I won't be needed again in America for quite a while after that."

"Oh, your money!" Scarlet said, sitting up quickly. "You must tell me where to send it as soon as possible!"

Thomas laughed.

"Keep it."

"You're kidding, right?"

"If I can't be here in person, I at least want to know that you're taken care of, no matter what needs may arise."

"I still have Sir Henry's bonds, you know," she replied, her eyes flashing as she gave him a devious smile.

"I'm absolutely certain you'll be able to think of some interesting ways to spend them!"

Scarlet leaned back on his shoulder again and he hugged her tightly. The last light of the sun had given way to the half moon that now reflected off the water between the islands. The clouds had passed with the rain and some of the stars shone brightly enough to be visible despite the moonlight.

A little later, they said goodnight to each other outside Scarlet's room.

"So we still have tomorrow, right?" she asked.

"Of course. I don't leave until the following afternoon."

"Good. Because Maria would be very unhappy if you weren't there for breakfast in the morning."

"Oh she would, would she?"

They hugged each other and kissed again, then Thomas gave her a little nod and said, "Goodnight, Miss Haslewood."

"Oh, wait!" Scarlet said suddenly.

"What is it?"

"I just realised something. When you figured out where I got my name, you never asked me what my real name was."

"Well, I thought perhaps you didn't want to go back there. That maybe you wanted to leave it behind."

"But aren't you just a little curious?" she said with a flick of her eyebrows.

"Ok then, let's have it!"

"Gina Parker. Do you love it?"

"Of course I --"

"Oh, I'm only teasing you! Don't answer me!" Scarlet laughed.

"Well then," Thomas replied, imitating her eyebrow gesture,

"what'll it be? Who are you, Signorina?"

Scarlet nodded and gave him a mischievous look.

"Goodnight, Mr. White."

Chapter 31

Venice
March-April 1926

"You're sure you don't want to come with me?"

"I'm sure. I mean, I do, but I really shouldn't just yet."

"I understand."

They had several minutes before Thomas had to board the train for Calais. Scarlet wasn't letting go of his hand. With the exception of a few brief moments when he needed to shift his luggage, she hadn't let go of it since they got on the water taxi outside the Danieli.

"Can I ask you something about the whole *Mona Lisa* arrangement?"

"Is that what we're going to call it now?" Scarlet laughed. "I like it."

"I think it works."

"Of course, ask me anything."

"Why the other two paintings? And why Berlin?" Thomas asked with a genuinely curious face. "Why not just send the *Mona Lisa* to England and let things play out however they will. You would still have gotten paid, right?"

"Are you familiar with thimble-rigging, Mr. White?"

Thomas gave her a confused look.

"It's also known as a shell game."

"Oh yes, of course. Moving the ball or whatever between

several containers until the spectator loses track, right?"

"Basically. I might also describe it as making noise."

"How do you mean?"

"You make one noise, or two, to cover the noise of the thing you're trying to hide. Like coughing as you open a door, or something like that."

"Ah, ok."

"I wanted Sir Henry to feel that there was something bigger going on than just a simple sale. An exhibit, a gesture of national solidarity, and so on. And I didn't want there to be any chance that the Louvre felt like the *Mona Lisa* was being targeted. I wanted her to sort of blend in with the crowd, if that makes sense."

"It does," Thomas said, nodding several times. "But I'm still not entirely clear on Berlin?"

"Ha!" Scarlet laughed, "Berlin, yes. Well, that was sort of just for me."

Thomas raised his eyebrow, waiting for her to elaborate.

"You see, Mr. White, the problem with stealing masterpieces is that it's darn near impossible to sell them. And if you can't turn a profit, well, what's the point? It's like hanging a million dollars on your wall and staring at it."

"Ok..." Thomas said slowly.

"At the same time, selling it just kind of felt... too simple."

"Oh really?" Thomas replied with a surprised laugh.

"Don't get me wrong," Scarlet said, "I think stealing it would have been just as easy. It's pulling off both, at the same time, that's the real trick."

"I see, I see. So basically you just wanted to see if you could?"

"Exactly," Scarlet replied, "and I did. Or at least, I could have. I wasn't really interested in the painting, hence why I sent it to Berlin for safe keeping. But don't worry, Mr. White," she added, giving him a playful, sneaky smile, "I'll behave myself while you're away."

"I'm sure you shall! Perhaps we'll have to talk about your version of 'behaving yourself' when I return."

"I'm more than willing," she said, giving his arm a squeeze as she spoke.

"I'm going to miss you. More than you can imagine," Thomas said.

"Of course you will!" Scarlet replied, elbowing him in the side and giving him another one of those mischievous smiles. Then her face changed back to the more anxious look she had been trying to suppress all morning.

"If you need me, ring me from the hotel. Obviously I can't just hop over here, but I do have a few friends in offices throughout Italy. I can always have one of them check on you and help you anyway you need it."

Scarlet held his arm tighter now and pulled him close to her side.

"Thank you... more than you can imagine," she said.

The conductor gave the final boarding call and Thomas turned toward Scarlet, hugged her, and gave her as long a kiss as he could spare without missing his train.

"Please tell Maria I'm sorry I'll be missing breakfast for a while! I know she'll be sad," he said with a wink. Then he jumped up onto the train while she followed behind him as closely as she could.

"Safe travels," she said, looking up at him from the platform.

"I will see you soon... Miss Haslewood."

Then the train began to crawl out of the station and they waved to one another as long as they could before the car vanished out of sight.

"You are alone today?" Maria asked, looking around as if Mr. White were going to pop out of a doorway somewhere.

"Yes," Scarlet said with a slightly exaggerated sad face. She was fishing for that doting big sister.

"Oh mia cara! I knew it! I knew he was a monster the moment I saw him!"

"No no no!" Scarlet said quickly. "He left but not like that!"

"Oh," Maria replied, calming down and letting go of the idea of killing Thomas in his sleep.

"Everything between us is fine. More than fine!"

"I see."

"He just has some very important business to attend to in America. He will be back as soon as possible."

"And you believe him?" Maria asked, still open to the idea of murdering Thomas.

"With all my heart."

Maria gave her a hug, a long hug.

"I'm so happy for you! He seemed like a lovely man. I can tell these things, you know!"

Scarlet sat down in the window and Maria got her a pastry and a coffee. Just then, as if they had agreed upon the time, Signora Rinaldi walked into the café.

"Miss Haslewood! Miss Haslewood!" she cried.

"Yes, it is me!"

"I thought... well, I thought... I mean, I didn't know what to think!"

"I'm very sorry, Signora Rinaldi. I couldn't write. It's very complicated but I'm ok. Everything is ok."

The old lady gave her a hug and then sat down opposite her at the same table.

"You know, I have had a new tenant in your rooms since the first of March. A very nice young man. I should introduce you to him. He is single and has a good job. And his mother is a lovely woman!"

Maria interrupted her.

"Oh, Signora, there is much to tell you! Our Scarlet here has found a nice young man already. All on her own!"

Signora Rinaldi's eyes widened and her mouth opened, though surprisingly she didn't make a sound.

"It's true," Scarlet said.

The old woman began to tear up. Then she got out of her chair and gave Scarlet a hug, perhaps the tightest of any tight embrace that has ever been exchanged between two people. Or at least, for Signora Rinaldi's part that is. Scarlet couldn't move her arms to hug her back.

"I am so happy for you, my dear girl! So where is he? Bring him to me! I must meet him!"

"And so you shall, I promise. But he will not be back to Venice for almost two months."

"Two months! Well, then I suppose I will have time to prepare the perfect evening for you two! Which reminds me. The celery has been absolutely terrible recently! Wouldn't you agree, Maria? I can hardly bring myself to buy it. But then, what does one use in place of celery?"

288

It was about forty-five minutes later but Signora Rinaldi eventually left Scarlet to her wilted pastry and cold coffee. As Maria came over to refresh them for her, she stopped her and asked her to sit down.

"What is it?" Maria asked.

"I need to talk to you about some things."

"Of course. Go ahead, my dear."

"It's going to take a while."

There was no one else in the café at the moment, so Maria got up, flipped the sign in the window to 'Chiuso', locked the door, removed her apron, and sat down again.

"Ok then," she said with a smile, "you have all the time you need."

Scarlet hesitated for a second.

"You don't want to do this later, after work? I don't want you to miss out on any business."

"Are you kidding? I'm the best!" Maria said. "If I'm closed for a while, it's not like they're going to find somewhere else to go."

Scarlet laughed.

"I have missed you, Maria!"

"Well then, get to it," she replied. "I'm trying to run a business here, you know!"

They talked for two hours that morning as customers came and went outside. A few of them knocked on the window when they saw Maria inside, but she shoed them away and told them to come back another time.

Scarlet shared her story from the *Mona Lisa*, working backwards to how she first came to Europe. She expected Maria to throw her out several times, and Maria's face expressed her shock and surprise more than once. But she never interrupted her, or questioned her. She just remained patient and attentive.

When she had finished, Maria was quiet for a while.

"It probably sounds crazy," Scarlet added, "but you've been one of the only steady things in my life for the last couple of years. Please know that I never wanted to hurt you."

"And you haven't, my dear," she replied, reaching out and taking her hand.

"Are you sure?"

"Yes, of course. I understand. You did things you thought you had to do."

"What do you mean?"

"I think you were like a wounded animal, mia stellina."

Scarlet felt herself starting to cry and she tried to wipe the first tears away before they ran down her face.

"Thank you, Maria."

"But can I ask you one thing?"

"Anything."

"Are you safe? I mean, you have made some enemies along the way, yes? Do you need to worry about any of them?"

"Only one, perhaps," Scarlet replied, looking out the window as she did. "But that is all speculation. I don't know anything for sure."

"Be careful, my dear," Maria said with a solemn expression, squeezing her hand as she did.

"Always."

"And if I can hep you with anything, ever, please ask."

"Thank you, Maria, but I would not want to get you caught up in any of this if something did happen."

"Pfft! Don't be ridiculous. If something did happen, that's

exactly when you would need your friends the most. And if I find out that you didn't ask me for help when I could have done something for you, then I'm the one you'll need to be afraid of!"

Scarlet thanked her again and gave her a long hug. Then Maria flipped her sign around and unlocked the door. A very old man was waiting there when she did.

"It's about time," he said with a huff and a growl.

Scarlet spent three more nights at the Danieli and then moved into her own rented accommodation. Signora Rinaldi's building was full but she thought it was better that way. She didn't want there to be any chance she might put her in danger, no matter how remote that chance may be.

The old landlady had put her in touch with a friend that was renting out an apartment atop a building not far from the Piazza, so Scarlet had gone to have a look. It was two rather large rooms but they were smaller than the overall footprint of the building, leaving space for an absolutely stunning rooftop patio.

"This is... perfect," Scarlet said as she leaned on the low wall that surrounded the patio. She took a deep breath, looking up at the sky and then down at the rooftops below. She could see the dome of the basilica and the campanile just a few streets away.

"Il Castello is always a popular building with tenants. It's very romantic, wouldn't you agree?" Signora Rinaldi's friend said.

"It certainly will be," she replied as she imagined sitting there with Thomas on a cool summer evening.

"So what do you think?"

"Oh, there's nothing to think about," Scarlet said with a big smile, "I'll definitely take it!"

By the time Thomas would return, she had furnished the large living room with two sumptuous couches, a stylish glass coffee table, and a deep, low-profile, button-tufted leather chair. She imagined him sitting there with a cup of coffee and a book on a quiet evening, while she lounged on the couch opposite him.

Maria had wanted to replace her outdoor tables at the café, so she gave Scarlet one, including the chairs, to set out on the patio. Scarlet couldn't have dreamed of a more perfect arrangement. She hired a local carpenter to build a simple pergola over part of it so that she could hang a sheet and create some shade on those hot summer days that were just around the corner. Then she completed the scene with several plants, including two that would hopefully creep up and over the pergola in due course.

The night she finished the final touches, she flopped down in one of the chairs on the patio and looked up at the stars. It was a moonless night and they were vibrant against the deep black sky.

Even though Thomas was still thousands of miles away and wouldn't be back for a couple of weeks, she was at peace. The rest that had settled upon her after their talk that afternoon in the little church hadn't left. It was like a roof over her head, a shelter amidst all the unknown that now swirled around her.

She sat there that night in her little aerie, looking up at the sky and feeling more in the moment and present than she ever had before. She felt patient and excited at the same time, content and yet full of anticipation.

She leaned back in her chair and put her feet up on the wall that surrounded the patio. As she hummed a song quietly to herself, she reached up and ran her fingers through the leaves of the vine that clung to the side of the pergola.

———————————————

———————————————

Outside *M. Fontaine* in the Rue de la Paix, a man paced back and forth, smoking a cigarette and looking in through the window. He dropped the smouldering remains on the ground, crushed them beneath his foot, and opened the door.

The owner was helping a customer, so the man waited patiently by the first display case near the door. It was filled with various pieces containing rubies of different shapes and sizes.

Fontaine noticed the man as soon as he entered the shop. He was tall and wore a long black coat over his dark grey suit. The only colour he projected was a red and blue striped tie, both in the darkest shades their respective palettes would allow. Fontaine tried to stay focused on the woman in front of him until she was finished. She decided to withhold her decision for the moment, thanked him for his time, and left.

"May I help you, Monsieur?"

"I hope so," the man said, walking over to the case where the jeweller stood.

"Are you looking for anyth--"

"You were robbed last year, is that correct?"

Fontaine was a little surprised by his forcefulness, but the anger he felt over the ordeal he had experienced last April had by no means abated.

"Yes. Why do you ask?"

The man glanced down at the case and took his time, reaching into his pocket and pulling out a card.

"I was wondering if we might be able to help each other," he said as he slid the card across the glass.

Fontaine picked it up and read it out loud.

"Mr. Neville Penwell. Associate at Culpepper Law."

The man stood quietly, staring at the jeweller.

"And how do you think we might be of service to one another, Mr. Penwell?"

TO BE CONTINUED...

Scarlet Haslewood and Mr. White will return in
ROSE.

Orléans
July 13, 1926

"Come on! Let's go!" her muffled voice called to him from the hall. He opened the door and Scarlet's eyes were wide with urgency.

"Ok ok," he replied, "I'm here."

"We need to hurry!"

"But she said she won't see us until dinner. I'm sure we have time."

"Better to be quick about it," Scarlet said as she started walking away without checking to see if he was following.

They hurried down the main stairs, through the dining room, then through the garden, across the lawn, and up to the front door of the cottage.

"Locked," Scarlet said as she tried the knob.

"Sooo... what happens now?" Thomas asked.

"Locks just make things interesting."

She slipped a thin, small, rectangular leather pouch from her pocket. Inside were what looked to Thomas like various pins or shims. Scarlet slid two of them from the pouch, then returned it to her pocket and crouched down slightly in front of the door.

"Keep an eye out, will you?"

Thomas turned around and tried to act casually as he paced back and forth on the tiny patio in front of the cottage. He could hear clicking, ticking, a little jangling, then the squeaking of the knob turning and the door opening.

"Voilà!" Scarlet said, motioning towards the cottage as though she were inviting Thomas in for a cup of tea. "After you, 'Mr. Watson'."

"I'm still a little uncomfortable with all of this," he said as he was the first to enter.

"Just remember, it's for Jacques."

Made in the USA
Middletown, DE
21 February 2021